HANA

T0266565

HANA

Alena Mornštajnová

Translated from the Czech by
Julia and Peter Sherwood

PARTHIAN

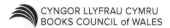

CYNGOR LLYFRAU CYMRU
BOOKS COUNCIL of WALES

Creative
Europe

Co-funded by the Creative Europe Programme of
the European Union

MINISTRY OF CULTURE
CZECH REPUBLIC

This translation was made possible by a grant
from the Ministry of Culture of the Czech Republic

Alena Mornštajnová is a Czech writer and translator. She made her debut in 2013 with the novel *Blind Map* followed by *The Little Hotel* in 2015. The publication of *Hana* in 2017 to huge critical and popular success confirmed Mornštajnová's position as one of the leading contemporary Czech writers.

Hana has sold over 100,000 copies and has been published in thirteen languages.

Alena Mornštajnová has won several awards including the National Czech Book Award. She lives in Valašské Meziříčí.

Julia Sherwood was born and grew up in Bratislava, Slovakia, and worked for Amnesty International in London for over twenty years.

Peter Sherwood taught Hungarian at the School of Slavonic and East European Studies (now part of University College London) and the University of North Carolina at Chapel Hill. They are based in London and work as freelance translators from and into English, Slovak, Czech, Hungarian, Polish and Russian. Their book-length translations include Peter Krištúfek's House of the Deaf Man (2014) and Uršuľa Kovalyk's The Equestrienne (2016) for Parthian, as well as works by Balla, Béla Hamvas, Hamid Ismailov, Daniela Kapitáňová, Hubert Klimko-Dobrzaniecki, Petra Procházková, Noémi Szécsi, Antal Szerb, Miklós Vámos, and Pavel Vilikovský.

For more information, see juliaandpetersherwood.com

Parthian, Cardigan SA43 1ED
www.parthianbooks.com
First published in Czech in 2017
© Alena Mornštajnová 2020
© This translation by Julia and Peter Sherwood
ISBN print: 978-1-912681-50-1
ISBN ebook: 978-1-913640-00-2
Editor: Carly Holmes
Cover Design: Syncopated Pandemonium
Cover image: Stephen Mulcahey
Typeset by Elaine Sharples
Printed by 4edge Limited
Published with the financial support of the Books Council of Wales and
the Ministry of Culture of the Czech Republic
Co-funded by the Creative Europe Programme of the European Union
British Library Cataloguing in Publication Data
A cataloguing record for this book is available from the British Library.

Table of Contents

PART ONE
I, Mira
1954-1963

Chapter One

February 1954

I've never understood why grown-ups tell children that it pays to be obedient. If I'd been a model daughter, my name would now be carved on a gravestone alongside those of my mother's parents – Grandma Elsa and Grandpa Ervin who died long before I was born. Or of Grandma Ludmila and Grandpa Mojmír, at whose grave my mother and I used to light candles in brown tubs at the far end of the cemetery.

On Sunday afternoons, if the weather was nice, my schoolfriends would go for a walk in the park or take a stroll around town with their families, while my mum would make Dagmar, Otto and me put on our Sunday best and push us out into the street outside the dark watchmaker's shop which used to be ours but where my father was, by then, only allowed to work for a pitiful salary and my mother could only mop the floor for no pay at all.

Every Sunday afternoon, after washing the dishes, Mum would put on her black hat, plonk Otto in his pram or, when he was a little older, grab him by the hand and head with us to the cemetery. It seemed miles away. First we had to pass the church, reach the river and cross the bridge, then walk through all of the lower town, which for some mysterious reason is known as Krásno, before trudging past the enormous castle park to where the houses ended, go through the cemetery gate and wait while Mum swept the gravestones clean, arranged the flowers in the vases and lit candles. As she worked, she talked to the dead, sharing with them the latest gossip from Meziříčí: who had been born, who had died, what rumours were going around, how the neighbours were doing and what mischief we, the children, had got up to again.

I never dared say anything, just sighed deeply to make Mum realise how the waiting annoyed me but even that was enough to prompt a reproach: 'Stop making that face. If it wasn't for them, you wouldn't be here today.'

After further names were added to the gravestones, including my Mum's, I often thought back on how she would stand by the graves every Sunday talking to her loved ones. It was comforting to know that she was now with those she had been missing so much.

The only reason my name is not among those inscribed on the gravestone in gold lettering is because it sometimes pays to be cheeky and disobedient. If you don't agree, you might as well stop reading right now. And don't let your children get hold of this book either, just to be on the safe side.

The winter of the year I turned nine and my entire life was turned upside down was frosty and fairy tale white but by February we had all had enough. Only in the last days of the month did it turn slightly warmer at last, with the snow starting to melt and the ice beginning to break up.

There are stretches of the river separating Meziříčí from Krásno where the current seems to drag along modestly and sluggishly rather than rushing down to merge with bigger rivers, and since the snow on the nearby mountains was melting only very gradually, it didn't make the river flow much faster and the water level barely rose. The conditions seemed perfect for a short ride on the ice floes that had come loose.

That February of 1954, as evil was already lurking deep in the town's underbelly, every day after school we ran straight to the river and impatiently checked if the ice was beginning to break up and if the current was strong enough for us to jump onto a passing floe, ride it for a few metres and enjoy the great adventure about which the sixth-formers, twins Eda and Marek Zedníček, raved to us in every school break. During a similarly freezing winter a few years ago they had first-hand experience of riding on a floe.

Eventually, after a few days, the ice cracked, the middle of the river broke free and ice floes started slowly floating downstream. This was the moment we had prayed and meticulously planned for.

I stood in the kitchen doorway, holding my bobbly red hat in one hand and gloves in the other.

'What's got into you?' Mum asked in surprise when I asked if I could go sledding with Jarmilka. The kitchen was warm and cosy, filled with the lovely smell of the tartlets my mother was baking for her birthday party. 'The snow has started to melt, you'll get all soaked.'

I reached for the baking sheet to take a tart but flinched as it was still hot. 'Yes, exactly! This may be our last ride this winter.'

Mum eyed me suspiciously. 'Mira, don't even think of going to the river.'

The fact that Mum had guessed what I was up to with Jarmilka Stejskalová and the Zedníček boys made me wonder if, before she grew up to be so extremely cautious, she too might have enjoyed riding on ice floes. But she wouldn't allow me to do so many things, just to keep me out of harm's way.

I wasn't allowed to go up to the attic, because I might trip on some junk or fall out of the window. I wasn't allowed to go down to the cellar, because I might slip and fall down the stairs. I wasn't allowed to go out onto the balcony because I might fall through the dilapidated floor onto the paved courtyard. And when you hear the words 'you mustn't do this and mustn't do that' all the time, it's no wonder that you stop taking them seriously.

'Of course not, Jarmilka and I are just going to the hill behind the Zedníčeks' garden,' I said, sneaking a tart into my pocket, hot as it was.

My mum was very pretty and when she hugged me, she gave off a warmth that was like a stove with the lovely smell of vanilla sugar. But at that moment her huge brown eyes, which always seemed so sad I was afraid to look into them, were fixed on me with such suspicion that they seemed to read my innermost thoughts.

'Jarmilka is waiting for me outside,' I said, buttoning up my coat, tying the laces of my warm ankle boots and pushing my hat deep down my forehead.

Mum handed me another tart. 'Take one for Jarmilka as well.'

I dashed out of the door, grabbed Jarmilka's sled by its strap and headed for the Square. I could feel Mum's eyes burning my back.

'Bye-bye, Mrs Karásková,' Jarmilka shouted, 'and thanks.' Tossing her long blonde plait, which I had always been jealous of because all the boys in our form used to tug at it with admiration, she shot my mum an innocent smile and bit into the tart.

At the end of the street I turned left.

'Where are you going?' asked Jarmilka, yanking the strap to stop me. 'We don't want to go around the whole town.'

'But I don't want my mum to see me heading for the river.'

'Oh, come on, she can't see around corners!'

I looked around. A curtain moved in the first-floor window of a house with peeling paint. Maybe I was just imagining it but perhaps it was old Mrs Benešová keeping watch so she did not miss anything that went on in the

Square. I quickened my pace. 'You never know. We might run into someone and then we'll be in trouble.'

'And you'll have to have peas for your supper,' laughed Jarmilka, scurrying after me in resignation.

She was right. I hated peas and Mum knew it too, so whenever I talked back or had been up to some mischief, she made me eat peas for lunch and supper. I would sit at the table with the rest of the family watching them enjoy potato pancakes with home-made jam or some other treat, while I forced down my peas. I pulled a face and said: 'That's not as bad as when my dad unbuckles his belt.' Something I also had to put up with every now and then, certainly more often than my younger sister and brother. And today's exploits would definitely qualify for the belt, I had no doubt about that.

My brown boots were soaked through even before we reached the river, and my gloves weren't thick enough to stop the cold from creeping under my fingernails. The Zedníček boys were already waiting for us on the riverbank under the whitewashed church with its wood-tiled roof. They scurried up and down in the mushy snow with long sticks trying to separate the floes that had drifted towards the bank. As soon as a floe slid into the river, the current would catch it and carry it, slowly at first but gradually faster and faster, towards a low weir some fifty metres away where an accumulation of broken-up ice would block it from going any further.

Courage suddenly deserted me. Jarmilka must have felt the same because she sat down on the sled and said: 'I'll just sit here and watch.'

'Scaredy-cat,' Eda Zedníček shouted contemptuously. I realised that courage, if not beauty, might be a way for me to get the better of Jarmilka. The boys might pull at her plait but I was the one who they would point to for years to come, telling their younger schoolfriends: 'That's the girl who rode down the river on an ice floe.'

I watched Eda skilfully free another chunk of ice, as large as the woven rug in my parents' bedroom, step right into the middle of it, push off the ground with a pole and start slowly drifting on the current towards the weir. We ran along the riverbank while Eda stood on the ice floe with his legs wide apart, using a pole to steer his impromptu vehicle into the slower current, sticking it into the ground and heading for the weir at a safe distance from the bank. After softening the impact with the pole, he walked back to the shore on the pile of ice.

How simple, I thought. Except for the bit where you have to cross from one floe to the other.

As we walked back to the sled the boys dispensed some well-meant advice that took my courage away again. 'The main thing is to step right into the middle of the floe so that you don't slip into the water. And to keep close to the shore, the water is shallower there. The current is really strong in the middle, it could sweep you along, even I couldn't handle that. And you have to push off with the pole on the side, don't hold it in front of you or you might fall off.'

Now my feet were shaking not just with the cold but also fear. Eda and Mirek helped me free a floe. 'Jump on,' Eda shouted and I jumped, except that in the meantime the ice had floated slightly further downstream. I landed on the edge; the ice swayed and I slipped.

I spread my arms in mid-flight and could feel my body hit the river and sink into the water. At first it didn't seem all that cold, but then it squeezed me like a pair of gigantic pliers, flooding my ears, eyes and nose, pressing me down into the shallows and pushing me to some dark place. Before I had time to get scared, someone's hand grabbed the lapels of my coat and lifted me out of the water.

'Didn't I tell you not to step on the edge?' Eda said, turning to Mirek and adding with a sneer: 'It was your stupid idea to bring the girls. We'll be in real trouble now.'

Jarmilka stood on the shore, whimpering. I scrambled out of my sodden coat as quickly as I could and tried to wring it out. I couldn't go home in that state, but I was terribly cold. It occurred to me that it might be an idea to make a fire so that I could dry my clothes and warm up a little. I was going to ask the boys for matches but my teeth were chattering so badly I couldn't say a word.

'Stop bawling, give her your coat and take her home,' Eda shouted at Jarmilka. Reluctantly, she unbuttoned her winter coat and threw it over my shoulders. It wasn't much help. Now both of us were shivering.

'If you dare blurt out that we were here with you, you'll get a proper hiding, even though you're girls,' Eda went on. 'And now clear off home,' he said, and with a nod to Mirek the two off them dashed up the hill.

I tossed the soaked coat onto the sled and we headed home, this time taking the shortest route. The cold was biting into my skin, forcing me to walk faster and faster. Two streets before our house I gave Jarmilka her damp coat back. She put it on, visibly relieved, gave me a sympathetic look and left me to it. I was still hoping that with a bit of luck I might be able to skulk up the stairs, slip past the kitchen, run up to the second floor to the room I shared with my brother and sister and secretly change into dry clothes without being spotted.

Never before had I noticed how badly our heavy front door needed oiling, how much the stairs creaked and how, unless you turned the light on, which was of course out of the question just now, you couldn't see as far as the next step.

'Is the light not working?' came a voice from above, then the lightbulb flickered and I stopped in my tracks halfway up the stairs. When I turned around, I realised I couldn't have avoided being found out anyway. I had left a small puddle behind on each step.

'I can't believe it!' Mum yelled, pouncing on me and dragging me up the stairs where she started to tear the wet clothes off me. 'What mischief have you been up to now? Didn't I tell you not to go to the river?'

She pulled my drenched tights off with one hand and thrashed my icy bottom with the other. I was shocked. This was the first time Mum had laid a hand on me. The blows weren't painful, just dreadfully humiliating.

'No,' I shouted. 'That's not true! I haven't been to the river. I went sledding with Jarmilka. It's the snow, it's really wet, that's why I'm all drenched.'

I started to cry with shame, from the cold and the shock of it all. My brother and sister appeared in the kitchen doorway but, seeing me getting a drubbing, beat a quick retreat. The front door opened, as the rumpus had now reached the watchmaker's shop, and my dad shouted out to ask what was happening.

'You liar, you,' Mum said angrily, rubbing my body with a towel so that it hurt, and pushing me into bed. 'Go and make some tea, quickly,' she called to Dad and threw an eiderdown over me. 'Do you want to catch pneumonia and die?'

What kind of question was that? Why should I want to die? 'I haven't been to the river, I fell into a puddle,' I sobbed. 'It's not my fault, it really isn't.'

Mum put a mug of tea on the bedside table, jammed a woolly hat on my head, tucked a hot water bottle under my feet and closed the door. I nestled into the bedding and pressed the soles of my frozen feet into the hot water bottle, whimpering quietly. I was cold and unhappy that Mummy and Daddy were cross with me. Perhaps I shouldn't have lied, perhaps I should have said that someone had pushed me into the river, perhaps...

Soon a pleasant warmth started to spread through my body and in half-sleep I heard the door open every now and then, felt a hand on my forehead and thought to myself that maybe Mummy wasn't all that angry with me after all, that instead of getting the belt it would only be mushy peas for dinner.

My dad had an uncanny ability of treading so softly that it sometimes seemed that he'd passed through walls and floors like a ghost rather than coming in through the door. He spent his days in the watchmaking workshop on the ground floor repairing clocks. His back was stooped from sitting all the time and when he walked, he bent slightly forward. With his thick but almost completely grey hair he looked more like my mum's father than her husband.

When I was very young, before I even went to school and my little brother Otto was still hiding under Mum's skirts, I wondered sometimes why my beautiful mum had married someone so old. One day I asked them about it.

'She had to marry me,' said Dad, 'after all, she's the reason my hair turned grey.'

'That's true,' Mum replied, patting him on his stooped back. 'But you're quite happy you did, aren't you? Who would bring you gallons of tea down to the workshop? You know how many steps it is?'

Eighteen. The narrow staircase had eighteen steps, and ever since the government had nationalised the family watchmaker's shop and had the connecting doors between the shop and the staircase bricked up, Mum had to go out into the street with every cup of tea and enter the little shop by the main door, which wasn't much fun, especially in winter or when it rained.

My dad would spend long hours down there with his clocks and watches, not just on weekdays when the shop was open, but even on Sundays. He would only go up to our first-floor flat to eat and sleep. At lunch and supper he would talk to Mum about the clocks he was working on and she would listen to him as if he were recounting some amazing adventures. He never said much to us children, and when Mum had to go away leaving Dad to look after us, he was rather put out. I'm sure it wasn't because he didn't love us. He just wasn't good with children and was waiting for us to grow up and find his clock stories as fascinating as Mum did.

On the Sunday when the world started turning in the wrong direction, Dad had been grumpy all day although he did his best not to show it. At first, I thought he was still angry with me because of my ice bath but in fact this time it had nothing to do with me. It was Mum's thirtieth birthday and Dad was ill at ease because his regular routine was disrupted by the celebrations. He couldn't go down to his workshop, sit at his bench and fix whatever needed fixing. He had to sit in the living room at the festively laid table alongside his wife, three children and sister-in-law Hana, with whom he simply couldn't get on even if he'd wanted to.

There was one simple reason – his sister-in-law was the embodiment of reproachfulness. Her every word, every gesture and every look showed clearly how much she disliked him. Dad found sharing a table with her just as unpleasant as I did.

As for me, I was scared of Aunt Hana. She would sit on a chair like a black moth, staring into the void. I never saw her in any bright clothes. Summer or winter, she wore the same black cardigan with deep pockets over a long-sleeved black dress, black tights and lace-up boots. I had never seen her without a headscarf, which I could understand as I had noticed her white hair sticking out from under the scarf, although she can't have been that old.

'Why doesn't she ever take that cardigan off?' I asked Mum.

'Can't you see how skinny she is?' she said. 'And skinny people are often sensitive to the cold.'

'If she ate properly, she wouldn't be so skinny. She just nibbles the bread she pulls out of her pockets. Why doesn't she eat some proper food instead?' It wasn't fair that grown-ups were allowed to strew breadcrumbs all over the place while children weren't.

'Why, why, why! Stop pestering me. It's none of your business. Does Aunt Hana tell you what you should or shouldn't do?'

That was quite true. Aunt Hana was the only grown-up I had never heard say "you mustn't". Actually, I had rarely heard her say anything at all, because Aunt Hana hardly ever spoke, she just stared. In that funny way of hers. As if she were looking but didn't see. As if she'd gone away and left her body on the chair. Sometimes I worried that she might suddenly slide down to the floor leaving only a pile of black clothes behind.

I should have known that Mum would stick up for Aunt Hana. Aunt Hana was her older sister; in fact, she was the only family we had. Mum loved her very much, which I found quite strange because my aunt had never given any sign of caring about any of us. Once I saw Mum try to hug her when she came to visit, but my aunt shrank back as if touching Mum had burnt her. Mum would always smile at her, speak to her in a soothing voice as if to a young child, and she would have moved mountains for her if my aunt had asked her to. But my aunt never asked her or anyone else for anything. She just sat in the living room staring into the void and would sometimes reply briefly in a voice that sounded exactly like Mum's.

As we sat down to the festive lunch, I was half expecting to find mushy peas on my plate instead of the hunter's stew. Although I hadn't noticed any signs of peas being cooked during my exploratory visits to the kitchen in the morning, I gathered from Mum's reserved behaviour that she had not yet drawn a line under my river adventure.

I was served the same food as everyone else. Maybe Mum was letting me off to mark her thirtieth birthday?

I had just got my hopes up when the time came for dessert. The lovely, fabulous cream puffs with their glittery sugar frosting and custard filling, specially bought for the celebrations from the patisserie in the Square.

One by one, my mum lifted the cream puffs off their tray with silver tongs and set them down on the gold-rimmed dessert plates she took out of the cupboard only on special occasions. She placed the first one before my aunt, then she served Dad, Dagmar and Otto. Then she looked around and said: 'And the last one is mine.'

'But what about me?' I asked, a little too quickly, as I knew what the answer would be.

'You don't deserve a dessert. You went down to the river even though you knew you weren't allowed to, and to cap it all you lied to me about it.'

I started to whimper. All eyes were on me. My brother and sister looked at me with sympathy, Aunt Hana uncomprehendingly. Dad just nodded and said: 'Stop bawling or I'll unbuckle my belt. You got away lightly as it is.'

'Well then, it's all yours,' I said, pushing my chair away so forcefully it nearly toppled over, and shot out of the room.

'And she's cheeky with it,' I heard Dad say. 'I should have given her a good thrashing.'

'Oh, come now, it's my birthday,' Mum said in a conciliatory voice. Those were the last words I heard before I ran up the wooden stairs to our second-floor room, where I slumped on the bed sobbing loudly.

So loudly that I didn't hear the evil that had hatched beneath our town and stolen into some of the houses, including ours, on that day. The tears welling up in my eyes stopped me from seeing it reach out towards us with its greedy claws, smothering hope and sowing death. I had no idea that it lurked unseen and unheard downstairs at the table, stealthily picking its victims.

Chapter Two

Next day, first thing in the morning, I sneaked into the pantry to check if there was a left-over cream puff for me, but there wasn't so much as a crumb. I wondered for a moment if I should go into a sulk but then thought better of it as that could have earned me the promised thrashing from Dad. I generously decided to forgive my parents and pretend that none of this had happened. By way of consolation, I snatched up a few pieces of hard gingerbread Mum kept on the top shelf for grating as a topping for plum dumplings, porridge and noodles. Mum would hide them behind the jars of stewed fruit and thought I didn't know about them. Then I found a bag of peas and pushed it into the furthest corner, just to be on the safe side.

By Friday Dagmar couldn't get out of bed. I urged and prodded her, pulled the duvet off her, but she just wouldn't get up. When she clutched her head and started crying, I realised she must be ill and not up to going to school. I ran downstairs to the kitchen and told Mum that Dagmar wasn't feeling well and that I had a headache coming on, too.

Mum felt my forehead. 'Have a bite to eat and off you go to school,' she said, pointing to a seat at the kitchen table next to Dad. I sat down, annoyed, and tried to force a cough but gave up when Dad shot me a menacing look.

I was famished by the time I came back from school at one o'clock because in the morning commotion I'd forgotten to pack myself something for elevenses. Dagmar was running a temperature and no one took any notice of me. My sister couldn't recognise anyone and kept shouting something about doorbells while Mum, with the help of old doctor Janotka, was applying compresses.

'It's probably mumps,' the doctor said. 'Be prepared, your other two will probably catch it too,' he said, pointing to me and Otto. To be honest, seeing how poorly Dagmar was, I'd much rather have gone to school.

The doctor was right. Otto also fell ill the next day and he seemed to be even worse than Dagmar. The doctor came every day and he seemed more and more concerned, since two days later their temperatures were not going down and although my two younger siblings still had a headache and were still too weak to get up, the bulges behind the ears, typical of mumps, failed to appear. The doctor tried to make them bend their heads to their chest to see if they had meningitis. Mum was crying with fear and exhaustion, Dad tried to do his best to help but just wandered aimlessly around the kitchen, while I kept waiting to fall ill as well.

In the end it wasn't me who fell ill but Mum and Dad. By then we knew that we weren't the only family afflicted by this strange disease, as the number of sick people in town kept growing. It became clear that this was some kind of infection and that the sick would have to be isolated from the healthy. Since there was no hospital in Meziříčí, my entire family was taken to the isolation ward in the district hospital in the nearest big town.

'Go to Aunt Hana's,' Mum said. Her cheeks were burning, she had difficulty talking and her tongue had taken on a strange brown hue. 'Don't forget to lock up. And don't get up to any mischief.' She stroked my cheek and let herself be taken down to the ambulance. Her head was bowed and the listless look in her eyes reminded me of Aunt Hana. She sat down next to Dad, resting her head on his shoulder. Dad opened his eyes and asked: 'Did you wind up the clock?' and closed them again. Mum closed her eyes without answering.

A man in a white coat slammed the ambulance door shut and I was left standing alone on the pavement in front of the watchmaker's. There was nobody around to stop me going to the attic, the cellar or down to the river. Nobody to care about me.

I climbed the stairs and sat down on the sofa in the empty kitchen which suddenly seemed huge, listening to the loud ticking of the clock. I didn't feel like going to Aunt Hana's, but what else was there for me to do? I took a deep, determined breath and then, all of a sudden, I heard shuffling upstairs. I froze, dug myself deeper into one corner of the kitchen sofa and pulled a cushion onto my lap. No, it was just my imagination. I realised I had never before been at home alone. I reached for the bag Mum had helped me pack, and then I heard the noises again. As if someone were walking up and down in the attic. I shot out of the kitchen, snatched my coat off the hook by the front door, grabbed my shoes and rushed out. Not until I got to the Square did it occur to me that I hadn't locked up.

Aunt Hana lived in the house where she and my mum were born and grew up with Grandma Elsa and Grandpa Ervin. Four large windows opened onto the Square and I used to envy her for being able to sit on the wide windowsill and watch the hustle and bustle outside. Our house had two floors but in order to see further than the narrow street I would have to climb to the attic from where you could see the whole town, but of course I wasn't allowed to go up there. Besides, I was quite sure that Aunt Hana never looked out of her window as she didn't like people and had not the slightest interest in them.

I dragged myself to my aunt's flat one step at a time,

imagining the face she would make when I told her I was going to stay with her for a few days. She wouldn't be best pleased, there was no doubt about that. She was so used to her solitude that she had almost lost her ability to speak. She never left the house except to buy the bare necessities or to pay a rare visit to my mum. Actually, I wasn't even sure she knew my name. I couldn't recall her ever addressing me by name. She couldn't have done, as a matter of fact – she had never spoken to me at all.

I rang the doorbell but there was no response. I rang again, this time more firmly. But no sound came from inside. I pressed my ear to the door. It would be just my luck not to find my aunt at home. I tried the handle. The door wasn't locked.

'Auntie?' I called through the door but there was no sound. 'Auntie, it's me, Mira. Mum told me to go to yours.' I imagined Aunt sitting at her table with that strange look in her eyes, not taking any notice of me. I went into the hallway, peered into the kitchen and, finally, the bedroom.

That was where I found her. She was lying in bed, in the same clothes she wore when she last came to our house, including her black headscarf, except that it had now slid off her white hair to her shoulders. She was lying on her back, strangely twisted, as if convulsed by pain, with her chin turned sideways, her eyes wide open and a strange rattle coming from her mouth.

I didn't know what to do. I edged forward a few steps. 'Auntie?' But by then I could see that her face was the same colour as Dagmar's. She was bleary-eyed and trembling all over – even more than I was after falling into the icy water.

'Mother,' she shouted all of a sudden. 'Mother, I knew... I knew you would come back.' She shook her head from side to side abruptly. 'They're not here, they're not here.' Tears rolled from her eyes. I had never seen anyone shed so many tears, even Otto who was really great at throwing tantrums.

I don't know what frightened me more, her violent feverish shivers, the convulsions of pain, her cries or her tears. I ran out of the flat, bounded down the stairs and once outside got hold of the first passer-by, pulling at his arm in desperation. 'Please, please, tell me what to do, tell me what to do! My aunt is really unwell!' To sound more serious, I added: 'She's fainted.'

The man in a long overcoat pushed me aside unceremoniously and moved away from me. By then everyone knew that the contagion had invaded our town. Stopping at a safe distance, he asked: 'Where is she?'

'Upstairs, in this house. She's there all alone and I don't know what to do.'

'Follow me,' he said and walked through the open door of a baker's. 'Don't touch anything.'

It was warm inside and the place smelled deliciously of freshly-baked bread. The bread that Aunt Hana used to buy here and cut into thin slices and carry in her pockets.

Ignoring the alarmed looks of the women in the queue, the man in the long overcoat went straight up to the counter and asked the shop assistant: 'Is there a phone I could use?'

'It's only for official business,' the woman snapped. 'This is not a post office.'

'Call an ambulance,' my rescuer said. 'The little girl will give you the name and address.'

The shop assistant was about to open her mouth, but the man yelled at her: 'Or do you want to go and take a look at the sick woman yourself first?'

The people in the queue shrank back to safety. I don't know what they were more scared of, the contagion or the angry man. The first thing that occurred to me was how lucky I was to have picked him to grab by the sleeve. I was sure he could tell me where I should go now that I'd been left all alone. Suddenly I felt safer.

Two women left their place in the queue, giving us a wide berth, and walked off. I told the shop assistant my aunt's name and she went into the office at the back to make the call. I was told to go and wait outside my aunt's house.

The ambulance arrived in no time. The front door opened, and a rotund doctor clambered out. He hesitated when he saw the stairs, gave a resigned sigh and started waddling towards the house, then stopped, took a deep breath and disappeared indoors, swearing under his breath. My aunt was carried out on a stretcher. I could tell she was still alive because the blanket they had thrown over her was trembling. The stretcher was loaded into the ambulance, the fat doctor climbed in, panting, slammed the door, the vehicle revved a few times, emitted a foul-smelling grey cloud and drove off jerkily.

I watched the white ambulance disappear and waited for the gentleman in the long overcoat to come back so I could ask his advice again. But he was nowhere to be seen.

I hung about for a good ten minutes, getting more and more chilled. It dawned on me that no one would help me and that it was up to me to find someone to look after me.

The first person who came to my mind was my golden-haired friend Jarmilka Stejskalová. Her equally fair-haired mother had always been very nice to me. I was sure she would let me stay at their house for a few days.

Once again I was standing in front of someone's flat with my hand on the doorknob, asking for help. This time the door opened after the first ring, but only just.

'Hello, Mira, Jarmilka is not going out today.'

'I haven't come to see Jarmilka. My Mummy and Daddy have been taken to hospital and I've been left alone. Could I stay with you until they come back?'

The gap grew even smaller. 'Not right now. We've all got a cold, you might catch it.'

'So where should I go?' I asked, but the door had already closed.

I looked up and down the street. In the windows, lights were being turned on; every now and then a shadow appeared behind the curtains, but I couldn't see anyone I knew anywhere. Slowly I started walking towards our house but slowed down even more as I remembered the strange shuffling noises I had heard coming from the attic. I passed the shop window of the watchmaker's, grown dark at the end of the day, stopped outside the front door and waited for something to happen. But nothing happened, except that the street was getting darker and on top of being cold I was getting increasingly scared of the approaching night.

I must lock up at least, I told myself. And once I've done that, all I can do is try knocking on a neighbour's door and ask for their advice. I'll go from house to house and hope someone will help me.

Having a plan gave me some courage. I pressed down the door handle. I was sure I wouldn't have to go in as the key was usually left in the lock. I would just have to reach inside, grab it quickly, slam the door shut again and turn the key in the lock. I felt for the other side of the door but the key wasn't there. How could that be? I was sure I'd seen it there. It could only mean that it was hanging on a coat hook a few steps from the door.

I poked my head into the unlit corridor. I didn't dare switch on the light for fear of attracting the attention of an intruder whose presence I sensed. The faint light from the darkening street suddenly made my shadow so long that it reached all the way to the narrow stairwell and seemed to climb the stairs with every step I took. The coat hook was barely visible in the dusk. If I didn't know it was Dad's winter coat on it I would have thought that a shadowy figure stood there, with his back pressed against the wall. What if there really was someone here?

I stood stock still and tried to make out the keys in the gloom. Suddenly I heard steps. They were coming closer and closer, and then another shadow joined mine on the stairs. Without trying to work out where the steps were coming from, I turned on my heels and made for the door. But the steps weren't approaching from upstairs as I thought. They were those of the figure that was now blocking my way out. I tried to slip past, but she grabbed me by the shoulder. 'Mira! You gave me a terrible fright.'

Chapter Three

March 1954

I once asked Mum, how come she didn't have a "real best friend". She was taken aback by my question and said that wasn't the way things worked with grown-ups.

'When people grow up, they don't go out with their best friend every afternoon like you do with Jarmilka,' she explained. 'They don't walk to work together or share their elevenses. They don't see each other every day; in fact, sometimes they might not see each other for weeks on end, but they always know that they're there for each other when needed.'

So Ivana Horáčková must have been a "real best friend" because the minute she heard that my family had been taken to hospital and I was left all alone, she came to see if I was all right.

The front door to our house was wide open and Ivana Horáčková noticed something moving in the dark hallway. Dashing out at her from the dusk, I gave her a bit of a fright but she quickly pulled herself together, switched on the light and helped me find the key to our house, transforming it into our safe and cosy home as if waving a magic wand. Then she got hold of my bag and led me to her house. I was still trembling.

She was a "real best friend" because, even though her husband Jaroslav shouted at her and insisted that she should hand me over to something called *the council*, she made up an old iron bed for me in the cubbyhole that used to be the servant's room. I was so exhausted that I managed just a sip of hot milk before climbing under the duvet. But before I fell asleep I heard Mr Horáček say: 'What did you bring her here for? Do you want us all to die?'

I didn't hear her reply but I thought it very strange that a big man like that should be frightened of a little girl.

The next day Ivana told me to call her Auntie, even though she wasn't my auntie at all, and explained that the town was in the grip of a typhoid epidemic and since my parents and siblings had been taken ill, it was quite likely that I was also a carrier. That was why I would have to go for a test and so would the Horáčeks, as they had come into contact with me.

I suppose Mr Horáček was still cross with me. Not only did he not suggest that I call him Uncle, he told Aunt Ivana in a huff that there was no way he would stick out his bottom just because of her. I didn't understand what he meant until we came to the doctor's surgery where the nurse took samples and said she would send them off for tests.

Aunt Ivana was really nice to me. She promised I could stay with her until my parents came home from hospital. The Horáčeks had plenty of room now because at the first sign that the epidemic was rampaging through the town, they had sent their two children to stay with relatives quite far away, in Kroměříž.

And it was just as well they had because Meziříčí was quickly sealed off. The two rivers running through town that share the same name and which usually hug the houses like a pair of friendly arms, now held the inhabitants in a tight grip. They turned into borders which no one was allowed to cross, to ensure that the contagion didn't spread to the surrounding villages.

Public notices and announcements on local radio requested the residents not to leave town but people were terrified and anyone who could, fled to stay with friends and relations. But they soon discovered that nobody would put them up for fear that the refugees might spread typhoid beyond the town limits.

All the families where someone had been taken ill were placed under strict quarantine. I wasn't allowed to go to school and the Horáčeks weren't permitted to go to work. We were told to avoid showing up anywhere we might spread the contagion and banned from going to restaurants. Mr Horáček, used to his pint of beer in the evening, defied this ban, just as he did the call for a medical examination.

Men and women in white coats went from house to house checking the sources of water and searching for the cause of the sudden disaster. Since Meziříčí had no mains water supply, local people used to draw water from wells in their courtyards and cellars. And it was in one of these wells, which had for centuries provided water for people who had once dug for it in a cellar, that death was hatched.

Whether a well had been contaminated by sewage, or the body of a dead rat had decomposed in the well, we never found out. What was certain, however, was that deadly bacteria started to breed in the water. And it happened to be the well that supplied water for the local patisserie. Every single bun, cream roll, slice of tart or cake, crescent roll and roulade carried germs of death.

The germs were lurking inside the cream puffs with the custard filling and the glittery sugar icing that my family enjoyed at my Mum's birthday celebration.

Here I was, sitting alone in someone else's kitchen. It smelled very different from my mum's kitchen. The floor, with its large brown tiles, felt cold to my feet. Four straight-backed wooden chairs stood around a white table and a saggy old sofa with a round cushion in a crocheted cover was pushed against the wall opposite the window. There was also a large cream-coloured chest of drawers with beautifully carved columns and cupboards with opaque glass.

I slipped off my chair, pushed it over to the sink, dipped my hands in the vinegary water and started to rinse the lunchtime dishes. I tried to make as little noise as possible and pricked up my ears to catch as much as I could of the conversation between Aunt Ivana and her husband next door. I knew they were discussing something important, something I was not supposed to hear even though it concerned me as well. Why else would Aunt Ivana have left the dishes in the sink and let the water go cold after heating it for a long time in a big pot, bringing it to a boil and then lugging it over to the sink and carefully pouring it in?

After scrubbing the last dish and placing it on the side of the sink to dry with the rest, I crept up to the door. I pressed my ear to the wood but still couldn't hear anything. Suddenly the door flew open, hitting me right in the face.

'Mira! What are you doing here?'

'What do you think she's doing? She's spying on us.' Mr Horáček still hadn't come to terms with my presence.

'I've washed the dishes,' I announced, rubbing my bruised face. I felt like crying but I knew I had only myself to blame for the pain. I reached for the tea towel. 'And now I'm going to dry them.'

Mr Horáček mumbled something, picked up a newspaper from the kitchen table and went back to the living room. Aunt Ivana stroked my back without saying a word.

'I wasn't spying,' I said as I started on the dishes. I'd never been too keen on helping with household chores at home but I knew from experience that adults tend to open up when you're doing something together with them. 'I'd just like to know if there's been any news of my family and Aunt Hana. Like when they'll let them out of hospital.'

Aunt Ivana shrugged her shoulders. 'Not so soon, I'm afraid.'

I thought that was strange. 'How can you be sure? I've never been sick for more than a week.' And that was only because I had dragged it out so I didn't have to go to school.

'Typhoid is not your common cold. But don't worry, I heard an announcement yesterday afternoon, it said that your family was in a satisfactory condition.'

That was news to me. 'Where did you hear that?'

Aunt Ivana faltered. 'In the Square.' When she saw my puzzled expression, she went on hesitantly. 'Lots of people are sick but no one is allowed to visit them in hospital so the local radio outside the town hall announces how people are doing.'

'Every day?'

'Yes.'

'Will there be an announcement this afternoon as well?'

'Sure. Uncle Jaroslav will go and tell us what they said.'

So this was the secret they had been whispering about behind the closed door. Why make such a fuss about it? Were they worried I might want to come along?

'Can I come today and listen to the announcement?'

'It's not suitable for children. And it's bitter out there, you might catch a cold.'

Aunt Ivana sounded so implacable that I gave up trying to persuade her and decided I'd have to come up with another idea if I wanted to go to the Square and find out more about my family.

That year, instead of the scent of spring it was the smell of disinfectant that filled the air. The houses huddled together as if trying to support each other in the gloom enveloping them as well as the people in the streets. All strife and arguments among neighbours that had seemed so important just a few weeks ago had been set aside and every conversation revolved around the people's sense of powerlessness, fear and illness.

Disinfection crews criss-crossed the town, stopping at every house where someone had been taken ill and leaving behind messed up beds stripped of bedding, a foul stench and white chalk marks on front doors.

Our house also had to be subjected to this humiliating procedure and I had to be present as the only member of the family not locked up in an infectious ward. At the appointed time I arrived in our street with Aunt Ivana, unlocked the door leading to the dark hallway and let two men in white coats and surgical masks over their mouths and noses into the house. We waited downstairs in the hallway for what to me seemed like an interminably long time while they got on with the job.

'All done?' Aunt Ivana asked when they came down the stairs.

'Only the watchmaker's left,' one of the men replied. 'The keys are supposed to be here somewhere.'

I pointed to a hook next to the front door and after they unlocked it and went in, I peeked in behind them. Everything was in its place in the shop, yet something was not quite right.

The silence. It was the alien, ominous silence that stunned me. I couldn't hear the clocks ticking. Their pendulums hung motionless, the hands on the clock faces showing the time when they stopped. There was no one left in the house to wind up the dozens or maybe even a hundred clocks; there was no one there who needed them. It was as if they had died.

When the men were finished, they asked Aunt Ivana to sign a piece of paper confirming they had done their job thoroughly and without a hitch, as if the horrible stench they left behind wasn't proof enough.

We locked up again, walked down the narrow street and turned into the Square. The streets were more crowded than usual and everyone was heading in the same direction.

'They're going to listen to the announcement,' said Aunt Ivana, squeezing my hand more firmly and quickening her pace. She evidently had no intention of lingering in the Square.

'Auntie,' I implored her, 'let's stay. Look, there are some other children over there.'

I'm sure it wasn't my pleading that made Ivana stop and listen to the endless litany of names and reports on the condition of the sick. What stopped her was the curiosity aroused by the sight of the silent crowd that stood facing the town hall. What prevented her from leaving was the murmur that ran through the crowd every now and then, ominous whispers and sobs at the news that somebody's condition had worsened. She stood still, listening out for any familiar names. She stood there even though she knew she ought to keep going, but curiosity glued her feet to the pavement.

A monotonous voice read out an endless list, articulating the names carefully and assigning them to categories. I heard the name Hana Helerová. I tugged at Aunt Ivana's sleeve and felt very important. They were talking about my Aunt Hana on the local radio.

'Condition very serious,' the announcer said. That didn't come as news to me as I'd seen for myself that she was very poorly. I kept listening. A name followed by a brief announcement. Condition moderately serious, condition critical, condition unchanged, condition satisfactory, out of danger... Then the announcer read out another name and it seemed to stick in his throat. 'Dead,' he said before he went on with the litany.

I was horror-struck. Until that moment it had never occurred to me that Mum, Dad, Dagmar or little Otto might die. I was sure that only old people died; Dad always used to say that it wasn't his age but worries that had made his hair turn grey, and Mum had not a single wrinkle on her face. And my siblings were only little. I felt Aunt Ivana's hand tightening its grip around my arm as she started dragging me away.

'But they've already got up to the letter J,' I howled, trying to hold Ivana back. 'It will soon be my family's turn.'

Aunt Ivana kept pulling me along. I dug my heels into the pavement and grabbed hold of the door frame of the bakery where I had stood two weeks earlier waiting for the ambulance to collect the sick Aunt Hana. Ivana prised my fingers away and dragged me along. She walked so fast she was almost running, but it was too late.

'Kalaš Jan,' the radio said. 'Condition satisfactory. Kalašová Marta, condition serious. Karásková Dagmar, condition unchanged, Karásek Karel, condition serious, Karásek Otto, condition unchanged, Karásková Rosa...' That was my mum. The voice went silent for a moment. Ivana kept dragging me away and I stopped resisting. Suddenly I wanted to run away as fast as I could to get away from the words I dreaded to hear.

'Dead,' said the voice and I heard nothing more because I broke down in tears. I sobbed uncontrollably as I bawled: 'No, not my mummy!'

People turned their heads and gave us indignant looks thinking I was some obstinate child refusing to obey her mother. I didn't care. Overwhelmed by terrible grief and loneliness I felt cold and wished I too could die. I became aware of someone picking me up and holding me to their chest and for a fraction of a second hoped it was all a terrible mistake and my mum had come to comfort me, but it was only Aunt Ivana. She carried me away from the Square, tears rolling down her face.

Chapter Four

I thought nothing could make me grieve and feel more helpless than Mum's death, but I was wrong. Within a week my sister Dagmar died, then little Otto and finally my dad, too. Not yet nine, I was left all alone. My life had come to a standstill just like the clocks on the walls of Dad's workshop. All I felt was grief, fear of the future and infinite loneliness.

Aunt Ivana moved me from the cubbyhole to the children's room. She let me sleep in the bed in which her older son Gustav normally slept, sat by my bedside and held my hand until I fell asleep. She was there when I woke up in the morning, drying the tears I couldn't stop and talking to me whenever she thought I was giving way to despair.

Mornings were the worst. Sleep made the present disappear and in my dreams I would return to the house where I was born. There was Mum, standing by the kitchen table again, baking a marble cake using Grandma Karásková's recipe, my Dad's favourite, or she would sit on the sofa reading one of her favourite romance paperbacks in the *Evenings Under the Lamp* series. She used to keep them in a shoe box on top of a wardrobe in the bedroom and Dad always had to take them down for her because she couldn't reach so high. Little Otto was building a tower of wooden blocks, and Dagmar and I were doing our homework.

The dream always ended in the same way. The door would open, Dad would come in and I'd say: 'I heard this announcement in the Square, it said that you've died.' And they would all look at me and laugh. 'That was just a dream, can't you see that we're all here?' and I felt happy. Except that I would then wake up and it was as if they had died all over again. Every morning I relived the grief until eventually I was afraid to go to sleep for fear of losing my dearest and nearest all over again.

The Horáčeks were very kind to me. Aunt Ivana's husband Jaroslav even said I could stay with them as long as I needed to, but that upset me even more because I wanted to go home. To my old life.

The typhoid epidemic was slowly receding. The hygiene regulations had been eased, the first people to recover were being discharged from the hospitals, Mr Horáček – actually, Uncle Jaroslav by now – was allowed to go to work again, Aunt Ivana went back to cooking in the school canteen and I went back to school.

At school everything was the same, yet different. I would sit next to Jarmilka Stejskalová and stare at the blackboard without seeing what was written there, I'd jot down numbers in my exercise book without understanding what they meant. I felt my schoolfriends' pitying glances and hated them for being able to go home to their mums, dads and siblings after school because I didn't have a home to go to. Jarmilka was at a loss as to what to say to me, so at least offered to share her elevenses at break. I just shook my head and kept staring straight ahead.

Over the course of the days that followed life resumed its course for most of our townspeople, with the sick and the dead becoming mere numbers in the hygiene mission's records. Altogether, some five hundred people had fallen ill and more than twenty had died.

I had no news of Aunt Hana but neither did I make any effort to find out anything about her. My mum's sister Hana Helerová was a stranger to me. More of a stranger than Aunt Ivana, who had shown me greater affection in the few weeks I had lived in her house than Aunt Hana had in my entire life.

I didn't even know if Hana was still alive. I understood that "condition very serious" was the first stage of dying. Without giving it much thought I assumed she had disappeared from my life just like my parents and siblings, and the Horáčeks didn't say anything so as not to make me feel more lonely.

Aunt Ivana was convinced that I needed to be kept busy so that I had no time to think and tried to involve me in doing the household chores. It seemed to work. I was still grieving, but the anxiety and fear that threatened to engulf me in the early days after the funeral started slowly to fade away. I was beginning to get used to the idea that I would stay with the Horáčeks.

After some time the Horáčeks concluded that the danger was over and it was safe for their two children to move back home from their grandparents. Aunt Ivana started making joyful preparations and I helped her change the bedding and do the laundry.

'Ida and Gustav will come back from their grandma soon and you'll all be great friends,' she promised as she sprinkled the clean pillowcases and duvet covers. We dipped our fingers in a bowl and sprinkled drops of water over the starched laundry as evenly as we could. Aunt Ivana was doing fine but I kept making huge puddles.

'My Ida has always wanted a little sister, she'll be so happy to have someone to play with. And Gustav is a lovely boy. I know you'll get on.' With a happy smile she handed me one end of a sprinkled sheet to help her stretch it out before passing it through a mangle. We grabbed the opposite corners and pulled away from each other. 'They will love you as their sister,' Aunt Ivana smiled, reaching for another sheet.

As it turned out, she couldn't have been more wrong.

I hadn't met Ida or Gustav before because the Horáčeks lived on the edge of town, in a street where single-storey villas were surrounded by pretty gardens and mature fruit trees. When the weather was nice Mum used to take us for walks to this part of town and always said that one day she'd love to live in a house with a garden like this. Sometimes she would stop to take a closer look at one of the houses as if she was seriously weighing up buying it, and say: 'This is where I'd put a hothouse.' Or: 'These trees need a trim.'

Dagmar and I would tag along just to get the obligatory family walk over with and be able to do something more fun, while Dad – when he came with us – would lean into the pram where little Otto was sitting and say: 'Come on, Rosa, our house isn't that bad either.' And Mum would invariably reply: 'That's true, but still, I wouldn't mind having a garden one day.'

The house wasn't the Horáčeks' own, they had been assigned the first-floor flat by the army because Uncle Jaroslav was a professional soldier, serving in the local barracks.

From afar the villa resembled a steamboat that had been washed up on the shore by a huge wave before it retreated into the sea. From one side it looked quite ordinary and rectangular, but the far corner was strangely rounded as if the architect had planned to build a turret there but had a change of heart. The villa had a flat roof and whitewashed walls. Seen from the street it was gleaming white but a closer look revealed that the plaster was dirty, going grey and peeling off in places. The windows were made of little glass squares, which looked like bars. On the ground floor a large glass door gave onto a garden. But nobody ever came out of that door, which was covered with thick drapes on the inside, something that made it seem sadly unnecessary.

An eccentric elderly couple lived on the ground floor. The man rarely went out because he was no longer able to get up from his armchair, and his wife only went out shopping and to church on Sundays. I wondered why she bothered going as she was quite deaf, and asked Aunt Ivana about it.

'What made you think Mrs Prášilová is deaf?'

'She never replies when I say hello to her. Or when you do.'

'But that's not because she's deaf. She just doesn't like us, that's why she won't talk to us.'

'Why doesn't she like us?'

I could tell from the look on Aunt Ivana's face that she didn't really feel like answering my question but eventually she said: 'The Prášils used to own this house but after the political takeover in 1948 they were told they could keep only the ground floor. The first floor was confiscated by the army and assigned to us. And the Prášils don't understand that it's not our fault. If it wasn't us living here, it would be someone else.'

That was what I liked about Aunt Ivana – she always answered my questions. When I had asked my mum something – for example, about my grandma or grandpa, or if Aunt Hana had always been so weird – she used to fob me off with "curiosity killed the cat" or some other grown-up nugget of wisdom, so I stopped asking.

Under different circumstances I would have made use of Aunt Ivana's openness and grilled her about everything, but the thought of Mum banished every question from my head.

Although Ida was only two months younger than me, she was more than half a head shorter. At first sight she was like a china doll, with a pellucid complexion, adorable pursed lips and hair braided into two neat plaits. She walked silently and looked so straight and perfect that I knew instantly we would never get along, even if those big eyes of hers, as blue as Aunt Ivana's, hadn't fixed me with such an icy look.

'So, this is Mira,' said Uncle Jaroslav following an excited welcome in the hallway, after Ida and Gustav had put down their bags and dashed into the kitchen, attracted by the delicious smell of jam buns. 'I told you about her,' he added when they stopped and gawped at me in silence.

'Hello,' I said, getting up from a chair and standing next to Aunt Ivana.

'That's my chair,' Ida said. 'That's where I always sit.'

'Ida!' her mother scolded her. 'It really doesn't matter who sits where.'

'See,' said Ida, turning to her older brother, the fourth-former Gustav, 'I told you so.'

Gustav gave me a blank look and turned to Aunt Ivana: 'Can I have a bun? What's the filling – poppy seed or plum jam?'

He stuffed himself with one bun after another and I wondered where it all went because he was so thin that clothes hung off him like from a hanger. As I stood next to Aunt Ivana, clinging to her hand like a safety net, watching this indifferent boy with cropped hair and his hostile china doll of a sister, I knew that my life had just taken another wrong turn.

'Gustav,' said Aunt Ivana. 'We have a surprise for you. Mira and I had emptied the cubbyhole and turned it into a lovely room for you – all your own. And Mira will share the children's room with Ida.'

'See,' said Ida again. 'I told you you'll end up in the cubbyhole.'

Aunt Ivana gave a sigh and gently freed her hand from mine.

The Horáčeks suggested that I switch schools to be in the same one as their children. I didn't want to, and Aunt Ivana admitted that I'd been through enough changes lately as it was. 'You can change schools from next September if you like,' she promised, but at the thought of being in the same form as the china doll Ida, I decided I wouldn't mind trudging to the other end of town.

Ida disliked me and didn't even try to hide it. She never spoke to me and whenever Gustav, who seemed to take no notice of me most of the time, happened to say a word to me, she was cross with him. She kept whispering to him, falling silent as soon as I came within earshot, and they would both eye me with suspicion.

Aunt Ivana came to read to us every night, but instead of sitting beside my bed she would now sit on a chair in the middle of the room. The first night, when her mother sat down next to me, Ida started to cry.

'You don't love us anymore, Mummy, you've forgotten us. You love her more now.'

'Ida, sweetheart,' Aunt Ivana said, 'you know that's not true. I love you both.'

'So why did you bring her here?'

'Mira doesn't have anyone,' Ivana said carefully.

'Why does she have to live with us, of all people? Say you love me more than you love her, say it.'

I could see Aunt Ivana was at a loss. She didn't know what to say. And I also spotted the spiteful glint in Ida's eye when Aunt Ivana stood up and said, 'All right, I'll sit in the middle.'

From then on Aunt Ivana took great care not to show me any favouritism, stroked my hair only when no one was looking and no longer talked to me as much as she used to. But one day, when Ida started to cry because Ivana had checked my homework before hers, she snapped at her: 'Now stop it! You're being a spoilt brat. Mira lives with us now, so you'd better get used to it.'

But Ida was determined not to get used to it.

'But Daddy said we didn't have to take her in, you could have taken her to the council. He said they would have put

her in a care home. Please Mum, let her go to a care home.'
She started sobbing loudly and Aunt Ivana grabbed her by
the hand, dragged her into the nursery, slammed the door
and left her there sobbing. I saw tears in Aunt Ivana's eyes,
too. I wondered if it hadn't also crossed her mind that this
might be the best solution for everyone.

The next day the elevenses in my schoolbag had been
broken into tiny crumbs, and the following day I found
some milk spilled on it. Then my school slippers went
missing and I had to go barefoot the whole morning at
school. The slippers were never found.

The buttons on my cardigan would get torn off and one
morning, as I was getting dressed for school, I found that a
hole had been cut in my tights. By now it was obvious to
Aunt Ivana that it couldn't have been a coincidence and she
gave Ida a proper dressing down. Ida denied everything, of
course, but to no avail. This time she got a thrashing.

I guessed that this development wouldn't help our
friendship. But I was so sick and tired of Ida by then that I
thought a bit of a spanking had served her right and
couldn't quite wipe a triumphant grin off my face. As I
glanced at Gustav I saw him giving me a suspicious look.

'What did I tell you,' Ida said to him, aggrieved, and ran
to the children's room, tears welling up in her eyes.

That evening, as I slipped under the duvet, I felt something
digging into my skin through my cotton nightie every time
I moved. I pulled the duvet away and discovered that my
bed was full of crumbs. Ida was clearly not giving up the
fight, but I had had enough and just climbed out of bed
and started collecting the crumbs into the palm of my hand
without a word. Just then Aunt Ivana walked in. 'What are
you doing?'

I said nothing.

'She's a pig, her bed is covered in breadcrumbs,' Ida said.

'It wasn't me,' I said.

'And she's a liar, to top it all,' Ida added.

Ivana didn't say anything, just gave a deep sigh, turned around and left. That night she didn't read us a story. I curled up on my side with my face to the wall and wished I could die and be with my Mum. Although Aunt Ivana said my family was in heaven, I found that hard to believe. Mum always used to say there was no such thing as heaven, that it was something people had invented. I really wished heaven did exist because I couldn't imagine that someone could just die and vanish without trace.

Later that night I was woken by a shadow flitting across my eyelids. I opened my eyes and stared into the darkness. Two figures were standing by my bed. I recognised them straight away. The china doll was holding a pillow in her hands, thrusting it at Gustav and whispering: 'You do it, you're stronger than me.'

'What do you want him to do?' I asked drowsily and the shadows disappeared. I switched on my bedside lamp and looked around. Ida was lying in bed and although her eyes were firmly shut, I could tell she wasn't asleep. The door had been left ajar and it was dark in the hallway. I turned off the light but the fright had startled me awake and I couldn't go back to sleep. I just lay there staring into the void. I couldn't wait for the morning to come.

Evil had crept upon me again. This time it wasn't lurking underground, looking for a random victim. This time it was hiding behind a delicate porcelain-doll face and was reaching out for me and me alone.

That year spring was very slow to arrive. It was the end of April but it was still grey and gloomy, as if the weather was in mourning for the victims of the typhoid epidemic. I spent a lot of time on my own because my school friends lived far away, Aunt Ivana was always tired after her shift in the school canteen, and Ida and Gustav avoided me. More and more often I saw them sitting with their heads together, whispering. Every now and then Gustav would raise his head, give me an inquisitive look, lower his head again and give a quiet reply.

One day they were sitting on a bench in the garden, deep in a conspiratorial conversation, and didn't notice that the window on the ground floor had been left open. That was when I got clear proof that Mrs Prášilová wasn't hard of hearing at all – on the contrary, her hearing was as sharp as a bat's. And what she heard either outraged her so much that she overcame her hatred of the Horáčeks, or confirmed her conviction that the Horáčeks were just a rabble, because she wasted no time, clambered up to the first floor on her feeble legs and informed Aunt Ivana and Uncle Jaroslav of what she had heard.

'She wanted her brother to push the little girl down the stairs,' she announced. 'She said she was like a cuckoo. She would push the fledglings out of the nest and keep it all to herself.' The old woman shook her head. 'What sort of people are you to have raised such nasty brats? You've got to be scared to be in your own house.' She turned on her heels, and holding on to the railing walked down the stairs gingerly, quietly repeating at each step: 'What nasty brats.'

Aunt Ivana started crying and Uncle Jaroslav shouted at her: 'It's all your fault! Because of your charitable spirit our children are about to turn into murderers. What are you doing to them? Why won't you let your own children enjoy a nice childhood?'

Aunt Ivana started to sob loudly, rushing past me to the bedroom and slamming its door. Without glancing at me Uncle Jaroslav lifted his cap off the hook and went out.

I was left standing in the hallway listening to the loud sobbing coming from the bedroom. I was terribly scared because I knew I couldn't stay at the Horáčeks' any longer.

I was scared they would take me to the council and have me placed in a care home. And the care home would be full of girls like Ida.

I curled up into a ball on my bed, weeping quietly and begging my mum in my mind not to leave me here alone, to come and fetch me. I must have fallen asleep for a while because I was woken by the doorbell ringing and Mum's voice in the hallway. 'I've come to get Mira.'

I leapt up and ran to the door. As Aunt Ivana stepped to one side, I spotted a gaunt figure in a big black cardigan.

Aunt Hana was back.

Chapter Five

A week after her sister's birthday party my Aunt Hana Helerová rose at seven, got dressed, made herself a cup of milky coffee and ate a slice of bread. After finishing her breakfast, she sat motionless for a while, staring into space, then started awake and, as her mind jolted back to the present, she cut a thin slice from last week's stale loaf and slipped it into the pocket of her black woolly cardigan.

She washed up thoroughly, wiped the table clean, swept the floor and looked around the kitchen to make sure everything was shipshape. Then she went to the bedroom to close the window and make the bed. As she plumped up the pillow she thought of her mother, my grandmother Elsa, who used to say that before making the bed one has to let it go completely cold.

She stroked the white duvet with her hand and suddenly the earth swayed beneath her. She took a deep breath, straightened up and headed to the pantry for a canvas bag. It was Monday, the day she normally went to the bakery next door to buy bread, and to the little shop at the bottom of the Square for a few other necessities.

These were the only places she ever went. She disliked people and distrusted them. The only exception was her sister whom she visited from time to time. Although Rosa dropped in on her nearly every day, she had a life of her own of which Hana was not a part.

Only on All Souls' Day, at Rosa's insistence, would she

accompany her sister to the cemetery to lay flowers on their mother's grave. She didn't see the point of going there more often as no one knew where their mother was actually buried anyway. What was the point of genuflecting in front of a name inscribed into cold marble in gold letters?

As she was taking the bag off the hook, she was overcome by sudden weakness. This didn't come as a surprise. Breathing difficulties, darkness before her eyes, trembling legs and arms, stomach cramps – none of this was new. She had come to terms with her ailments and grown accustomed to the idea that while other women had a husband and children, what she had were her illnesses.

She sat down and waited for the moment of faintness to pass. It always disappeared sooner or later. Out of habit she reached into her pocket, broke off a bit of bread crust and stuck it into her mouth. She felt queasy, her head started spinning and the kitchen swayed around in wild circles. Gingerly she stood up, felt her way from the table to the wall holding on to the furniture, and inched her way towards the bedroom. The swaying worsened, tossing her from side to side and making her knees wobble. Finally, her hands touched the side rail and she slumped down onto the bed she had carefully made. She reached it at the last moment before her mind clouded over and fell through into another world.

All of a sudden, she was no longer at home but on a train. The train was hooting, pitching and tossing, ice-cold air streamed in through its open windows and Hana started to shiver with cold. All she was aware of was the cold and the rhythmic clanking of the iron wheels hurtling down the tracks and carrying her to a place of no return. Then someone turned the lights off on the train and everything was swallowed by darkness. Figures emerged from the gloom and spoke to her, dragging her to a place she never wanted to return to. She stopped up her ears, running away from the figures, but there was nowhere to hide.

Later that evening the woman at the bakers' remembered that Helerová, the peculiar old hag who couldn't even say hello properly, hadn't come to buy her bread today, but her thoughts swiftly moved to the twenty-three crowns missing from the till at the end of the day.

The assistant at the little grocery shop didn't miss Hana Helerová either, even though she used to come regularly every Monday morning after nine. What vexed her far more was that her customers kept touching up the goods despite notices from the Department of Hygiene and despite being repeatedly told not to, forcing her to keep an eye on the chaotic scenes and tell them off in case she got into trouble.

The townspeople were absorbed by their own problems and nobody noticed that the windows in the flat of their neighbour, Hana Helerová, had remained dark and the curtains had been left open for two nights in a row.

As I climbed the stairs to her flat, Hana was delirious, feverishly wrestling with her demons. She was not aware of the arrival of the chubby doctor or the drive to the hospital. She was standing in the doorway and only a few short steps separated her from the invisible wall, on the other side of which she would be reunited with her loved ones and would finally learn where the lives of her mother Elsa and her grandparents had come to an end.

While I was hanging around the pavement, in what was then called Stalingrad Square, looking out for the tall figure of my saviour, Aunt Hana was being driven to the district hospital. The isolation ward was so crowded that some of the sick had to be left lying in corridors. The hospital staff were just as exhausted and terrified as their patients, and the ambulance was sent straight from the reception to the hospital in the nearby town of Hradiště. The chubby doctor got off, after concluding that his presence was not necessary as this patient was half dead and, unlike many others, beyond help. The sick woman had been so enfeebled by running a high temperature for two days, without any food or drink, that he held out little hope for her.

As I desperately fumbled for keys in the dark entrance hall of our house, Aunt Hana was being admitted to the hospital in Hradiště. The nurses took off her black cardigan, dress, stockings and underwear, stuffed everything into a bag and sent it off to be disinfected. Then they washed her, put a cotton nightdress on her, forced some sweet tea down her throat and took her to a ward to await her death.

That night, as I went to sleep in a tiny cubbyhole on the first floor of a villa that resembled a boat, the thought that I would never again return home never even crossed my mind.

In a small hospital room she shared with two other dying people, Aunt Hana was fleeing from her nightmares. Over and over again, she warded off arms that tried to push her out of a railway carriage, she was desperate to grip the metal doors but there was no strength left in her fingers. Her whole body was one gigantic ache, tears of despair streamed down her cheeks, her mouth was distended by fear and a single thought pounded in her head: No, anywhere but that place again, I'd rather die than go back there.

Then someone gave her a push and Hana dropped onto a cold, concrete platform. Mustering all her strength, she scrambled up to her feet and hobbled away from the train. The screaming behind her was still loud but when she turned around, she no longer saw anyone. She knew that in order to escape she had to get away as fast as she could. The door of the railway station stood open and Hana started running down the long hall looking for an exit. But all the doors were locked and all the windows barred. Her strength was fading fast. Her legs were weak, her knees wobbled and her hands trembled. She stumbled from one door to another until one finally gave way.

She found herself in a small, white-tiled room. There was a row of sinks on the right and toilet cubicles on the left. The window in the middle of the far wall was open and there were no bars on it. She slammed the door shut from the inside but could still hear her pursuers' voices. She knew they were on the other side of the door, would burst in any minute and capture her. She had only one option left.

She took a chair standing in the corner, dragged it under the window, climbed onto it, sat on the windowsill and threw one leg over. As she looked out of the window, she saw the outline of the Meziříčí Square in the darkness below. All she had to do was run across the Square and she would soon be in the safety of her home. There she would lock the door and never let anyone in.

She threw her other leg over, slid down to the ledge running the length of the building and slowly, pressing her back into the rough wall, edged away from the window. Only after taking a few steps did she look down. The Square was gone. A bottomless pit opened beneath her feet. She closed her eyes but it was too late. An invisible force grabbed hold of her, dragging her down into the depths.

Hana's bed stood at the far end of the room, separated from the door by the beds of two gravely ill women. Once every hour the nurse would look in, listen to the laboured breathing and moaning of the dying patients. But the ward was filled to the rafters with people who were in greater need of her help, and the nurse stayed outside and didn't notice Hana wasn't in her bed.

It wasn't until early morning that a boilerman leaving after his night shift nearly tripped over the lifeless body of a woman. Once he got over the initial shock, he sprinted to the emergency room on the ground floor, knocked on the door and barged in. 'You've got a corpse outside,' he stuttered. 'Looks like she fell out of your window.'

The sleepy doctor Jarolím whose nightshift was about to finish and who had managed to snatch only an hour's sleep after dealing with his last patient of the day, knew instantly from the boilerman's terrified look that this time the old man wasn't drunk, although that was not an infrequent occurrence. He gestured to the nurse to call an orderly, and they both hurried outside.

Hana was lying on her back, spreadeagled, her nightdress rolled up and her white-haired head turned to one side. Without checking if she was alive the doctor grabbed her under the arms and with the help of the orderly hoisted the stone-cold, emaciated body onto a stretcher, threw a sheet over it and carried it indoors. Then they pushed the boilerman out of the door and under threat of sacking forbade him to tell anyone what he had just witnessed.

'You think I don't know what a medical secret is? I won't breathe a word,' swore the boilerman but by midday, under the influence of several shots that he had imbibed to get over the shock, he forgot all about his promise and recounted his dreadful experience in all its gory detail not just to his wife and neighbours but also to his pals in the pub by the railway station.

Dr Jarolím had been working in the hospital for years. In the course of his long practice his idea of the virtues and benefits of the medical profession had been crushed by his daily routine, but he still loved his job. It was his stubbornness, his main characteristic, that made him fight the fate already imprinted on the gaunt white-haired woman's half-dead face. He wasn't prepared to let her die, as suggested by the nurses and some of his colleagues, weary of being blamed for letting a patient fall out of a window, which might be used against them sooner or later.

'It's pointless,' they said. 'She was already condemned to death when she was brought in.'

Dr Jarolím examined the bony female body marked by

the kind of suffering no living being should ever endure and, as he rolled up the sleeve of her grubby nightdress, he detected a faint pulse. He moved Hana's head from side to side, felt her arms and legs and immediately ordered an X-ray. He personally accompanied the gurney to the lift, pushed it all the way to the X-ray room and got them to open up by banging anxiously on the door. Then he urged the X-ray operators to work faster, as if it was in their power to speed up chemical processes, and after thoroughly examining the images he concluded that this person with the hair of an old woman and a martyred body was, in fact, no more than thirty-five years old, and that the fall from the second floor resulted only in fractures of both shinbones, her right arm, and a few broken ribs.

It was nearly midday by the time he personally took Hana, covered in plaster and still unconscious, back to the isolation ward and handed her over to the consultant with the wry comment: 'She's not likely to run away from you anytime soon.'

'You ought to know, doctor, that people who run a high fever...'

'Yes, I know,' Jarolím interrupted. 'But if she dies, I'm not going to cover for you, even though we are colleagues.'

Whenever a patient lost their battle with typhoid and the nurse covered their body with a sheet and drove it away, fear made the patients of every faith and every political hue turn to the One in whose existence they suddenly wanted to believe. Clasping their hands together, they implored Him to let them be the ones He spared and return to their old lives.

After a few days Aunt Hana's fever subsided, she regained consciousness and started taking in her surroundings. But the plaster on her right hand prevented her from clasping her hands together. She wouldn't have prayed anyway. She couldn't understand how you could ask something of a being who didn't exist at best and who, at worst, was the one to have visited the suffering on them in the first place or – being omnipotent – failed to stop it.

As the typhoid epidemic abated, fewer and fewer people were dying and the patients were gradually discharged. Hana, who everyone thought beyond hope a few weeks ago, was also recovering fast, but was not yet able to look after herself as her legs were imprisoned in a carapace of plaster.

Although she had no news of her sister's family, she didn't think it strange that no one had come to visit her throughout her illness as no visitors were allowed in the isolation ward. She couldn't remember how she came by her fractures, learning only gradually, from the other patients more than from hospital staff, how she had roamed the hospital corridors in a fever and fell out of the second-floor window trying to escape her imaginary pursuers. Since no one had actually seen her wandering about or falling out, several versions emerged. Some believed that Hana wanted to kill herself while others claimed the opposite, that she was the victim of a crime. Another version involved supernatural beings, since many of the sick people, like Hana, also suffered from delusions and were not sure which of their recollections were real and which were just a dream. Fear spread among the patients and soon they would go to the toilet only in pairs. Eventually Dr Jarolím had to intervene and give Hana the official explanation of what had really happened.

As it became clear that she had not the slightest intention of blaming anyone but herself for her fall, the nurses were extremely grateful and started looking after the taciturn woman as if she were their dearest friend.

It wasn't until mid-May that the fractures healed sufficiently for her legs to bear the weight of Hana's skinny body, that she could move her arm, even if not straighten it out completely, and her ribs grew back together, letting her turn to one side at night and sigh deeply during the day. Hana had long ago learned not to dwell on her feelings and mastered the art of forgetting her past and not thinking about the future. Only now and then a sudden memory would flash up and catch her unawares, enveloping her like a dark blanket and making her freeze on the spot. She had trained herself not to get attached to objects or people, which helped to make her hospital stay bearable, and also not to expect too much when she returned home.

An ambulance drove her all the way to her house. She gave the driver a nod by way of goodbye. He slammed the door shut and drove off, relieved to be rid of the weird female. He liked chatting to his passengers, but this one sat there the whole time without moving or uttering a word. If she hadn't sat up straight, he would have thought she had died. He kept glancing in her direction and found her so disconcerting that he nearly crashed the ambulance several times. He decided never to let anyone sit in the passenger seat again. Let them stew in the back.

Hana clutched her bag and started towards the house. It didn't occurr to her to relish the spring air or to look around the Square of her hometown. She wasn't looking for news, wasn't interested in finding out how her neighbours and acquaintances had coped with the epidemic. She headed straight for her first-floor flat and opened the windows to get rid of the stale air. Seeing the unmade bed and the withered clivia, the only plant she owned, a birthday present her sister had brought her years ago, she wondered for the first time why Rosa had never dropped by. She sat down at the kitchen table staring at the canvas bag that was in the exact same place she had left it almost three months ago, and started to think.

Rosa was the only relative she had left – apart from her sister's annoying offspring, that is. She was a few years younger and many years ago their mother had got it into her head that Rosa was sickly and constantly fretted about her, entrusting her to Hana's care for most of her childhood. But then things took a different turn. Once the two of them were the only ones left in this world, Hana had no strength left to look after herself, let alone anyone else. But Rosa suddenly had masses of strength and love to spare. She loved her children and her husband and still had plenty of love left for her sister. She looked after Hana as if she were her fourth child, even though she didn't want to be looked after at all. Hana refused to let herself be in thrall to her sister's feelings and insisted on keeping herself to herself. But Rosa wouldn't be pushed away and imposed herself, enmeshing her in her love and not allowing her to cut herself off from the world completely and sink into a liberating indifference.

Hana looked around the floor, furniture and windowsills with their grey layer of dust and at that moment it dawned on her why she had never received any letters in hospital, why no one had enquired about her condition or sent her a basket of fruit. She felt a sharp twinge of pain, her chest burst open, its contents spilling onto the floor like sand from a torn sack, and everything that bound her to the world slowly evaporated.

She realised that Rosa was dead.

She got up and left the flat, walking faster than she had done for years. Her sore legs carried her down the stairs, across the paved Square, passing the plague column, the House of the Twelve Apostles, and turned into the narrow alley leading to the river. The watchmaker's shopfront was dirty, the hands on the faces of the dusty clocks not moving. She pressed down the wrought-iron door handle, rattling the locked door. She tried again and then looked around the street helplessly. She thought she saw someone peer out of a window in the house across the street, then quickly pull their head back.

For a moment she stood there uncertainly, then crossed the street. 'Hello,' she resolved to call out towards the window.

No one appeared so she banged her fist on the door. A bespectacled face appeared among freshly planted geraniums.

'Hello,' she repeated the greeting. 'I'm Mrs Karasková's sister.' She stopped to think what to say next. 'Do you know where I might find her?'

'You'll have to ask at the council, I suppose,' a woman's voice replied. The eyes behind the spectacles examined her inquisitively and Hana still felt their gaze on her back when she turned into the street leading back to the Square.

And there, in the building with the beautiful vaulted ceilings, a registrar pushed a long alphabetical list towards her and left the room. The piece of paper contained the names of those who had fallen ill during the epidemic, the names of the hospitals they had been taken to and the dates of admission and discharge. Twenty names had little crosses next to the dates.

This is how Hana Helerová learned that Rosa, Karel and their two children had died. When the registrar returned, Hana was still sitting at the table staring at her sister's typed name. Her eyes were dry and her head completely empty. No sound reached her, there was just this icy coldness growing inside her chest and spreading throughout her body. She stood up.

'Ehm, there's also the issue of the funeral,' the registrar said. 'They were buried at the town's expense because we didn't know when... if... But now that a next of kin has come forward...' She cleared her throat uneasily. 'It's the law, you see... These bills need to be paid.' She pushed an envelope towards Hana.

Without favouring her with a glance, Hana left the envelope on the table and headed for the door.

'Very well then, we'll put it in the post for you,' the registrar shouted after her.

Hana closed the door. She didn't even think to ask about me, her only living relative.

Chapter Six

May 1954

Jaroslav Horáček had known he wanted to be a soldier since the age of four. He had a clear memory of sitting high up on his father's shoulders and watching the military parade that marked the first anniversary of the foundation of the new Czechoslovak Republic, and was sure all those people in the packed Square could only envy him. He was so spellbound by the straight lines of the soldiers and their perfectly coordinated movements that he marched all the way home, continuing to march when he went shopping with his mother and, despite his parents' protests, he also marched to church with them on Sundays. When I was still living with the Horáčeks and Uncle Jaroslav was in a good mood, he would sometimes tell us at dinner, laughing, how wonderful it was to hear his little feet echo beneath the stone arches. 'But then my dad said that the statue of the Virgin Mary had frowned at me. That stopped me stomping my feet, and every time I was about to enter the church I would start bawling. And that's how I became an atheist.' I didn't know what an atheist was but thought it was some kind of military rank because Uncle Jaroslav did indeed become a soldier. But first he was apprenticed to his uncle, a butcher.

Come to think of it, that was quite a suitable grounding for a soldier. Whenever meat was on the menu at the Horáčeks, Uncle Jaroslav was in charge of carving. He would pick up a knife – always the biggest one he could find in the drawer – and I had to look away because in my head his butcher's profession got mixed up with his military one, conjuring up strange fantasies in my mind's eye.

'And then I was called up and I stayed on in the army. Because the army will always look after you.' Whenever we heard these words, we all knew that the next statement would be aimed at Gustav, and we turned to look at him. Gustav pretended he wasn't in the room, withdrew into himself, and his eyes took on an impassive expression similar to Aunt Hana's.

'The army teaches you discipline and becomes your second family.'

The more worked up Uncle Jaroslav got, the more Gustav would disappear into his shell, in anticipation of the inevitable conclusion. 'I didn't get a chance to go to military academy, Gustav. But I'm sure you will make an officer one day.' And he patted his son on the back, ignoring Gustav's lack of enthusiasm. He was probably hoping that by repeating his wish every night he would wear down his son's resistance, the way a drop of water wears down a stone over the years.

Aunt Ivana didn't feel quite the same way about the army and I was fairly certain that the thought of Gustav becoming a soldier didn't particularly appeal to her. But she didn't want to argue with her husband and have him repeat for the hundredth time that everything they had they owed to the army.

As far as I could tell Aunt Ivana was the only person – at least of those I knew – who benefited from the war in any way. This was because before the war Uncle Jaroslav had served as a non-commissioned officer, and as such he needed the permission of the army to get married. And he wasn't going to get permission because his chosen bride didn't have a big enough dowry. But after the country was invaded by the Germans, Uncle Jaroslav left the army and went back to work for his uncle as a butcher. And since butchers could marry whoever they liked, he was finally able to marry Ivana and make her Mrs Horáčková. After the war the butcher Horáček went back to being sergeant Horáček but times had changed and he was a married man now, so in due course the army allocated him a flat on the first floor of a bourgeois villa, and he returned to marching with his comrades-in-arms.

I have no idea what else his job involved, but I do know what he did the day he learned that his two children were planning to push me off the stairs. He put on his flat cap and marched in the direction of the Square. When he got to Aunt Hana's house he hesitated for a moment, not quite sure if what he was about to do was the right thing, but then resolutely ran up the stairs. I'm sure he took two steps at a time because he was extremely proud of his fitness, working out whenever he got a chance.

After he rang the bell, he had to wait for a while. Aunt Hana never had any visitors and must have thought someone had got the wrong door and didn't even bother to answer it.

Jaroslav Horáček rang the bell again and this time he heard muffled noises from inside. Aunt Hana awoke from her half-sleep, pushed the chair aside and made for the door. For a fraction of a second she thought it was her sister Rosa but then she remembered that Rosa was dead and would never come again. And unlike me she wasn't foolish enough to think it was just a bad dream, so she was in no hurry.

Jaroslav Horáček had known Hana many years earlier, and although he had heard that she had turned into a weirdo, the sight of the crone dressed in black who answered the door terrified him.

After my mother Rosa died, Hana would only leave the house if she ran out of bread. She stopped buying anything else. She spent all day sitting at the kitchen table, breaking off a piece of crust every now and then and putting it in her mouth. She had always been skinny but had put on some weight during her long stay in hospital. By now, however, she had lost all of it; her black clothes hung on her, her cheeks were hollow and her eyes dead.

'It was the look in her eyes, that's what terrified me most,' Uncle Jaroslav would say later, but what hit him first was the foul smell coming from the flat, which made him recoil. 'The first thing that occurred to me was that we can't let Mira live there,' he would say.

But the look in Hana's eyes suddenly changed. 'Why are you here?'

At this point in the story Jaroslav Horáček's voice turned belligerent. 'What was I supposed to say? I told her we had Mira living with us and that she couldn't stay any longer. She should look after her, or take her to the council and let them do whatever they wanted with her. We're not a care home, after all.'

He turned on his heels to get away as fast as possible. He had to get away from the acrid smell coming from the doorway, and the black crone and her dead eyes.

'Wait a minute.'

He stopped.

'Where is she?'

He gave her the address. Then he ran for the pub. He didn't want to be there when the black Hana turned up on their doorstep.

I imagine that the day Aunt Hana came to fetch me, Ivana Horáčková was as surprised and as terrified as I was. She stood in the door staring at Aunt Hana as if she knew that she had to say something but couldn't think of anything. Standing behind her I knew only one thing for sure – that I didn't want to go with Aunt Hana but that I had no choice because the Horáčeks wouldn't let me stay with them any longer.

Aunt Hana shifted from one foot to another. Her broken legs were still swollen and sore. She looked at me as if she had never seen me before and inspected me carefully. It occurred to me that she wanted to see if I bore any resemblance to her sister Rosa, now that she was going to be stuck with me. In those days all I had inherited from my mum, I thought, were my eyes. Only in later years did I start to detect some of her features in my face and now I have some idea of what she might have looked like had she been given a chance to grow older.

'Let's go.' Hana's voice sounded so tired that Ivana Horáčková stopped being scared and forced herself to speak up.

'Hana, I'm so sorry about what's happened...'

'Let's go,' Aunt Hana said again, this time sounding crestfallen and impatient. As if she didn't want to hear what Ivana was about to say.

'I wish I could have...'

Back then I thought she was referring to the death of my loved ones, that she wanted to express her condolences to Aunt Hana. It wasn't until much later that I understood what she was really talking about.

All of a sudden Aunt Hana straightened up and anger replaced the despair emanating from her emaciated, black-clad body. She pounced on me, grabbing me by the shoulders. Her bony fingers dug into my skin painfully, the force of my aunt's rage dragging me away. 'You certainly could have...' I heard my mum's voice screaming from Hana's lips. 'You could have!'

I was so frightened I started to cry. Even life with Ida and Gustav seemed preferable to living with Aunt Hana. At least I knew them well and was aware that I couldn't expect anything nice from them. But what could I expect from crazy Hana? I kept hoping Aunt Ivana would say I could stay with them. She must have known that Hana Helerová wasn't quite right in the head. But Ivana Horáčková just stood there, covering her face with her hands. I stumbled along by Hana's side, feeling the same despair I saw reflected in Hana's face for reasons I could not understand.

Outside the house Aunt Hana slowed down and let go of me. Exhausted by this brief altercation she headed for the house in the Square at the other end of town with slow, painful steps. I followed her obediently. What else could I do? I didn't have the courage to tell her that I had left all my stuff at the Horáčeks – everything from my toothbrush and pyjamas to my school bag. We didn't exchange a single word throughout the walk. Back then I thought that Aunt Hana was angry but now I know she was as frightened as I was. Barely able to look after herself she had just lumbered herself with a little girl.

We made a strange pair. A weary woman in a shapeless black cardigan, long skirt, lace-up boots and headscarf pushed halfway down her forehead, leading a tearful nine-year-old girl with dishevelled hair and dressed only in a light button-through pinafore and house slippers on her feet. By the time we reached my aunt's house I was shivering with cold.

On the first floor of the house in the Square Aunt Hana sat down at the table and, although I was numb with cold, I rushed to throw open all the windows to get rid of the stale air that was making me nauseous.

'I don't have my toothbrush or my pyjamas,' I said to Hana's back.

She didn't move.

'I have to go to school tomorrow but my bag is still at the Horáčeks',' I continued.

Aunt Hana reached into her pocket and placed a slice of bread on the table. Even from where I was standing, I could see bits of black wool clinging to it. I turned to the window that I had always envied Aunt Hana for, wrapped a bedspread from the kitchen couch around my shoulders, sat down on the windowsill and watched the people criss-crossing the Square.

In the morning I was woken by the cold. I was lying on the kitchen sofa, its springs digging into my ribs. I was wearing the same pinafore I had on when I arrived at my aunt's flat and covered only by the crocheted bedspread I had wrapped myself in before falling asleep. The windows were still open and the cold morning air was streaming in, chafing against my skin. I got up, closed the windows and curled up on the sofa again to keep at least a bit warm. The clock in the kitchen had stopped months ago but from the noises in the Square I guessed it was time to get up and go to school. This must have been the first time in my life I was keen to go to school.

The church clock started to chime and I counted seven strokes. I thought I heard some rustling next door, then the door opened and after a while Aunt Hana emerged.

She paused in surprise when she saw me as if she'd forgotten I was there, and gaped at me, just like I did at her. I couldn't tear my eyes off her because this was the first time I saw her in something that wasn't black. She was wearing a long white canvas nightshirt which made her look even skinnier and more wretched than her black cardigan. Her white hair was plaited and the only thing that was black were her eyes. She must have had a wash the night before because she no longer smelled so awful, but I wasn't sure as I didn't dare take a deep breath.

'You've got to go to school,' she said.

Coming from someone as confused as Aunt Hana this was a surprisingly sensible statement.

'I can't go to school like this,' I sniffled because at that moment I was genuinely sorry about it. 'I don't have any shoes, or my school bag.'

Aunt Hana turned on the stove and put on a kettle to

make tea. She found a cup in a cupboard and stared at it intently. 'You can go and pick it up in the afternoon.'

I realised it was me she was talking to about my stuff, not the cup, and pictured myself dragging the heavy wooden suitcase and my school bag across town. But I didn't dare object. I moved over to the kitchen table, still wrapped in the crocheted bedspread. Aunt Hana pushed a basket with stale bread towards me. 'It's Monday, I'll go shopping today.'

Although the bread was old, at least it didn't come from her pocket and wasn't all crumbled with bits of wool stuck to it. As I hadn't eaten anything since Sunday lunch, I didn't protest. Aunt Hana went off to get changed, then she made the tea and sat down across the table from me. I tried not to stare as she broke off bits of bread, dunked the crust in the cup and put it in her mouth. This is what all my mornings will be like from now on, I thought to myself, as Aunt Hana swept the crumbs into the palm of her hand and raised it to her mouth.

Not a word was uttered during breakfast. My aunt had finished eating now but she kept sitting there, somehow looking right through me in that strange way of hers. I didn't know what to do so I picked up the empty cup, carried it to the kitchen sink and curled up on the sofa again. My aunt suddenly got up, poured some water into a tub and started washing the dishes. There wasn't a lot but it must have sat in the sink for quite some time. I shuffled over to her and picked up a tea towel. She gave me a surprised look but said nothing. Then she wiped the table, swept the floor and disappeared into the bedroom.

I took my time drying the dishes to keep myself busy but even so I was finished long before my aunt reappeared. Without looking at me she took a canvas bag off a hook in the hallway and made for the door. She reached for the handle and that was probably when she remembered that she wasn't alone.

She turned around and gave me one of her strange looks. 'All right, I'll get some potatoes,' she announced as if this decision had been the outcome of a lengthy discussion, and opened the door. A big suitcase sat outside with my red schoolbag on top of it. I was relieved not to have to lug all the heavy stuff across town but at the same time it dawned on me that my move to Aunt Hana's was now irreversible. The Horáčeks had packed my suitcase and brought it all the way to the door so that they wouldn't have to see me or Hana again.

'I didn't even say thank you to Aunt Ivana.' I slipped past Hana and dragged the suitcase inside. I only just managed it. I wouldn't have been able to carry it all the way from the Horáčeks for sure.

Aunt Hana said nothing. She just gave a contemptuous snort and closed the door behind her.

I unloaded my things onto the sofa and wondered if there was anywhere I could put my underwear, tights, tops and dresses. And whether I would find room for the odd toy and book Aunt Ivana had let me bring. Most of my things and all my winter clothes had stayed in the old house because – as Aunt Ivana put it – the Horáčeks' flat wasn't infinitely expandable.

I made use of my aunt's absence to peek into every drawer and cupboard in the kitchen, look around her bedroom and explore the pantry, and was surprised to see how little she had. The sideboard contained two pots, and a few plates and cups. All the drawers except one were empty and the only thing hanging in the wardrobe was a coat and a couple of cardigans – both black, of course. A thin slice of bread was hidden in the bedside table drawer. A shelf in the pantry held canvas bags filled with pearl barley, flour and dried peas. I pushed the peas into a far corner, to be on the safe side, and walked from the kitchen to the hallway to find out what was hidden behind the wooden doors.

There were four doors in the dark hallway. The one facing the front door was never closed and led straight into the big kitchen. But opposite the bathroom door on the left there was a mysterious white door. That used to be Grandma's room, that was the only thing I had learned during our rare visits to Aunt Hana's flat. Only Grandma's because Grandma's husband, my Grandpa Ervin, had died when my mum and aunt were still very young. I could never understand why I wasn't allowed to take a look inside. Surely Grandma Elsa wouldn't have minded, seeing as she was dead, but my mum would always give me a warning slap on the back and say that we mustn't remind Aunt Hana of Grandma because it would make her sad. As if Aunt Hana had ever been jolly.

I tiptoed over to the door of the forbidden room and quietly pressed down the handle. It was locked. I gave the door an angry kick and then went back to the table. Aunt Hana found me sitting there like a good girl.

She came over to the table and started to unload the shopping. A big bag of potatoes – at least three kilos – some celeriac, onions, carrots, and another bag of peas. I gave her a quizzical look. 'Vitamins are good for you,' she said. 'I mean for children,' she added and took a loaf of bread and a bottle of milk from the bag. She looked around helplessly as if hoping someone would tell her what to do next. I was beginning to understand why Aunt Hana was so skinny and why my mum would sometimes bring her cooked meals in a pot.

While I was stowing the vegetables away in the pantry, shoving the peas into the darkest corner again, my aunt sat down at the table and buried her head in her hands. I wasn't so scared of her anymore, but what frightened me was her helplessness.

'We will manage,' I said, more to convince myself, and sat down next to her. I was wary of touching her because I remembered that my mum wasn't allowed to do that either.

A sigh escaped from under the hands hiding her face. Hana nodded.

'So why are you sighing?' I asked.

Aunt Hana sniffled, took her hands from her eyes and looked at me. I was annoyed by a droplet slowly rolling down from her nose. I was tempted to give her my handkerchief but it didn't seem appropriate.

My aunt remained silent for a while and then said: 'Because now I can't die anymore.'

Chapter Seven

May 1954 - September 1955

Aunt Hana got up, went over to the cupboard and found a key. After holding it in her hand for a while, as if she couldn't remember which door it opened, she bent over, gave a sigh, and headed for Grandma's room. I slid off my chair double quick and followed her.

My aunt unlocked the door and without looking around walked straight to the window and threw both panes wide open. I was disappointed. Why had they been so secretive about this room? I saw a bed by the wall, next to it a wardrobe, and two chests of drawers opposite. No carpet, curtains, doilies or pictures. Just yellow walls and a window opening onto the courtyard. While my aunt went to fetch bed linen, I had a quick peek in the drawers. At the bottom of one I found some starched crochet doilies sticking out of their paper wrapping. Other than that, there was nothing, nothing at all.

'Why was this room locked?' I asked but my aunt either didn't hear me or her mind was elsewhere again. I was getting used to the fact that there wouldn't be much chatting with Aunt Hana.

I brought my things in and when everything was unpacked, it filled three whole drawers. My favourite teddy bear, whose eyes Ida had gouged out and Aunt Ivana had sewn back, found its place on the bed. Then I sat down next to it and surveyed my new home. The third in a very short space of time.

I had the whole room to myself, but it didn't make me happy at all.

I took me several days to persuade Aunt Hana to come with me to our old house in the little alley leading to the church. I wanted to take a few things I needed badly and for which there was no room at the Horáčeks'. Things like my own cup, a walking doll with blinking eyes and hair you could brush, which I got last Christmas, and an almost new set of paints. I was also planning to take Dagmar's toy dishes, which I could play with only in secret, when she was out, because ever since I broke a miniature cup she wouldn't let me play with it. But now, seeing the tiny cups on the shelf in our room, suddenly I didn't feel like taking it anymore and started to understand why Aunt Hana had kept Grandma Elsa's room under lock and key and had rarely gone in.

I stuffed my underwear, pyjamas and winter clothes into a big canvas shopper and locked the door of the house which still belonged to me but was no longer my home.

It probably wasn't a good idea to go back there because the short time we spent in the old flat above the watchmaker's made me really sad and my aunt, who stayed on the stairs waiting for me, stopped responding to me again after we came back to her kitchen, and just sat there staring into space.

But apart from that, I have to say that Aunt Hana made a real effort. For supper we usually had potatoes with milk, or potato pancakes, or potato dumplings or something else made of potatoes, some vegetables or pulses – except peas – and when I noticed my aunt gazing at her battered wallet I realised it was not so much a lack of imagination as a shortage of money. I ate lunch at the school canteen, so I didn't go hungry, but Aunt Hana had to make do with bread and potatoes.

It troubled me to see how little she cared for herself.

I felt very self-conscious walking around town with my aunt dressed in her shapeless black cardigan and worn-out shoes, and always tried to find an excuse to avoid going out with her. I was embarrassed when people turned their heads after us, some even looked away in disgust and others – especially children – shouted abuse at us. But she didn't care in the least.

'Why do you always wear black?' I would pester her. 'And when you go to a shop, why can't you at least say hello? Why do you just sit here like this?'

She didn't reply. My questions washed off her like water off oilcloth, and after a while I stopped asking.

Our financial difficulties weighed on us more and more. My aunt didn't have a job. Nor could she have had one. What kind of work could she do? A shop assistant? I tried to imagine what it would look like if she suddenly froze in the middle of a shop and stared straight ahead. A teacher? Who would let a weirdo like this look after their children? A cleaner or cook? She was as weak as a kitten.

She would clutch at her heart, her back or her stomach and sometimes her breathing was so laboured I was scared she would choke. I don't think she would have been able to hold down a job even if she hadn't been out of her mind. It was my dad who used to say she was out of her mind, but my mum would always stick up for her. 'She's not out of her mind,' she would argue, 'she is just mentally exhausted.' Living with Aunt Hana I tended to agree with my dad.

Aunt Hana was getting a small pension but after a woman from the council, who sported the tallest top knot I had ever seen, came for a home visit, she also started to receive some money for me and things became a little less tight. Although my aunt did not spend any more on food for herself, she made sure to always set some money aside in case I needed a new pair of tights or crayons. I remember the day the lady from the council turned up at our house as if it was yesterday. By then I had been living with Aunt Hana for three months. I had almost got used to being there and was scared that I might have to move again.

Living with Aunt Hana had its pros and cons. Her cooking wasn't particularly varied, and she was too eccentric for a normal chat. But after a while the fact she wasn't responding stopped bothering me. I would sit at the table opposite her and prattle on about every detail of my day at school: who said what, what Jarmilka Stejskalová had for her elevenses – about anything that came to my mind, really. My aunt never interrupted me although sometimes she got up and went to her bedroom.

Another advantage was that she never told me what I must and must not do. Had I decided to skip school or go barefoot, she wouldn't even have noticed. But surprisingly enough, I never did any such thing.

Perching on the edge of a chair, the lady from the council put on her glasses and looked around the kitchen. She must have been satisfied with what she saw as my aunt kept the place clean and tidy. She probably expected to be offered some tea at the very least, but Hana just shifted her chair to face the visitor and sat there waiting in silence. The official spread her papers out on the table and began.

She explained the guidelines, listed the laws, asked some questions that she answered herself, enquired why we hadn't applied for orphan's benefit for me and completed the form for us there and then, pushing it in front of my aunt to sign, while the two of us just stared at her. I think my aunt's face bore the same uncomprehending expression as mine, so it didn't strike the officer as odd.

After a monologue lasting fifteen minutes, from which I remember only that I could stay at my aunt's and that the postwoman would deliver our money on the fifteenth of every month, the woman gathered up her papers, briskly sprang to her feet and pinched my cheek. 'So, you like it here at your auntie's?'

I started to open my mouth to answer but the officer patted me on the cheek and answered herself: 'Of course you do, my dear,' and was gone.

I turned to my aunt to tell her what was on my mind but she got up and headed for her bedroom, which I took to mean that she had had enough contact with other people for the day and needed a rest. It was raining outside so I took a cushion to the windowsill and brought my book about the orphan girl Pollyanna from the bottom drawer in my bedroom. This was the book I turned to whenever I was feeling sad. I loved it so much I couldn't face returning it to the library and told the librarian I had lost it. I hoped she wouldn't be too cross if I looked sufficiently contrite. She wasn't and let me get away with a fine, commenting that these things happen. I paid the fine out of my school lunch money and survived for a few days solely on bread, which made me feel as if I had atoned for my offence and no longer had to feel guilty.

I sat down on the cushion, found my favourite chapter in which Pollyanna explains the rules of her "glad game" and wished that my life might take a similar turn for the better, that I might be able to see only the good in the world and that Aunt Hana would, by some miracle, turn into a loving auntie similar to Pollyanna's aunt Polly. But when I raised my head from the book I was all alone in the kitchen and it was still raining outside.

Soon I learned that my aunt's days followed a routine. She would get up, eat and go to bed at a regular time. She always did her shopping on the same day and in the same shops, laundry had to be done on Saturdays and any disruption of her routine would induce in her the strange torpor I remembered from her visits to our house. Her states of silent numbness no longer terrified me, they just made me cross. Why can't she control herself like everyone else? I would ask myself. Is she too cowardly or lazy? Likewise, I couldn't understand my aunt's permanent exhaustion. I was bursting with life and my aunt's sighing annoyed me although eventually I learned to ignore it.

On colder days, I would go to Jarmilka's house after school and spend the rest of the day there. But after a while I noticed that Mrs Stejskalová, Jarmilka's mother, wasn't all that happy to see me. In the old days she would chat to me, offer me a snack, ask about my mum and send her regards to my dad, but ever since I moved in with my aunt she stopped asking me any questions and didn't even offer me a drink. Then Jarmilka stopped inviting me to her house altogether. That really upset me but I was afraid to ask why, fearing that I might learn something unpleasant. Eventually I couldn't contain myself. It was raining, we couldn't play outside and ended up under an arcade entertaining ourselves by counting umbrellas.

'Jarmilka,' I began, 'why don't you ever invite me back to your house anymore?'

Jarmilka blushed.

'To do what?'

'So we could play when it's raining outside.'

'Why can't we go to your place?' Jarmilka tried to weasel out of an answer. She knew very well we couldn't go there.

'You mean Aunt Hana's? You know she's scared of visitors.'

'Exactly.'

I looked at my best friend, astonished.

'What do you mean?'

'Your aunt's crazy.'

'No, she's not, she's just mentally exhausted.' My mum's coy term came in handy now.

Jarmilka hesitated before going on: 'My mum says your aunt is crazy and that we shouldn't be seen with people like that.'

I felt as if she had poured a bucket of cold water over me. 'But you're my friend, not Aunt Hana's. What's that got to do with me?' I snapped.

Jarmilka was on the verge of tears. 'I don't believe it but my mum said it's beginning to show on you. That you've been running wild since you moved in with your aunt and she doesn't want you to be my best friend anymore. And on top of that, she says you're a Jew.'

'I'm certainly not,' I objected. How could I possibly be a Jew if I didn't even know what the word meant?

Jarmilka took my hand. 'I don't care, I really don't. You'll always be my best friend – forever and ever.' She wiped her nose on her sleeve and I thought there might be something to the suggestion that I was a bad influence on her because before she would have blown her nose into a handkerchief like a good girl.

Although it was raining, Jarmilka walked me all the way to my front door and promised to come and play with me the following day after school. I climbed up the stairs, rolling the strange new word on my tongue.

Aunt Hana was sitting at the table in her impeccably tidy kitchen. She must have heard me come in but didn't even glance at me. I took off my school bag, stopped in the doorway and watched her peel potatoes with total concentration. Her headscarf, which she had tied too loosely, slipped off at the back, exposing her hair. It was completely white but just as thick as mine. Either I had grown used to her or she had put on some weight lately because her cheeks didn't seem so hollow, or her chin as pointed as before. If she'd had all her teeth, she might not look so pathetic. But she didn't seem to care.

I went closer and sat down next to her. 'Auntie?'

It took her a while to turn to me.

'What does it mean to be a Jew?'

She looked at me without a word, put the knife down,

rolled up her sleeve and revealed a long number tattooed on her wrist.

Then she got up without washing her hands, dirty from peeling the potatoes, and went to her room.

The next day I could tell Jarmilka with a clear conscience that I wasn't a Jew because I didn't have a number written on my wrist.

Except that this didn't solve all our problems. I still wasn't welcome at the Stejskals, we couldn't go and play at my aunt's and it was raining outside. We hung around under the arcades, in the same spot as the day before and I was beginning to dread another lonely afternoon. I raised my eyes heavenwards, but the clouds that had settled low upon the roofs were gloomy and grey, just like my prospects for the future.

And that's when the idea came to me. Why, I have a whole house! More than a year had passed since my family had died, but my parents' house still stood empty. The shop on the ground floor was deserted because the town had found more suitable premises for a new workshop and the tiny room where my dad had fixed and cleaned hundreds of clocks was too dark and no one had any use for it. The rest of the house still belonged to me. When the woman from the council came to see us, she said I could sell the house and that the town would buy it from us. Then, sounding a bit sheepish, she added that, although obviously it was up to me, she wouldn't recommend it. 'Not that I think there will be another currency reform like the one we had last year...' she said and that was the only time she paused briefly. 'Well, it's your decision.'

We didn't sell the house, of course, but not because of the advice of the top-knotted lady from the council, rather because my aunt was unable to cope with this kind of business.

So I was the owner of a house in the street by the church and I knew exactly where the key was. 'Wait here,' I said to Jarmilka and ran home. 'I'll be right back,' I called to her over my shoulder.

I dashed up the stairs, dumped my schoolbag on the floor in Grandma Elsa's room and poked my head around the kitchen door. My aunt wasn't there. She must have been sitting in her room staring at the wall or lying down nursing one of her unfathomable ailments. I pushed a chair to the sideboard and reached up for the key. I was quite sure my aunt wouldn't have come up with a new hiding place.

I jumped down, put the chair back – so as not to upset my aunt by leaving things in a different place than usual – slipped my wellies back on and scooted off to join Jarmilka, who was waiting for me. However, on my way back to her I slowed down. I remembered the strange noises coming from the attic of our old house that had alarmed me so much that day, and the oppressive feeling I couldn't shake off when I returned to our house to collect my stuff after I moved in with Aunt Hana. But I was more frightened of anxiety and despair than the rustling noises in the attic.

Then I told myself that I was ten years old now, not a scaredy-cat little girl anymore, and it would be less scary if I went back there with Jarmilka. And deep down, I hoped that my sensible girlfriend wouldn't be keen on this idea.

But Jarmilka was thrilled and so, with the hoods of our raincoats pulled down on our heads, we waded through puddles towards my old house.

The key turned in the lock as easily as I had remembered, the light in the stairwell came on, but there was a chill and a dank dampness hanging in the air. We peered into the flat but didn't venture further. The chairs had been placed on the table upside down, as if someone had just cleaned the floor, and there were no curtains on the windows. The house was exactly as the disinfection crew had left it. 'Yuck, the place smells awful,' said Jarmilka. 'Why don't we go to the attic? You said there's a view of the whole town from there.'

I had indeed said that, but as a matter of fact I only supposed that you could see the whole town from the attic because I'd never actually been up there. My mum had said I would get dirty because the place was covered in dust, and that I could hurt myself because the attic was quite dark, or that I might even fall out of the window, careless as I was. The fact was, she herself never went up to the attic. She put it down to fear of heights.

Jarmilka and I climbed to the second floor, passed the room I used to share with my younger sister who was now... I quickly forced myself to think of something else.

Some steep narrow steps led to the attic. 'You go first,' Jarmilka urged me. 'You're less clumsy than me.'

I wasn't so sure about that, but I started climbing up to the hatch-door that barred the entry to the attic. Maybe it would be locked: I hoped so. Or I wouldn't be able to lift it.

But the wooden hatch proved very easy to open. I looked inside and stopped being afraid. Although it was raining outside, the attic was very bright. Light came in through windows in the gables and the two light wells. I decided that my mum had never been in the attic, or she would have known that the windows were so high it was impossible to fall out of them.

I clambered up and Jarmilka squeezed through after me. The dust we kicked up with our feet swirled in the air. 'It's not so smelly up here,' she said, and she was right. Some roof tiles had come loose and didn't fit tightly, letting fresh air in. The attic smelled old but there was no trace of the mustiness that reigned in the living quarters lower down.

Pushed against the slanted walls stood some old chests of drawers, a heavy wooden chest, a bedside table with a door missing and chairs stacked up to take up as little space as possible. In the middle of the attic, under the highest point of the roof, blocking the way, were two tall wardrobes. Under the window, under the gable facing the town, stood a wooden bed with a saggy wire mattress. There were also three grey horsehair mattresses next to the bed, and an eiderdown and some plump pillows with striped covers hung from lines strung up between the beams.

I opened the largest wardrobe. It was stuffed full of coats, discarded clothes and wide-brimmed hats, and at the bottom and also on the top shelf a few boxes had been shoved in higgledy-piggledy one on top of the other. The contents of the other wardrobes looked similar, only instead of wide-brimmed hats, muffs and fur hats spilled out on me from the top shelf. Jarmilka and I joined forces to lift the heavy lid of the wooden chest, where we discovered a real treasure. The chest was crammed full of books and magazines you couldn't find in any bookshops in those days. We spent some time looking at the books and browsing through yellowing magazines and while I pulled out thin paperbacks with the adventures of *Tarzan the Ape Man* from among some heavy volumes, crowing with delight over the *Mammoth Hunters* and piled up instalments of the *Gabra and Málinka* series, Jarmilka stood in front of the mirror mounted on the wardrobe door, trying on hats.

Next we pushed two chairs under the window overlooking the lower part of town. We stood there watching the swollen river flowing below in the rain. We could see the right-hand bank overgrown with shrubs and Water Street along it, some low houses in the background, the sawmill with its tall brick chimney, the railway tracks running from the station, the tall trees in the city park and wooded hills in the distance behind the town.

We stood there watching figures hiding under umbrellas or huddling in their raincoats as they rushed home in the late afternoon.

Back then I had no idea that exactly thirteen years ago my Mum had stood in this same spot, trying to catch sight of figures walking across town, and that it was tears rather than raindrops that obscured her view.

Chapter Eight

I don't recall Aunt Hana ever asking me anything. I'm sure she had never asked where I was spending entire afternoons, or why I only came home after dark. But she didn't really need to ask as I volunteered to tell her everything. I was exhilarated by all the unexpected discoveries and opportunities for play and adventure offered by my old attic and simply had to share my joy. I would bring home old books, show them to Hana and read out passages that caught my interest.

It was not just the autumn and winter of that year as well as the rainy days of spring and summer that Jarmilka and I spent in the attic, but also many afternoons in the following years. We explored every wardrobe and drawer, appraised each item of abandoned clothing and examined all the discarded dishes. We spent hours examining objects whose purpose we had no idea about, but our exploration always ended with us chatting on the horsehair mattresses on the old iron bed. Our topics of conversation were inexhaustible, as every day brought some new experience.

When Jarmilka shot up twenty centimetres in a single year and my chest started to itch before sprouting something resembling two buttons on a winter coat, our conversations would revolve around our rosy futures. I was determined to make my mark in literature while Jarmilka planned to become a famous actress. Originally she had dreamt of a career as a ballet dancer but she was the first to admit that she had grown so tall no dancing partner could lift her.

That gave us the idea that I would write theatre plays for her to act in, and capture her life in a sort of biographical novel, as by then I had ditched adventure novels as too contrived and divorced from reality, immersing myself instead in what I then regarded as real literature, from *Svéhlavička*, Eliška Krásnohorská's story of a stubborn girl, to my Mum's favourite romances in the *Evenings Under the Lamp* series.

By the time my hips got rounder and the two buttons on my chest turned into scoops of vanilla ice-cream, I would be sitting on the iron bed on my own, with one of the fat volumes that I had put aside during our first exploration for company. While I devoured Stendhal, Balzac and Tolstoy and dreamt of meeting my very own Lucien, Julien or Prince Bolkonsky one day, the pretty Jarmilka chose to focus on practical rather than theoretical preparations and spent her afternoons walking by the river with a young man a couple of years her senior, a student at the engineering college, all within the bounds of decency, of course.

We were by now students at the secondary school, and still best friends. We both knew now what it meant to be a Jew but neither of us thought it was important.

Although the recent war was still vivid in people's memories, people were not keen to recall the past. And while fallen resistance fighters, partisan commanders and their helpers were being commemorated and fresh monuments to the Soviet liberators were being unveiled on every anniversary, there was never any mention of where Grandma Elsa had disappeared and what Aunt Hana had been through.

As I pieced together a picture of what had happened from various scraps and snippets, I began to gain some appreciation of the horrors that had been branded onto

Aunt Hana's wrist along with the number, leaving her unable to live and reducing her to a mere shadow. I understood why she always kept a slice of bread in her pocket and turned away whenever she saw a uniform in the street. And I realised why in the first year of living with her, I once caught her burning my striped pyjamas in the kitchen stove.

'I left it to be washed, not burned,' I yelled but all that was left of the pyjamas were the scorched buttons. 'You don't understand! These are the pyjamas my mum bought me!' Tears of rage welled up in my eyes. My aunt said nothing to defend herself, and that annoyed me even more. 'Why won't you answer me?'

Hana frowned and slowly opened her mouth to reply but no sound came out. She opened her toothless mouth a few more times, like a carp out of water. Her lifeless eyes started rolling round strangely and on that occasion I was the one who ran out of the kitchen. The look on her face told me that my aunt was right and I was wrong, and I felt guilty.

At thirteen, I applied to go to the secondary school because Jarmilka wanted to go there and also because I didn't know what other school I should choose to become a writer. I was by no means an enthusiastic student but my grades were quite decent and being an orphan must have compensated for my father's bourgeois background, so nothing stood in the way of my secondary education.

On our first day as secondary school students Jarmilka waited for me outside our house as usual. I noticed immediately that she wasn't wearing her Young Pioneer scarf. A festive occasion such as the first day of school undoubtedly called for the wearing of the red scarf. We all had one, apart from those considered unworthy of it, I never found out why, and those people certainly didn't go to secondary school.

'Can't you see that it would clash with my dress?' said Jarmilka, opening her school bag slightly to show me her carefully pressed scarf. 'I'll put it on once we're at school.' And smoothing down her wide skirt and adjusting the strap of the schoolbag she carried on her forearm she added a bit self-consciously: 'Oh, there's one more thing. Please call me Jarmila, not Jarmilka, I'm not a little girl anymore. Nobody calls you Mirunka either.'

'I'll try,' I said, thinking how nice it would be to have someone address me affectionately by a diminutive.

But I only had Aunt Hana, who rarely addressed me at all and managed to string a whole sentence together only in a genuine emergency.

I often thought that she might not even notice if I vanished from her life. Day after day I would return to a silent flat and a taciturn woman who didn't even look at me. Needless to say, we never celebrated birthdays or name days, and whenever I suggested that we should have at least a little celebration or a present, I was rebuffed. And when I dropped hints about my upcoming birthday weeks in advance and went on and on about the presents my friends got for their birthdays, my aunt didn't even wish me a happy birthday. The day I turned thirteen my aunt's indifference made me feel so sorry for myself that I sought refuge in our old attic, determined never to return voluntarily to my aunt's place. 'I'll stay in the attic forever and I will die here,' I sobbed.

'Don't worry, I'll come and visit you and bring you some food,' Jarmilka comforted me.

My friend's response disappointed me, as I assumed that Jarmilka would try to talk me out of it. The only thing I could do in order not to lose face was stay put.

The attic looked very different at night. Fortunately, it was now June so it didn't get dark until quite late and the nights were warm, but I hope I'd never have to relive the terror that seized me at the slightest rustle and squeak. Moonlight came in through the skylights, objects cast sinister shadows and the ancient wood of the floors and the furniture creaked. I would have fled if I hadn't been too scared to walk the length of the attic and then down the stairs past the deserted flat and shop. Instead I lay curled up on the iron bed without moving to prevent it squeaking and attracting the attention of the horrors lurking in the shadows. I was too scared to fall asleep and as soon as the next day dawned, I shot out of the house and ran home down the deserted street, hoping faintly that Aunt Hana hadn't noticed my absence. All of a sudden my behaviour seemed very childish and foolish.

Aunt Hana wasn't asleep. She hadn't even put her nightie on. She was sitting at the kitchen table and although she didn't say a word, I knew she had stayed up waiting for me. And that she'd been worried about me.

I knelt down in front of her, threw my arms around her skinny waist and started crying. 'I'm so sorry, please forgive me.' I pressed my forehead against her bony legs in the black skirt and sobs shook my entire body.

My aunt didn't say a word. Then she raised her hand and stroked my hair.

Knowing how terrified she was of touching or being touched I appreciated that this was the greatest token of affection I could expect from her. That morning, after my thirteenth birthday, I came to realise that there was, after all, someone who cared for me.

Our school was almost at the other end of town and there were two ways of getting there. In the mornings, when we were in a hurry, from the Square we took the street to the Institute for the Deaf. The tall building at the top of the hill with its beautiful façade and turrets loomed above the trees like an enchanted castle. But we much preferred rambling along Zádruha, the workers' colony with its little houses and picket fences that opened onto tiny courtyards and front gardens. The fifteen-minute walk often took us a good half hour.

But then something strange happened and made me get up early enough to take the longer route, via Zádruha. One of the students at my new school and my new classmate turned out to be Ida Horáčková, the china doll.

Of course, I had caught a glimpse of her now and then since she had hounded me out of their house almost five years before. Meziříčí was too small a place for people not to run into one another. Sometimes we would spot each other in the street or in a shop but we both pretended the other didn't exist. And we continued this pretence once we became classmates. We never exchanged a word and looked through each other as if we were transparent.

And then that strange thing happened. Ida started to dance attendance on Jarmilka, by then known to one and all as Jarmila. She would wax lyrical about her blonde tresses, which really were a thing of beauty, swoon about her plaited skirt, which I thought made Jarmila look like a balloon because she was no stick insect, and offered to lend her the fluffy light-blue jumper she was wearing. 'It will go soooo well with your skirt,' she cooed.

Before I knew it she attached herself to us on our walk home. She walked alongside Jarmilka, prattling away merrily as if I weren't there at all.

'I'm so glad we're in the same class,' she chirruped. 'I could tell straight away that you have style. The only one who has style, in fact. I'm sure we'll be good friends.'

'I've always had an interest in fashion,' Jarmilka replied hesitantly. 'When we were little, Mira and I used to go to the attic and...'

'I can lend you the journal *Woman and Fashion* if you like.' Ida pretended not to have heard my name being mentioned. 'My mum has a subscription and we have several years of it at home.'

That did the trick. Jarmilka wavered. 'Well, I wouldn't mind taking a look.'

'You know what, I live around the corner, I can lend them to you right now if you like.'

We had come to the crossroads where Ida was supposed to say good-bye and sashay off home. Jarmilka paused, unsure how to react. 'Maybe some other time, my parents are waiting for me.'

Ida gave a forced smile and warbled: 'Whatever is best for you. Should we say tomorrow then?'

'Oh well, maybe,' Jarmilka said uncertainly. When Ida finally sauntered off, she turned to me. 'Why is it that you don't you like Ida? She seems quite nice.'

'Quite nice?' I saw stars before my eyes. 'Don't you remember that she almost killed me?'

'Come off it, Mira, you're exaggerating. You were only kids. It was just a game.'

That rang alarm bells for me. I realised that Ida was winning again and that I would need to be on my guard or she would rob me of my best friend. So I made Jarmilka walk via Zádruha both there and back to school.

But it wasn't much use. Ida kept making up to Jarmila at breaks and at lunchtime and she didn't mind taking a detour and walking with us the longer way. Until one day the inevitable happened. Bewitched by her flattery Jarmila could no longer resist temptation and chose Ida and her fashion magazines instead of me. 'You are still my best friend,' she assured me, but I knew that Ida would poison our friendship and things would never be the same again.

Jarmila started to visit Ida more and more often, leaving me to walk slowly home alone. I would peer into the gardens in Zádruha; in the town centre I would walk past dusty shop windows and watch passers-by in the Square, wondering about their comings and goings, whether anyone was waiting for them at home and trying to imagine their wishes and dreams.

I must have been lost in thought and got into people's way because, all of a sudden, a tall figure blocked my way.

'Where are your girlfriends?'

I raised my head and instantly recognised Gustav even though he was no longer so skinny and his hair was much longer. There was a friendly smile on his face and he seemed pleased to see me.

'What girlfriends?' I asked. I must have sounded somewhat suspicious.

'You know who I mean, Ida and the blonde girl.'

'Ida has never been a friend of mine,' I said. 'You might have noticed that when I was living at your house.'

He laughed and rubbed his chin as if trying to check if a beard was sprouting there. 'She was jealous of you. She was only little and she was being silly.'

'Well, she wasn't all that little.' I liked Gustav's laugh very much. It made the world seem a less sad place. 'But you also wanted to get rid of me,' I added, so he wouldn't think I'd forgotten.

He raised his eyebrows and threw up his arms. 'Well, wasn't it understandable? I had to move into the cubbyhole because of you.' He chuckled. 'But actually, Ida is so mean that a few days after you left I moved back into the cubbyhole of my own accord. Oh well,' he shrugged his shoulders and pulled a tragic face, 'darling Ida has given both of us hell.'

I had to smile, in spite of myself. But then he turned serious and looked at me. 'So Ida has stolen your friend? Why don't you take revenge for all these wrongs?'

'Revenge? But how?' I was a bit scared. I'm no saint but I didn't like the sound of the word.

Gustav bent down to me and whispered: 'Well, to start with, how about coming to the cinema with me on Saturday?'

Chapter Nine

1961-1963

After dusk the streets of our town were unusually lively. Figures wrapped in warm coats and scarves plodded wearily towards the designated meeting points in front of schools, offices and factories. Schoolkids – who had more spring in their step – got under their feet, swinging their unlit Chinese lanterns.

By now the nasty drizzle had eased off and people were hanging about impatiently, stamping their feet, looking for matches for their lanterns, and waiting for the signal to start marching in the direction of the Square where all the streams of the lantern procession were to come together and listen to speeches marking yet another anniversary of the Great October Revolution before collectively winding their way, like some gigantic glittering cobra, to various spots in the lower town to watch the pitiful fireworks, as they had the year before, and the years before that.

This was my first lantern march. The slow river of humanity flowing down the streets of our town reminded me of a funeral procession and the flickering flames of candles on graves. I had seen enough funerals. More than enough for my age. When you're sixteen the last thing you want is sad memories and thoughts of death. You want to live for the present and the future.

I looked at my classmates. Gathered in front of the school, they were all waiting for the first opportunity to sneak away, just like me. 'Mira, get in line. Make sure you don't go straying off like you did on May Day!'

My form teacher, Miss Máslová, wagged her finger at me but she was smiling. She was a teacher, and awfully old to boot, but we knew she would stick up for us. She was about as keen on these compulsory extracurricular activities as we were, but the only thing she could do for us was tick off our names on the register and then pretend she didn't notice when we disappeared.

I looked over at the final year students stamping their feet and gave Gustav a wave. We had agreed to stay with the school procession until it reached the Square. Then we would slowly slip away unnoticed and watch the fireworks display from the attic window of my old house.

'Time to light the lanterns and start,' roared a male voice probably belonging to a PE teacher: they have the best trained vocal cords. The lights on the lanterns started to come on, some flaring up with a tall flame.

'Didn't I tell you to trim the wicks?' the voice thundered amid the loud stamping, but by then the procession had started to inch forward. 'Watch your step! Keep your distance!' A hint of hysteria crept into the PE teacher's voice. I was glad we'd started moving at last as we'd been standing at the gathering point for a good thirty minutes and my feet were getting numb with cold. I walked alongside Jarmila and didn't really mind that she was chatting to Ida because I was thinking of Gustav, my main preoccupation throughout the past year.

We met every day. We'd walk around town, sit on benches and later on in the old attic, and talk and talk. I would tell him about Aunt Hana, school and the books I was reading. Gustav talked mainly about the secrets of the past, of things that had happened long ago as well as more recently, which some people still remembered. He was the one who helped me understand the significance of the number tattooed on Hana's forearm, although even he couldn't have had an idea of all that had happened to her.

'We need to learn as much as we can about our past so we don't make the same mistakes again. Events are always connected one way or another, giving rise to new developments. Understanding the context is the only way for mankind to move forward.'

I listened to his impassioned speeches. If only things could be that straightforward, I thought to myself. I was only sixteen, but I already knew that people would always be people, with their flaws and desires, that they would never learn any lessons and no amount of scientific calculation would ever change them. I admired Gustav's fervour but didn't share it.

'Let me give you an example – not a single egalitarian society lasted more than a few years. Every endeavour of this kind has ended in failure. Our egalitarian society is just another such experiment and is doomed to fail.'

I wasn't too keen on this kind of talk. For one thing, I thought it was pointless, even if uttered by the lips I adored. And secondly, it was undoubtedly dangerous. 'I hope you'll keep these theories to yourself,' I warned him every time.

'But how can the world ever become a better place if we all keep our mouths shut?'

He furrowed his brow and narrowed his eyes which were an even deeper shade of blue than mine. He narrowed his eyes quite often because he needed glasses but didn't wear any as they would have got in his way. He wasn't as tall as his father and still had a slender boyish figure. The serious expression didn't suit him at all. I much preferred him when he was smiling.

That evening, after climbing up to the attic, we didn't discuss what was best for mankind. We stood side by side on the edge of the old bed, our elbows on the narrow windowsill, and stared into the darkness that was from time to time illuminated by the bright lights of the fireworks. I was frightened by the noisy flares which to me suggested a city under siege.

'I wonder if this is how the town looked when it was liberated by the Russians at the end of the war?' I sat down on the bed, covering my ears with my hands.

Gustav put his arms around me. 'I guess so.' He smiled. 'Not something I can remember, as I was only a year old.'

I snuggled up to him but even though I pressed my hands to my ears with such force that I could hear the rumbling of a sea hundreds of kilometres away it still wasn't enough to drown out the explosions. I closed my eyes and lay down on the bed. Gustav stretched out beside me and gently ran his hands up and down my body. It felt soothing and scary at the same time. I could feel him kissing my lips and neck, undoing the buttons of my coat and cardigan. By then I forgot all about my fear and helped him with both hands to loosen the buttons, take off my top and pull down my tights. The attic was chilly, there was a cold wind blowing and the dampness of autumn filtered through the gaps between roof tiles, but we were oblivious to it all. We pulled the big striped eiderdown over our heads, cuddled up close and forgot about the fireworks, the people in the streets, and our desire to save the world.

Jarmila and I continued to see each other at school but I could no longer blame her for spending her time poring over fashion magazines with Ida. It was me, after all, who had less and less time for our friendship as I preferred to be with Gustav. Even though Jarmila was now friends with Ida and was on her third consecutive boyfriend from the engineering college, she always found time for me when I needed her. And I needed to talk to her about Gustav. How witty and wonderful he was, in other words, how fabulous. I needed to tell someone that we had become a couple.

Ida knew it too and couldn't bear the thought. She was

still ignoring me, looking through me as if I were made of glass and making the odd wry remark to Jarmila, but at home she gave Gustav hell. 'You're an idiot, can't you see that she's chasing after you just to take revenge on me?'

Gustav had no desire to argue with her, so he would simply leave the room without a word and go to his cubbyhole. Ida followed hard on his heels, dripping poison. 'Don't you remember the horrid things she used to do to spite us when she lived with us? The hard time she gave us?'

Gustav turned around. 'I think you've got it slightly mixed up. As far as I remember, we were the ones who gave Mira a hard time. You in particular – you couldn't stand her.'

'Come on, it was because of her that you had to move to the cubbyhole.'

Gustav looked around his tiny room. 'And do you know why I've stayed here? Because you're unbearable. So clear off now and leave me alone.'

He was laughing when he told me about this, but it was sad laughter. He said Ida had taken offence and went off to complain to her mother. Knowing Aunt Ivana, she wouldn't have had much time for her complaints, but they certainly didn't fall on deaf ears with Jaroslav. He had pinned great hopes on his son, spent years trying to persuade him to follow in his footsteps and become a soldier, and dreamed of the pips and stars on his son's military epaulettes. Gustav always heard him out, without letting on that he had very different ideas about his future. Then, one day, he announced out of the blue that he wanted to go to university and study history.

'History? What kind of future is in that? You'll end up wiping dust off exhibits in a museum. That's not a job for a real man. And it's no way to provide for a family.' His father shook his head in despair.

'Well, at least he'll get to enjoy his family,' chipped in

Aunt Ivana, who had a soft spot for her son as mothers always do. She rarely contradicted her husband but on this occasion she felt she had to intervene. 'Unlike you, who are forever being transferred from one place to the next.' That was quite true, as just then Uncle Jaroslav was deployed in Kroměříž and he only came to visit his family at weekends.

'You could have moved and lived with me, but you refused.'

'Oh, so you want the whole family to up sticks every couple of years?'

Taking advantage of the fact that the argument had strayed off the original topic, Gustav skulked off. But his father didn't forgive him for having his own way and enrolling at a secondary school instead of the military academy. He kept dropping disdainful comments in his son's presence and when he found out about Gustav's friendship with me, Ida had gained a powerful ally.

In the years I had spent living with Aunt Hana nothing changed in the flat with the windows opening onto the Square. Everything had its fixed place and Hana clung to her immutable habits. Only me and the clock on the wall offered proof that time was moving forward.

I no longer bore any resemblance to the scrawny little girl with a messy plait and scuffed knees and elbows. I hadn't grown very tall, but I now wore my hair pulled back in a long ponytail. I didn't have a fringe as there was no one to trim it and it gradually disappeared quite naturally. Jarmila used to say that I had a heart-shaped face but I was much harsher on myself. I thought my face was as round as an apple with a pointy chin jutting out of it. I was beginning to resemble my mother as I knew her from that photo taken on a walk in the park. Except that my eyes weren't brown but deep blue, after my dad's, and instead of my mother's frail appearance I was quite chunky, like my father.

Sometimes before going to sleep, I would open the drawer where I kept the photo, hidden from Aunt Hana, and just like my mum used to share her news with the gravestones, I confided my innermost thoughts to the yellowing picture, which was by now more than fifteen years old. Looking at the young couple pushing the pram I felt more and more sad that a more mature image of my parents had disappeared from my memory.

Even though there were many things in my family's past I would have liked to ask my aunt about, I had never mentioned my parents to her because I knew it would have been pointless. She wouldn't have replied and would just have withdrawn to her bedroom like she did when she got tired of my jabbering. I got into the habit of telling her everything, or almost everything, that happened to me every day and was just as used to her never showing any sign that she'd heard what I said. That is why I was taken aback by her vehement response when she realised that Gustav, whose praises I'd been singing for months and with whom I had been spending so much time, was the son of Ivana and Jaroslav Horáček.

She started beating the devil's tattoo on the table to make herself heard, and when I paused in astonishment, she said over and over again, breathing heavily: 'No, not him, not a Horáček.'

'All right, I won't mention him anymore,' I said, rather hurt, but instead of calming down, Hana kept yelling:

'You can't trust these people, you mustn't trust them an inch!'

'All right,' I repeated, but by then Aunt Hana had got up and shuffled off to her bedroom on those swollen legs of hers.

When I looked in on her a few minutes later, she was lying in bed, the duvet over her head, trembling all over.

I knew my aunt's fits only too well by now. I knew that

any mention of our family would thrust her into deepest silence, that occasional news from the outside world could upset her so much that she had to lie down and the slightest change to her established routine could make her spend the whole day in bed. But this time I had no idea what might have upset her so much.

Right, this means that I can't bring Gustav home, I thought to myself. I made a cup of herb tea, put it on my aunt's bedside table and went to my room to do my homework.

Whereas Aunt Hana would be thrown off balance by the slightest departure from her daily routine, I was longing for change. Gustav became my escape from the dullness of life: my friend and lover. I stopped talking to Jarmila and Aunt Hana about the time I spent with him. I knew neither of them would understand. Although Jarmila had taken walks by the river with quite a few boys, she had never let anyone as much as hold her hand. 'I'm too young to plight my troth,' she would say and we'd both laugh at this old-fashioned expression.

I, on the other hand, was not that careful. I longed to have someone close, someone I could love and cherish and who would return my love. That was one of the reasons why I invited Gustav up to the old attic and why the old squeaky iron bed, where I had spent one of the scariest nights of my life on my thirteenth birthday, now became the place I found the greatest happiness that, I hoped, would last forever. Both of us had very clear ideas of our future. I had fallen under the spell of stories and was going to devote myself to literature. Gustav preferred facts and was determined to study history.

Except that what he regarded as discussion, his young history teacher, Bohumil Brouček – or Buggie to his students, as his surname meant little bug – regarded as an attempt to undermine his authority. Buggie was unable to answer many of Gustav's probing questions since for him, unlike for his fascinated student, history was just a subject he had to take while studying for an arts degree.

Instead of admitting that he didn't know the answers and offering to look them up together with Gustav, he got tangled up in meaningless evasions. As he struggled desperately to find satisfactory answers for Gustav he noticed the amused looks on the faces of his students who, although they didn't have a fraction of his knowledge, relished the sight of their teacher being put on the spot. At moments like these his aversion to Gustav bordered on hatred.

And although Gustav eventually realised that it was pointless asking the young teacher questions that went beyond the textbook and stopped asking him about anything, Buggie felt jittery every time he entered any classroom Gustav was in. He mistook the lad's silence for contempt and would have done anything to make the disdainful student disappear from his class.

Gustav was very good at spotting connections between historical events but when it came to today's world, he was hopelessly at sea. Being straight as a die and free of malice, he failed to detect signs of malice in others. Just as he had fallen for Ida's insinuations as a ten-year-old because he couldn't imagine why his sister could have told lies, so it didn't occur to the eighteen-year-old Gustav that he ought to be more careful in his dealings with the world around him. It hadn't dawned on him that there were certain things he could think but under no account was he to speak or write about: this was the basic idea that parents in every kind of dictatorship hammer into their children from the day they utter their first word. And he failed to understand that the last place he could say those things was at school, especially if he was already in his teacher's bad books.

It happened a few days after the death of the communist

minister of culture Zdeněk Nejedlý. The school magazine published a gushing obituary penned by the young teacher Buggie. 'What a great man has left us!' he lamented. 'What an oeuvre comrade Nejedlý has left as his legacy and how much he has taught us! It was he who opened our eyes to the importance of the Hussite movement and to the discovery of the inexhaustible wellspring of knowledge that is Alois Jirásek's work, *The Old Czech Legends*.' This was the spirit of the brief article which most students didn't deem interesting enough to read beyond the headline.

Except for Gustav. He saw it as his duty to put the record straight and correct all the errors and untruths he believed to have found in the obituary. He got so carried away that in his zeal he not only tore into Buggie but exposed also comrade Nejedlý's unscholarly approach to the facts of history.

I can easily imagine the awkward position the young teacher found himself in when Gustav approached him with his own article and asked him to publish it. He must have realised at once that his student was about to make a fatal mistake and so, more to avoid getting into trouble than out of sympathy for Gustav, he ventured a suggestion: 'How about rephrasing some of these statements, Gustav?'

'Which ones, for example?' Gustav asked, stunned.

'Well, the one about comrade Nejedlý's unscholarly approach, for example. You must realise that it's not appropriate for you, a student, to criticise a famous scholar, professor and former minister of culture.'

'But surely not even you believe that using old Czech legends as a source of factual information is serious scholarship?'

The young teacher thought he detected a note of sarcasm in the way Gustav said the words 'not even you' and gave up. 'All right, if you insist, I will take your article to comrade headmaster for approval.'

He went to see his superior and presented Gustav's treatment of the tricky subject with the requisite indignation. Comrade headmaster could feel his headmaster's chair quake under him. He knew that to keep his job he had to tackle the criticism of the great comrade head on and find a scapegoat. He summoned the school board and with its approval carried out a ritual sacrifice. Gustav was expelled from school three months before graduation.

For a long time that was the end of peace and quiet for the Horáčeks. Instead of going to university Gustav was conscripted into the army, the paterfamilias, Uncle Jaroslav, had to say goodbye to the promotion he'd been promised and Ida worried that she might not get a good reference for university. Gustav sought refuge from his mother's sighs and his father's and sister's reproaches with me in the attic. We made love and hashed over the limited options the future had in store for us.

What depressed me most was that Gustav would have to spend two long years serving our socialist motherland, which meant that we couldn't go to university together. Gustav insisted I continue with my studies and I had every intention of doing so, but in the end I had to give up the idea of university for a very simple reason. Before Gustav left for the army I discovered that I was pregnant.

The pregnancy by itself would have been grounds for expulsion and since everyone knew I was going out with Gustav, it was inevitable that I would have been kicked out. That was why I didn't confide in anyone, not even Jarmila or Hana, and Gustav waited until I graduated – though not with the top grades I had hoped for, as I couldn't properly focus on studying – before informing his parents that we were getting married.

By then I was of age. Gustav was doing his military service and came to our wedding in an ugly and horribly scratchy green uniform that smelled of disinfectant, and no dress could hide my belly anymore. The Horáčeks were too furious with Gustav to attend our wedding and Aunt Hana didn't come either as she never went to unfamiliar places.

We had no money for a wedding party so after the ceremony we just invited our two witnesses, Jarmila and Gustav's friend Štěpán, to my parents' house for lunch and a cake I baked myself. We decided to move there since I couldn't live at my aunt's with a baby. Even a raised voice was enough to upset Aunt Hana, let alone a baby crying.

Before he started his military service, Gustav and a few friends whitewashed the walls and helped me clear out the wardrobes that hadn't been opened for years. I didn't recognise much of their contents. The only things I kept were the furniture, some pots and pans and photos stacked in an old hat box.

It felt strange to return to my old childhood home. Nearly a decade had passed since my parents died and time had transmuted profound grief into quiet sorrow. I walked through rooms I had rarely entered before to avoid painful memories, only to find that the past had almost completely evaporated. I no longer saw my mother's shadow in the kitchen or heard my father's soft footsteps on the stairs, and couldn't even recall what colour my brother's and sister's eyes were.

After the wedding we spent only one night together in our new home as Gustav had to return to his unit the very next day. I watched my husband run down the narrow street and when he turned the corner, I closed the window and looked around the kitchen.

I took a deep breath. No trace of the mustiness remained. I reached out and ran my fingers along the freshly-painted table, caressed the cool whitewashed wall of my old-new home, and I knew we would get on well.

PART TWO
Those who came before me
1933-1945

Chapter Ten

1933-1937

I have never understood how it is possible for people not to be interested in what happened before they were born, why they don't grill their parents and grandparents about their lives, what had made them happy and what they would do differently now if they could.

When my parents and siblings departed this world and forgot to take me along with them, I was too young to ask any questions, and over the years that I lived with my Aunt Hana the secret of her grief and the reasons for her eccentricity were revealed to me only slowly and gradually like the bed of a river that was drying up.

'You wouldn't be here if it weren't for them,' my mum used to say reproachfully when I skulked around the cemetery bored stiff as I waited for her to clean the gravestones and share her news with the dead. Had I listened more attentively back then and asked her to tell me the stories that lay beneath the gilded lettering, it would have made it much easier for me to piece together the events preceding my birth, from the fragments of a thousand memories.

My grandma Elsa Helerová was widowed after fifteen years of marriage. She claimed to have had a quiet and happy life with Ervin Heler, whom she married at the age of twenty-one, which was why throughout her marriage not a single line had furrowed her brow and not a single hair on her head had turned white.

She conveniently forgot that she found her husband noisy and messy, how Ervin's habit of interrupting people when they spoke had driven her mad, and she never dwelled on her late husband's unbelievable stubbornness and the fact that he always had to have the last word – qualities which, in Elsa's opinion at least, had driven him to his grave.

If he had listened to his wife's advice and insisted on storing his stacks of paper on the topmost shelves he would have noticed a nail sticking out of the wood and wouldn't have pricked his thumb. If, instead of cursing and swearing at the sloppy builders, he had followed her advice and attended to his wound, it wouldn't have become infected. And if he hadn't stubbornly insisted that thyme infusions would draw the infection out and had gone to see doctor Janotka instead, as Elsa had implored him to do for days on end, the poison wouldn't have spread through his entire body and Ervin would surely have lived beyond a mere forty-one years.

Her husband's death left Elsa helpless. She reigned supreme in the kitchen, made sure the doilies on the polished coffee tables and cupboards were always starched stiff and she raised her two daughters to respect their elders. But practical matters, such as buying coal, dealing with official business or running her husband's stationery shop were all terrifying, unknown territory for her.

She didn't even know how to go about arranging the funeral and whether to have a church ceremony for her dearly departed husband or follow the Jewish rite, as her family demanded.

The problem was that Ervin had renounced his Jewish faith soon after they wed under the canopy. Elsa's parents had never forgiven him for abandoning his faith. Especially Elsa's mother. On the rare occasions when she came to visit her daughter in Meziříčí from her hometown of Nový Jičín ten miles up north, Elsa's mother would speak only

German just to irk her ardent Czech patriot of a son-in-law, who looked up to President Masaryk and his republic. She wouldn't swallow a single morsel of Elsa's food, as she didn't believe it was really kosher, which was unfair to her daughter who still used two sets of dishes, one for dairy and one for meat, and never touched rabbit meat or pork, even if her attitude to religion cooled off considerably under her husband's influence. Nevertheless, Elsa would go to the synagogue only when visiting her parents in her hometown and the only holiday she continued to observe was Hanukkah. Her daughters thought this was just another Christmas custom and looked forward to lighting the candles and especially the small change they would be given by their parents on the occasion.

In line with Masaryk's humanist ideals Ervin decided that it was up to his daughters to decide what religion to choose when they grew up. Elsa accepted that this was for their own good out of respect for the husband her parents had chosen for her, which they had come to regret bitterly. As a result, the visits from Elsa's parents became increasingly rare.

Following Ervin's death, however, Elsa's whole family congregated in the widow's house on the east side of the Square and demanded that he be buried as soon as possible according to the ancient rite. As she knelt on the floor by her late husband's body, covered by a white sheet and with a candle by his head, vaguely aware of her parents taking a white shroud out of a canvas bag and quietly discussing with Ervin's siblings who should fetch the cantor, organise a wooden coffin, and what needed to be done for the funeral to be held as soon as possible, the devastated Elsa realised that, despite being surrounded by all these people, from now one she had only herself to rely on.

She would need to shoulder the responsibility of looking after the house and running the household as well as the stationery shop on the ground floor. She was now the family's breadwinner. There would be no one else to ensure that her older daughter Hana, who was growing dangerously more beautiful by the day, didn't become too vain and that her younger one, the sickly Rosa, would never want for food and affection.

Her train of thought was interrupted by her mother's loud sobbing, which suddenly broke the silence. Elsa was stunned. Her mother had not been fond of Ervin and while she now showed the respect for the deceased that was due, refraining from making any comments about him, her grief over her son-in-law's demise certainly didn't warrant such loud wailing. Elsa looked around. Every eye was fixed on her.

'I've talked to the cantor,' Ervin's brother said in a low voice. 'He said we can't bury him amongst us because Ervin had renounced the faith.'

Elsa's mother sobbed in despair. Ervin's body would now be covered by stones or burned to ashes. But what would happen to his soul? Would it be resurrected? She had wanted her daughter to marry a businessman who was firm in his faith but had instead thrown her into the clutches of an apostate. Because of her Elsa and her children were in danger of being denied the grace of redemption when the Redeemer arrived. Horrified by this thought, she buried her head in her hands.

The news brought by her brother-in-law neither surprised nor shocked Elsa. Ervin was gone. It didn't make any difference where his body would rest. She shrugged her shoulders. 'What do we do now?' she asked.

'It'll have to be a civil funeral,' her brother-in-law replied, and her mother groaned.

Even years later Elsa could clearly recall that groan which sounded like the wailing of a mother-to-be in labour, because it was this desperate lament that transformed the delicate and carefree Elsa into a resolute and independent person.

'Fine,' she said. She ran her fingers down the hem of the sheet that covered her Ervin's body, changed beyond recognition by sepsis, stood up and turned to her husband's elder brother. 'Brother-in-law, I'd be grateful if you would make the necessary arrangements. I will cover all the expenses.'

Her mother was about to open her mouth for another desperate scream but seeing Elsa's anguished but resolute expression she closed it again.

And so it was that the widow Helerová bought a grave for herself and for her husband at the town cemetery that she was never to lie in, even though her name was on the gravestone. And while Elsa's mother was shedding tears over the souls of her daughter's family, furtively rending her stunned granddaughters' best clothes at the funeral and praying for the deceased instead of his closest relatives for the next few months, Elsa turned her attention to more practical matters than sitting shiva which required her to stay at home behind closed doors for a week, grieving and doing nothing.

Since she had spent most of the family's savings on the funeral and on purchasing the grave, she decided to economise by sacking Urbánek, her husband's shop assistant. She had never been too keen on the handsome young fellow with the thick eyebrows and an arrogant look in his eyes. She felt he was just loafing around the shop and had several times asked her husband to get rid of him. But Ervin always came to the young man's defence: 'My female customers like him,' he insisted. 'He's willing to chat to them and he's good at it, too. And besides, I'm the one running the business. I don't stick my nose into your cooking either.'

It took her less than a day to realise that she had made a

big mistake. She had no idea of where everything was in the shop, where Ervin got his supplies from, she wasn't strong enough to lift the heavy boxes with notebooks and calendars and didn't have a clue about book-keeping. After a week of chaos and despair she swallowed her pride, went to see the sacked assistant and asked him to come back.

'But there's a problem, Mrs Helerová,' the young man said, gazing at a point behind Elsa's back. He realised straight away that the widow was at her wits' end and wanted to make the most of the situation. 'I've already found a job in the glassworks. I'll be making two hundred a week. So you'd have to give me a rise.'

But Elsa wasn't born yesterday either, she knew that unemployment was rife and didn't believe his story of a factory job. 'I can't give you a rise, you know very well that we're really hard up now that my husband has died.'

'Exactly,' Urbánek said, not giving up. 'I'll be left to do all the hard work now that Mr Heler is no longer with us.'

'I'll be there too.'

Urbánek gave such a disdainful snort that she nearly took offence. 'I'll have to tell you where everything is. You should give me a rise, the shop is making profit and you own the house, so you have no rent to pay.'

'How much extra are we talking about?' asked Elsa, already planning to get rid of the lad as soon as he showed her the ropes.

'Thirty crowns a week, Mrs Helerová.'

The exorbitant sum so infuriated Elsa that she turned on her heels and when the assistant realised he'd gone too far and shouted after her: 'Or ten, at least,' she didn't even look back.

Elsa entrusted the care of her younger daughter Rosa to the fourteen-year-old Hana, and directed all her energies and skills into running the stationer's. During the day she stood at the counter serving customers, in the evenings she reorganised the storeroom to clear out two rooms on the ground floor that could be rented out as a tobacconist's, and at night she tried to get her head around the books and orders. She would rise early in the morning, wake up Hana and make her help with the cooking. She wanted to teach her older daughter all the skills necessary to run a household. 'Rosa needs hot meals and regular walks,' she kept repeating. 'So please see to it.'

And Hana obeyed her mother because she was used to obeying. Early in the morning she did the cooking, and in the afternoon, after coming home from school, she looked after the frail Rosa. She made sure that her sister ate properly, dressed warmly and didn't catch a cold. But best of all she loved sitting down on the kitchen sofa, picking up her needles and yarn, and knitting or crocheting collars, blankets, sweaters, bed linen and pillowcases. With each stitch she dreamt of the life she would have one day. Of a husband who would shower her with love, the children she would carry around wrapped in crocheted blankets, of a flat with the loveliest crocheted curtains in town. The fame of her skilful hands soon spread and her friends and even the odd neighbour, much older and experienced, flocked to their house to admire her creations, copy her ingenious patterns and seek her advice.

Her younger sister Rosa wasn't much trouble at all. She was a quiet, solitary creature. In her early years she created her own world filled with silence and fantasies, a world devoid of illness, fortifying pills, constitutionals, and the much-hated cod liver oil.

She used to play as quietly as a mouse and developed an uncanny ability to disappear noiselessly into some dark corner where she was difficult to find and where she would daydream of sunshine, flowers and faraway places. Her mother and sister always found her after a while but occasionally Rosa managed to come up with a new hiding place, making her mother panic and rummage frantically through every wardrobe, terrified that Rosa had suffocated in one of her perfect hideaways. Only when she found her daughter sleeping behind a sack of flour in the pantry or under the coats hanging in the hallway would Elsa calm down.

By the time Ervin Heler died, Rosa was nine and although she still preferred to be alone, she no longer sought out dark hiding places and made her relatives fret about her sudden disappearances. This wasn't because she grew wiser and didn't want to frighten her mother but rather because she had grown bigger and it was no longer as easy to find a secluded spot she could squeeze into. She got on with people because she had to, but she didn't really need them.

She had loved her father but soon after he died, she found that her life was easier without him. She no longer had to endure the noise he generated – his heavy footsteps, the slamming of doors, his booming voice, the sound of cutlery banging on plates and the disagreeable lip smacking. Her mother had less time for her now and no longer burdened her with attention, so Rosa had more time left for daydreaming.

She'd never had close friends and when Hana asked her if she didn't miss having any, she replied, surprised: 'But I have Mummy and you,' and gazed at her with those enormous brown eyes so like Hana's. Except that Rosa's eyes gave the impression that she could see deep down to where others concealed their innermost secrets, making people who didn't know her well look away and change the subject.

At home everyone was used to Rosa's piercing eyes. Only occasionally would her mother point out that it was impolite to stare at others so intently, but whenever Hana felt her sister's gaze as she sat bent over her work, she would just tell her off laconically: 'Stop staring, Rosa.'

As both her daughters grew older and more beautiful, Elsa's hair turned grey and tiredness lined her face. In spite of that the idea was raised every now and then that she ought to remarry and let a husband look after the business. But Elsa wouldn't dream of it. She lived only for her daughters, who were on her mind from the minute she woke up and whose future was in her thoughts as she went to bed at night. She scrimped and saved, dreaming of raising two beautiful brides with big dowries and finding them kind and well-to-do husbands. Then Elsa would finally rest, look after her grandchildren, bake apple strudel and relax in the evenings with her white wool, knitting blankets for babies.

Chapter Eleven

1937

Ludmila Karásková had never been sick in her life but in September 1937 she felt a sudden weakness in her legs and some tingling in the arms. At first she thought she had overexerted herself. Then she started to trip over thresholds and the edges of rugs, and drop things, breaking four plates and two china cups from a set inherited from her grandmother, and her knees were so heavy that she could barely climb up the stairs. One chilly morning Karel Karásek took his mother to see a doctor and for the next few days Ludmila was kept in hospital in Vsetín.

Ludmila Karásková was born in the second-floor bedroom of a house near the Square and ever since – that is, throughout the sixty years of her life – she had only once slept under a roof different from the one where she had come into this world. That was when she reached the age of Jesus and made a pilgrimage to St Hostýn to beg the Virgin Mary for a child that still hadn't materialised after ten years of married life.

Her neighbours said it was pointless, that once past thirty the body begins to shrivel and age but Ludmila had become wedded to the idea and wouldn't be talked out of it. I don't know what she promised the Mother of God but before a year was over, she gave birth to a son, Karel. He remained an only child since her husband Mojmír hadn't come back from the Great War. Ludmila's dream of a daughter never came true, so at least she liked to imagine what her daughter might have been like. She would have been petite and had Mojmír's blue eyes and her blonde hair.

Elsa Helerová, who moved to town after her marriage, was exactly twenty years Ludmila's junior and although she bore no resemblance to her dreamed-of daughter, the older woman grew very fond of her. The young bride didn't know anyone in Meziříčí and felt quite lost. All of a sudden, she didn't belong anywhere. People exchanged friendly greetings with her but eyed her with suspicion.

She was Jewish but neither she nor her handsome husband Ervin went to the Meziříčí synagogue on the riverbank. Some members of the Jewish community held it against them. You shouldn't turn away from your faith, they said. Not keeping to it is clearly a sign of a fickle and flawed character.

Once the newly arrived couple had been sized up by their neighbours' prying eyes, the verdict was that Ervin was a hard-working man and Elsa was quite nice. Until someone pointed out that Jews were beginning to throw their weight about Meziříčí. Taking jobs away from the locals. The papers said that even the poorest Jew was wealthier than an honestly toiling peasant. And Jews shouldn't be allowed to serve in the army anyway because they spoke German, so they were not proper Czechs. Come to think of it, Schön and Rosenfeld shouldn't really be members of the local Sokol sports club. However, not many people shared this view, if for no other reason than that Mr Reichl, the factory owner, who was also Jewish, employed many local people. But then again, let's face it, there's always been something fishy about the Jews, hasn't there? Don't we all remember what happened in the autumn of 1899? The anti-Jewish riots in Meziříčí may not have been quite as violent as those in Vsetín which claimed few casualties, but the odd window in the synagogue did get broken.

But Ludmila Karásková, by then a widow, either didn't

hear this talk or turned a deaf ear to it. Either way, she took Elsa, a complete stranger, under her wing. She was the one who advised Elsa to speak only Czech, even though in her native Nový Jičín she had been used to speaking German. She explained that the good citizens of Meziříčí were weary of hearing what they mockingly referred to as the 'sacred' language. She told Elsa where to do her shopping and which stores to avoid, which neighbour to stop for a chat with and with whom to just exchange pleasantries.

When Elsa was widowed, her mother would toss and turn in bed at night in Nový Vsetín, consumed with worry about what lay in wait for her daughter, and prayed for her, her granddaughters and the soul of her godless son-in-law in the local synagogue. But it was Ludmila Karásková that Elsa turned to when she didn't know how to deal with officialdom or book-keeping in the shop.

It was Ludmila Karásková who witnessed Elsa's transformation at first hand. Day after day, month after month she watched her young friend – so helpless and insecure to begin with – turn into an independent, resolute and far-sighted woman, ready to face anything the world threw at her.

But she also saw the deep lines around her brown eyes and her mouth, and spotted the first grey hairs on Elsa's temples, even though they were skilfully concealed under a knotted scarf. She noticed that Elsa had forgotten how to smile, that her mouth was frozen in a permanent frown and a stern expression had settled on her face, but she was convinced that somewhere below the layers of sorrow and anxiety the old Elsa she used to know was still there. A loving, supportive woman, always ready to lend a helping hand.

That September, when she she became too frail to leave the house and enjoying the warm sunshine, when she found every movement so exhausting that she let the geraniums in their wooden window boxes wither, Ludmila

Karásková found that she hadn't been mistaken. While she was in hospital undergoing unpleasant medical tests that proved inconclusive anyway, Elsa would stop by the ground-floor shop where Karel Karásek sat stooped over his clocks twice a week. She enquired after his mother's health and left a small container with a cooked lunch on the counter.

You might have thought that Ludmila's son would appreciate the nice gesture, but it wasn't the case. Karel Karásek couldn't stand Elsa Helerová. He wasn't keen on the stern look in her eyes, the way her lips were firmly pressed together, and the tone of her voice which suggested that Elsa thought him a fool. And in fact, that was exactly what Elsa did think, because it was true. What else could one say about a twenty-six-year-old man whose sole interest were tiny cogwheels and miniature springs, while the world had so much beauty and joy to offer? What else should one call a young man who couldn't even find himself a wife, although the town was teeming with dozens of pretty women keen to marry?

Ludmila felt a little better after being discharged from hospital, but they all knew that her condition would deteriorate. She felt tired all the time, her skin acquired a greyish hue and it rustled like paper. She barely managed to do the cooking and spent a great deal of time just lying flat on her back.

And all this time Elsa's visits continued. Sometimes she would drop by for a quick chat at the end of the day, and on Sunday afternoons she would bring a piece of cake or a strudel. Whenever she came, Karel would disappear to his workbench downstairs. He didn't care for women's talk, their endless complaints about badly ground flour, stale coffee and exorbitant prices. He wasn't interested in Elsa's moaning about the tobacconist who had set up shop in the two ground-floor rooms next to her stationer's, who stank the whole house out with the smell of tobacco and paid the rent only when threatened with eviction. So, luckily, Karel had no idea that after covering less important subjects, such as appraising a neighbour's new dress or reminiscing about their late husbands, the women usually moved to discussing his bachelordom.

'Even the Hanáks' son Josef is getting married,' sighed Ludmila. 'And he's two years younger than my Karel. I keep telling him to find someone so that he's not left alone when I'm no longer here, but he won't hear of it.'

Elsa said nothing and just stroked Ludmila's hand. Seeing her friend's increasingly hollow cheeks she couldn't bring herself to lie to her face and assure her that she would indeed be around for much longer.

'Such a shame that you're not ten years younger,' said Ludmila with a smile. 'You would make a wonderful daughter-in-law. But as things are, I'll just have to last a bit longer and wait for your daughters to grow up.'

Elsa gave a laugh but said nothing. In fact, that was the last thing she wanted. However much she loved Ludmila she would never let her daughter marry a dolt like Karel.

Hana stood in the bedroom in front of the dressing table combing her hair. She had opened out the three-winged mirror so as to see herself from every side and relished the sight of her glossy black tresses flowing down her back all the way to her waist.

Yes, she had beautiful hair, no doubt about that, but she would much rather wear it short, after the latest fashion, if only her mother let her. She would definitely get a bob as soon as she could.

She positioned herself sideways to the dressing table, straightened up and pushed her chest out. She was as slim as a movie star, with a narrow waist and flat tummy, but thought that her breasts were too big. She bent down a little to see if she could hide them. Much better. She went closer to the mirror, examining her reflection and trying on a smile. The gap between her teeth was still there. Small but visible. Her mother assured her that the chink would become smaller with age, but Hana thought it was getting wider, if anything. She bared her teeth and pushed the tip of her tongue between her incisors.

She heard laughter from the kitchen. 'You're baring your teeth like a dog.'

Hana didn't bother to turn around. 'Stop looking at me and do your homework. I'll come and check it in a minute.'

Rosa was thirteen now and went to the middle school. She wasn't too keen on studying but her mother wanted her to go on to teaching college, like Hana. 'It's important to have a profession,' she said when Rosa protested. 'You might never get to be a teacher but a little education won't do you any harm.'

Rosa pursed her lips, stared at the exercise book in front of her and mumbled in Hana's direction: 'It's Sunday and you're making me sit here doing maths. You'll obviously make a good teacher.' She tried to add up a column of figures, but her eyes kept turning towards her sister. 'You look lovely, don't worry, he'll like you.'

'Who?' asked Hana, although she knew very well who her sister meant.

'Don't pretend. Jaroslav, of course. I know he hasn't been taking walks with us because of me.'

Hana gathered up her hair into a ponytail. 'Maybe it's because of Ivana.'

'Hah! So is that why he always walks all the way to our front door with us?' Rosa gave a laugh. 'You fancy him, don't you?'

'He's not bad,' Hana, said trying to sound indifferent, and ran a finger wetted with saliva along her eyebrows. In actual fact, she thought Jaroslav was the best-looking man she had ever met. Whenever she thought of him, she had butterflies in her stomach – and she thought of him almost all the time.

'You'd better stop preening in front of the mirror. Mummy will be home any minute and if she sees you dolling yourself up again, she'll be cross.'

'Am I not allowed to comb my hair?' said Hana, but just in case, she put the mirror back the way it had been, closed the bedroom door, sat down next to Rosa and peered over her shoulder. 'You got it all wrong. You have to write down the numbers neatly one below the other.'

While Rosa sighed and started to redo the exercise for the third time, Hana ran her eyes over the kitchen to make sure everything was as tidy as her mother expected it to be. If everything was the way it should be, Mother might allow her to go to the pictures in the evening. She'd told her mother she was going with Ivana Zítková, an old schoolfriend of hers. If she knew it was Jaroslav who'd invited her to the pictures, she would certainly not let her go or would insist that she take Rosa along.

Elsa Helerová loved her daughters, neither of them had any doubt about that, but she did keep them on a tight leash. Since she herself slaved from morning till night, she wouldn't put up with any slacking by Hana or Rosa.

Hana bent her head to one side and pricked up her ears to hear if her mother was coming up the stairs. Jaroslav would be waiting and she didn't want to be late. They saw each other very rarely because just now Jaroslav was serving in Hranice, and they had never been alone as little Rosa always had to tag along.

Actually, Rosa wasn't so little anymore. Only her mother thought she needed to be looked after all the time and handled with kid gloves. Rosa was quite thin but otherwise no different from other girls her age. But in their mother's eyes she was always pale and tired and she worried about leaving her on her own even for a moment.

Mother had always been an anxious person, but lately she'd been overdoing it. She saved every penny she made from the stationer's and the rent of the ground-floor rooms for darker times. What darker times? Why should the times get darker?

Night after night mother sat by the radio listening to the news and then the next day she had a moan with her customers about how terrible the world was and how that awful man Hitler was throwing his weight around.

It frightened Elsa that her brother Rudolf and his family had to flee from Germany because Hitler didn't want any Jews or aliens in is country, and Hana's uncle ticked both boxes. He had lost his textile shop and the family had to move to Czechoslovakia, or rather to the Helers in Moravia, and stayed in Meziříčí for a while. They didn't want to stay with Grandma and Grandpa in Nový Jičín because Uncle Rudolf's wife wasn't Jewish, something Grandma couldn't stomach.

Uncle Rudolf said that in Germany everyone who hadn't voted for Hitler had lost their job, and the prisons were full of Bolsheviks. 'All the Germans wear the swastika and they want a new war. You'll soon have Hitler here as well. And my advice to you, Elsa, is to sell this house before it's too late, take the girls and get out too. Who knows how things will pan out in this country?'

'This is the twentieth century,' Mother replied. 'The time of pogroms is long gone. And even if a war did start, nobody would harm women or children.'

That was what she said out loud, but her brother's words did alarm her. After Rudolf's family left, Elsa's economising turned into stinginess and listening to the evening news on the radio became an obsession.

Hana couldn't understand it. Why should anyone want war? What was the point of worrying unnecessarily? Old people were frightened because they remembered the Great

War and generally had a pessimistic outlook. But Hitler was in Germany and the Helers lived here, in Czechoslovakia. And even if he wanted to throw his weight about, our army and our allies would take him down a peg. That was what Jaroslav had said. Jaroslav...

She stretched her arm to take the end of Rosa's plait out of her mouth where she had stuck it, absorbed in her homework. 'Stop sucking your hair.'

Rosa smiled. 'I'm done. Will you check it for me?'

The door opened at last and the way it slammed shut told Hana straight away that Mother wasn't in the best of moods. Either Mrs Karásková's condition had deteriorated, or they'd heard more bad news on the radio. Hana steeled herself for an indignant lecture of the kind she was subjected to whenever she rolled her eyes at her mother's emotional account of civilians suffering and being executed in Spain, where Spanish people were killing one another for reasons Hana couldn't fathom.

'How can you be so selfish?' Mother fumed on that occasion. 'You only think of yourself. Innocent people are dying and you are rolling your eyes. Just hearing about it annoys you.'

'Oh, but that's not true, Mummy,' Hana said defensively. 'I do sympathise. But why should I listen to this and worry about it when there's nothing I can do to help?'

However, this time Elsa Helerová wasn't upset about injustice in distant countries but the mess in the hallway. 'As if it wasn't enough that the whole house stinks like a pub because of him, he leaves his boxes piled up in the hallway and it's impossible to get past. And the mud he's dragged in! He owes me four months' rent and won't even sweep the floor after himself. If your father was alive, he wouldn't stand for it. But everyone thinks they can do whatever they like to a poor widow.'

Mr Skácel the tobacconist was a constant source of

trouble and the cause of Elsa's complaints. She wished she could give him notice but didn't have the heart to deprive the father of three and the only breadwinner in the family of his income. So she kept threatening to have him evicted and Skácel kept making promises, occasionally making small payments, but his rent arrears for the two small rooms on the ground floor where he had his tobacconist's shop continued to mount.

Hana realised that the situation wasn't developing in her favour. If her mother started talking about money and how much their tenant owed them, how low last month's takings at the shop had been, and the increasing cost of bread and milk, it would make it hard for Hana to pluck up the courage to ask her for money for the cinema. She didn't actually need the money since Jaroslav knew what was right and proper and she was sure he would pay for the tickets, but since she had told her mother she was going with Ivana...

But Elsa sat down on the sofa and buried her face in her hands. All her anger and hardness were suddenly gone. She was sitting with her shoulders hunched, a greying strand of hair peeking out from under her headscarf. Hana snuggled up to her and put her arm around her shoulders.

'Ludmila is more and more poorly,' Elsa whispered into the palms of her hands. 'And once she's gone... I'll have no one left.' Her shoulders shook.

Hana pressed herself to her mother. 'Why, you have me and Rosa, Mummy. You'll never be alone. I promise.'

Elsa took a deep breath, straightened up and ran her hands over her face. Then she raised her head and looked at Rosa who was still sitting at the table bent over her exercise book. The girl seemed confused and alarmed. She had never seen her mother not knowing what to do or, indeed, crying. Elsa forced herself to smile. 'Hana is going to the cinema with Ivana. Would you like to go with them? It's not much fun sitting here with me.'

Rosa glanced at Hana who was sitting by her mother's side looking helpless and lost for words.

'I'd rather stay here with you, Mummy. It's too cold outside, I don't feel like going out,' Rosa begged.

'Thank you,' Hana whispered to her a little later as she was putting on her coat in the hallway.

Rosa smiled. 'You owe me.'

Although Hana was slightly late and had been running most of the way to the cinema, she stopped on the corner to catch her breath, smooth down her coat and rearrange her hair. Then she furtively looked out around the corner.

Jaroslav was waiting at the cinema entrance. A couple had just come up to him and Hana watched as he said hello, gently bowing his head to kiss the hand of a fair-haired woman with a little hat fashionably tilted on her head, and shook hands with a stocky man by her side. She was proud that this handsome and gallant man was waiting for her.

It was dark and the light from the lamp above the entrance lit up only a small area, surrounding Jaroslav like a halo and making his army coat turn grey and glint with gold. This must be a first, a soldier with a halo, she laughed to herself. Suddenly a foul stench hit her nostrils. She stepped away from the corner, which must have been used as a public toilet by drunkards at night. But the stench was still there. She looked at her shoes and in the dark it was her nose rather than her eyes that told her she had stepped into some dog excrement. Queasily, she tried to wipe her shoe on the kerb. Jaroslav raised a hand and waved. Then he said something to his companions and set out towards Hana. She felt like crying with anger and humiliation. If she could, she would have turned around and run away but that would only have made things worse.

So she just stood still and tried to smile. When Jaroslav was a few steps away, she held out her hand to stop him coming closer. 'Please don't come too close to me.'

He stopped in his tracks, baffled. 'Is something wrong?'

'Oh, I've had a mishap.'

'What kind of mishap?' He ran his eyes from her head to her toes but didn't see anything wrong.

'I've stepped into something.' She felt her cheeks burning and was glad that it was dark.

Jaroslav took a good look at her ankle boots. 'Don't worry, it will be fine,' he said.

Yes, Hana had long fancied Jaroslav and thought she had never met a more handsome man. But on that night in early December, when he sat her down on a bench and took it upon himself to dash down the steep bank to the river to clean her foul-smelling shoe, she fell in love with him for real. She didn't mind that they didn't make it to the cinema until after the newsreel ended, in fact she wouldn't have minded even if they had missed half the film, as she could not concentrate on the screen anyway. All her thoughts were on the man sitting next to her, his hand gently squeezing hers and the common future that she was certain awaited them.

Chapter Twelve

1938

Jaroslav Horáček was not an evil man. He may have been somewhat selfish and self-centred but he genuinely longed to find someone to love and cherish. And even though money had been decisive in his initial hesitation between Ivana and Hana, it would have been unfair to accuse the young man of being mercenary.

Jaroslav needed to find a bride with money because he was a professional soldier. And in those days if an officer in the Czechoslovak army wished to marry he needed the permission of his superiors, which was given only if the bride-to-be had enough of a dowry.

Ivana, though not exactly a dazzling beauty, was quite pretty, had a ready smile and was more easy-going than Hana, who didn't talk much. But what really mattered was that Hana's mother Elsa Helerová owned a house on the Square, ran the only stationer's in town and also rented out a couple of rooms. Hana wasn't a poor bride while Ivana couldn't afford to continue her studies because she had to help her family make ends meet. And that settled the matter.

While Hana knew after six months of courtship that she was going to marry Jaroslav and started preparing her trousseau, designing her wedding dress in her head after going to bed, and losing sleep trying to choose between satin and lace, Jaroslav – who was by then genuinely in love – faced an insoluble problem. Hana was a Jew.

Initially, he hadn't ascribed great importance to this fact but as time went by he started to wonder why so many people around him had a problem with Hana's background.

They both had a secret. Hana didn't want her mother to know that she was going out with Jaroslav and tried to find the least painful – at least for her – way of breaking the news that she had been seeing a man for several months without ever having mentioned him.

Jaroslav, meanwhile, was hoping that the moment would never come when he would have to choose between the sweet Hana and his future in the army.

He came to see Hana as often as his duties allowed. If it bothered him that Hana was trying to keep their 'friendship' secret from her mother, he never showed it. On the contrary, he seemed to enjoy playing along.

He would wait for her in side streets and take her for walks by the river or in the fields and meadows on the outskirts of town. He particularly relished it when someone appeared in the bend of the road. Then he would pull Hana into the bushes or into a dark corner and hold her very close. 'We wouldn't want anyone to recognise us, would we?' he whispered in her ear, kissing her hair and lips, and Hana would snuggle up to him happily, stifling her laughter into his coat lapels. It had never crossed her mind that there could be something more to Jaroslav's behaviour than his wish to accommodate her and have a little fun while he was at it.

In fact, Jaroslav welcomed Hana's secretiveness. It allowed him to put off the seemingly inevitable decision and hope that something might happen. What exactly, he really didn't know: anything – a miracle. The first vague warning came soon after he went to the cinema with Hana.

That night, as he waited for her apprehensively, stamping his feet on the pavement to keep warm, he heard a familiar voice: 'So she's late, is she?'

Jaroslav turned around, instinctively raising his arm to

salute his superior, but Horník smiled at him and signalled to a plump blonde at his side. 'Marie, have you met Warrant Officer Horáček?'

Marie shook her head. 'No, darling, I don't think I have. Pleased to meet you.' And she reached her hand out to him.

Jaroslav bent down to kiss her hand, grateful for the social mores that gave him a chance to hide the amused smile he couldn't suppress. He had never seen his superior wear anything but a uniform. In an overlong coat and a hat that barely covered his high forehead he looked like a door-to-door insecticide salesman and the intimate way his wife addressed him only reinforced the impression of a salesman who had just come home from a successful business trip and was now taking his better half out.

Jaroslav shook the captain's hand, which was almost too warm in the chilly weather, involuntarily glancing at the last stragglers hurrying to the cinema. He spotted Hana standing at the end of a narrow alley and even in the dark he could see that she was embarrassed, apparently too shy to come closer, seeing him with people she didn't know.

'There she is,' he said, and the captain and his wife Marie turned their heads in Hana's direction.

'Ah, Hanička Helerová,' said Marie Horníková, visibly pleased to have some gossip to share at the next tea party.

'But isn't she Jewish?' asked the captain and fixed Jaroslav with an inquisitive look.

Jaroslav didn't know what to say so he just stuttered an awkward: 'Will you excuse me?' He made a slight bow. 'Mrs Horníková.' And started walking towards Hana.

But the captain's question stuck in his head and kept nagging at him all evening – as he was greeting Hana, helping to clean her shoe after the malodorous mishap and later in the cinema, as he plucked up the courage to hold her hand. He managed to shake it off only when he kissed her goodnight.

But he wasn't allowed to forget the matter altogether. Some two months later, after a few more dates with Hana, when her dark eyes and feminine scent had got deep under his skin, Captain Horník summoned him to his cramped office with tall windows and an uncomfortable wooden chair. After dealing with some official business that clearly didn't merit a private meeting and following a long-winded introduction that emphasised the importance of family life and included a reference to the captain's own exemplary twenty-year marriage to Marie, Horník finally cut to the chase.

'Still going out with Miss Helerová?' he asked as if the question had just crossed his mind, rapping his fingers on the desk and staring out of the window.

'Yes, I am, sir.' Jaroslav knew immediately that the question was no polite formality.

Neither man spoke for a while.

'Jaroslav,' said Horník, finally looking his subordinate in the eye and clearing his throat as if a fishbone had got stuck there. 'You're a promising young man. You have a great future ahead of you,' he said, and cleared his throat again. 'You must take care that you don't make any mistakes that you might regret.'

Jaroslav was beginning to suspect where this was going but didn't know what to say. 'But Captain Jirák's wife is also... like Hana, and nobody seems to mind...' he stuttered self-consciously.

'Well, for the time being, for the time being. But you don't need me to tell you what kind of times we live in, just look at what's happening in other countries – like Germany. It's not that I'm prejudiced against anyone, Jaroslav. But the Jews have always caused trouble and it can't be a coincidence that Hitler has taken against them. I'm telling you this as a friend. The world is full of pretty girls, so why make your life difficult? You get my drift?'

Jaroslav was silent for a while. He felt as if a mouldy

fungus had sprouted in his mouth and tried to enter his lungs. 'Yes, sir, I do.'

'I'm glad to hear that,' said Horník, seemingly with genuine relief.

'May I go now, sir?' asked Jaroslav. The walls of the room seemed to close around him, the ceiling was pressing down on him, and the air had had all the oxygen sucked out of it. There was a nasty acrid taste in his mouth. He hurried out of the officers' building, turned the corner and as soon as he found a place he couldn't be seen he bent down, planted his hands on his knees and took a deep breath of the chilly winter air.

He gazed at the muddy ground before him in horror. Was Horník really suggesting that he would have to choose between Hana and his military career? He leaned back against the grey wall of the office building and stayed there for a long time, even after his queasiness had passed.

At midday Elsa threw a knitted shawl over her shoulders, locked up the shop and in the sunshine that signalled the coming of spring dashed across the Square and down a narrow alley. As she walked past the watchmaker's, through the shop window she caught a glimpse of Karel Karásek bent over his labours by the light of a table lamp. She went up the stairs, gently tapped on the kitchen door and went in.

She found Ludmila Karásková sitting at the dining table with a tea towel on her knees and some potatoes in front of her. Under the table, around the chair and all over the kitchen floor potato peelings lay scattered next to some half-peeled tubers that had rolled away. Ludmila was holding down a potato on a chopping board with her left hand, while her right, which held a knife, was flailing in the air wildly, as if it didn't belong to her. Only now and then, by sheer luck rather than force of will, did she manage to cut off some peel, but more often than not she missed.

Elsa gently took Ludmila's forearm and prised the knife from her hand. It surprised her how much strength that required. She didn't need to ask why Ludmila hadn't asked her son to help. Karel invariably spent most of his time at his workbench down in the shop and since his mother had fallen ill and her condition got steadily worse, he went up to the flat only if he absolutely had to. Treading gingerly, he avoided his mother's eyes and pretended not to notice how poorly she was.

Ludmila, too, was aware that her condition was deteriorating every day but her way of fighting the disease was by ignoring it. She never mentioned that the ground swayed beneath her feet and that the right side of her body no longer obeyed her brain's commands and led a life of its own. But her fear of the future and the feeling of powerlessness continued to grow inside her, bubbling up to the surface more and more often.

She gazed at Elsa. Tears welled up in her eyes and stifled sobs broke from her lips. 'How can I go on, how can I go on?' she whispered hoarsely.

Elsa sat down next to her and picked up the knife and the nearest potato. 'You have to get home help.'

Ludmila nodded. 'Yes, I've been thinking about that, too.' She spoke slowly, the words struggling to emerge from far back in her throat.

'Should I look for someone for you? I know a few families that have just arrived from Austria, they managed to escape from Hitler. Someone will surely be glad to have a job.'

Ludmila shook her head.

'Oh, I see, you don't want them because they're Jewish?'

Ludmila looked at her with a barely concealed reproach. 'You know very well,' she said slowly, 'that has never bothered me. But these people won't go into domestic service. They don't need to. I'm sure they have enough money if they managed to get away from Hitler. And anyway, they're not going to stay. They'll go as far away as they can, just like your brother and his family.' She paused. 'And you should leave too. Sell the house, or at least let it, until this blows over. Karel and I will keep an eye on it for you. Take the girls and go to live with your brother and his family. There's nothing good in store for you here.' She gave an exhausted sigh and opened and closed her mouth several times as if struggling for air.

Elsa threw the peeled potatoes into a pot, got up and filled the pot with water. Ludmila was giving voice to fears that had plagued her for months.

'All right, I'll ask around for a home help,' she said as if she hadn't heard Ludmila.

'That would be nice of you.' Ludmila swallowed a few times with great difficulty, got hold of her disobedient right hand with her left, lifted herself heavily from the chair and moved unsteadily over to the sofa. 'But you must promise me that you will at least think about my suggestion.'

Elsa, whose back was turned to Ludmila, nodded lightly. And while her hands chopped vegetables for the soup, dozens of contradictory thoughts raced through her head. She knew that Ludmila Karásková was right, all those evenings listening to the news had left their mark, but letting the house and moving to a country whose language and customs she didn't know seemed too much of a leap into the unknown. I have to think it through and make a plan. Rosa hasn't even finished middle school and Hana is due to graduate from teacher training college this year. First, I'd have to find a reliable tenant for the house, to have an income. But where will I find such a person? And how much rent can I charge? How could I leave my parents behind? And who will look after Ervin's grave? But then again, what if Hitler really does invade this country as he has threatened? What will become of us?

She couldn't shake these thoughts off. After leaving the

Karáseks she was so troubled by Ludmila's increasing infirmity and paralysed by fear of the future that instead of going home she headed for the river. Today she would open the shop late and her customers would have to wait for their napkins, notebooks and pencils. She needed a walk; she had to convince herself that the river was still running in its bed and green shoots were starting to appear on the trees on its banks.

Slowly she walked down to the river, leaned against the trunk of an ancient tree and let her face bathe in the early spring sunshine. The soothing murmur of the river drowned out the noises of the town. How she wished she could lie in the water and drift away, far away from all her grief and worries. Away from the responsibility and the urgent need to take a decision.

She turned around and, taking care not to slip, clambered slowly back to the path. As she looked back at the river whose only concern was how to keep its waters within its bed, and at the trees waiting for the spring with more patience than she had, Rosa spotted two figures at the end of the path disappearing into the distance.

Although she only saw their backs, she immediately knew that the girl walking arm in arm with a young man in uniform was Hana. How could she not recognise her daughter's beautiful long hair and the distinctive coat with its seam across the waistline they had bought together? But to make sure she wasn't mistaken, she craned her neck and watched the couple intently as they vanished from view.

Hana is still supposed to be at school. She said she had classes until four on Thursdays... She's lied to me. What other secrets does she have from me?

Elsa started to walk back to town. Sadness and disappointment melded with fear and grew into a morass of powerlessness. But she couldn't afford to be powerless or to give way to despair. She had two daughters to look after. She was the one who would need to make a decision about their future and secure their happiness, against their will if need be.

She hung a *CLOSED* sign on the shop door, something she had done only once since Ervin died, on the day when she couldn't stand up straight because of agonizing back pain. She sat down on the windowsill overlooking the Square and waited for Hana to come home.

Hana was out of breath after racing up the stairs. She spotted the sign on the shop and thought instantly that something terrible must have happened to her mother or Rosa.

'What's happened?' she burst out, still in the doorway.

Elsa didn't even turn her head and continued to gaze out of the window as if interested only in the people criss-crossing the Square. 'I'm going to write to your uncle in England and ask him to find us somewhere to live,' she said instead of answering her question.

Hana felt the ground falling away under her feet. She gripped the table with one hand. 'But why?'

'Why? You are asking why?' Elsa turned from the window and Hana noticed that her eyes were red. 'Because I'm frightened. I'm frightened that Hitler will come and take our shop away, just like he did Uncle Rudolf's. That we will be beaten up in the street simply because we're Jewish, as he was.'

With every word she spoke Elsa grew more certain that leaving was the right thing to do.

Hana also remembered the fading bruise on her uncle's face but couldn't believe that anything like that could happen in Meziříčí. 'Who knows what happened there... This is not Germany, after all.'

'Not yet. But if Hitler keeps going at this rate, this will indeed soon be part of Germany.' Elsa looked out into the Square again. The sun had disappeared behind a cloud and the promise of spring was gone. 'But I wonder if the reason you want to stay here might be the soldier you went walking with by the river this afternoon.'

As Hana said nothing, Elsa continued. 'You're too young to have a boyfriend. You are supposed to be going to school and helping me to look after Rosa, so why are you gallivanting about with a man of whom you're obviously ashamed, since you've never even mentioned him to me?' Elsa's indignation grew, she raised her voice and was beginning to sound angry. 'How long have you been lying to me?'

'Mother...'

Hana was now crying but Elsa could no longer control herself. All her fears and sense of insecurity and anger at a world that had let her down and forced her to take difficult decisions were concentrated in her voice. She turned on her daughter: 'You're a liar, nothing but a liar.'

She walked past the sobbing Hana and stopped in the doorway. 'You and Rosa will finish this year at school, and I will try to find a tenant for the house. As soon as we get visas, we'll leave. That is all I have to say and you might as well tell that admirer of yours.' She picked up the key to the shop and slammed the door.

Chapter Thirteen

1938

Hana was an obedient child. She took care of the household and looked after her younger sister Rosa and she did it gladly, because she was keen to make her mother's life easier. She went to teacher training college although she had no desire to become a teacher and couldn't picture herself standing in front of a classroom full of gawping children. She always went straight home from her Sokol training or rehearsals at the amateur drama company, where she had taken on the responsible role of prompter, to devote herself to Rosa, even though she knew that Rosa was quite capable of looking after herself.

But despite being an obedient child, on this occasion she decided to go against her mother's wishes. Nothing in the world would make her give up Jaroslav and leave for England. Her mother and Rosa would have to go without her.

Elsa Helerová wasted no time and that same evening sat down at the kitchen table. After folding away the starched tablecloth, she took a sheet of paper and started to write a letter to her brother in a meticulous hand. She began by passing on regards from various friends and acquaintances, listed all those who had died and had been born, gave an account of the business and complained about how expensive everything had become. After filling up almost the whole page, when there was room left only for one final paragraph, she got to the request she had been putting off for so long.

I think, she wrote, *I may have to take your advice and leave this country. We no longer feel safe here. My dear brother, will you help us find a place to live? Best regards to my sister-in-law and your children. Your sister, Elsa Helerová.*

She quickly folded the letter without re-reading it, stuffed it into an envelope and sealed it. As she carefully copied the complicated looking foreign address, she was again gripped by panic. She could hardly read the name of the city where her brother was living. She would barely be able to ask for a loaf of bread in England. How would she make a living? She stared at the sealed envelope for a while, then got up, took a few resolute steps to the hallway where her coat was hanging and put the envelope in its pocket. That is where the letter sat for a week before she resolved to buy a stamp, and it took her a further two days to bring herself to drop it into a letterbox and make the first enquiries about passports and visas.

Hana, on the other hand, did not hesitate. The next time she saw Jaroslav she told him how serious the situation was.

'My mother wants us to leave the country,' she complained, glancing around apprehensively and wondering who could have spotted them the last time they had gone out and told her mother. She was convinced that Jaroslav would find a way to solve the problem. He would go and see her mother, tell her that he was in love with Hana and didn't want her to leave. He would take care of her and make sure she was out of harm's way.

The sudden revelation put Jaroslav quite out of countenance. Of course, he knew that he and Hana couldn't keep their relationship hidden forever. But he was still hoping for *something* to happen, for *some* turn of events that would make Hana's mother agree to her daughter marrying so young, and Captain Horník and the rest of his army superiors to accept that his future wife was Jewish.

Yes, his wife-to-be. That was how he had always thought of Hana. But now he was no longer sure. All of a sudden, his life had become more complicated, like a maths problem without a correct solution. However he chose to act, he would be making a mistake. But there were big mistakes and small ones. Which would this be?

He realised that Hana was looking at him questioningly, expecting an answer. He didn't even hear what she had asked him. 'What did you say?'

She eyed him suspiciously. 'What are we going to do?' she repeated.

What are *we* going to do? How was he to know? Surely she wasn't expecting him to decide for her? Didn't she understand that this was the end? He'd made it clear to her that he was allowed to marry only a girl with a suitable dowry. But her mother would refuse. No dowry, no wedding. Did she really need him to spell it out in words of one syllable?

'We'll think of something,' he said. More time, he told himself, I need more time to think. There had to be a way out.

As a matter of fact, he already knew what the solution was but was not prepared to admit it to himself. Under normal circumstances he would have liked to marry Hana, would even have been prepared to fight for it, but these were not normal circumstances.

And for Hana, too, it was safer to leave, he thought. It was quite likely that war would break out and how would she manage here, all alone, if the rest of her family moved abroad and he had to go and fight in the war? That was what he'd have to do, being a soldier... However, if he married Hana, he would no longer be a soldier... Perish the thought. They had been seeing each other for just over six months and, luckily, nothing had happened that would have tied him to her. A few kisses, that was all. Hana would have to understand that he couldn't give up his career for the sake of a brief romance.

'So what are we going to think of?' she asked. He knew that she was hoping for something less vague by way of an answer. But he couldn't bring himself to tell her the truth.

That this might be best for both of them.

Hana would disappear somewhere nobody would mind her being Jewish and he, after a while, would marry a girl whose background wouldn't ruin his chances of rising through the ranks.

'I'm finishing teacher training college in a few months,' she said, and Jaroslav took this as a hint. Hana really seemed to expect him to propose to her now. But fortunately she continued: 'My mother said we would leave after my graduation. In the meantime, she'll try to rent out our house and we'd join my uncle in England after the summer holidays.'

Jaroslav was relieved. He had until the summer to end their relationship. He could do it slowly, gradually, painlessly. He'd find less and less time for her until the romance just withered away.

'See,' he said, taking her face in his hands and looking into her eyes that only recently seemed so irresistible. Now he found their gaze annoying. He kissed her on the forehead. 'No need to worry. All sorts of things might happen by then. Maybe your mother will change her mind.'

That wasn't quite the reply Hana was hoping for, but she found it reassuring nevertheless. Jaroslav was right. Maybe it was too early to panic. There was plenty of time before the summer holidays.

She threw herself into studying with renewed resolve, determined to graduate with the best possible results and to convince her mother as well as herself that she longed to be a teacher and teach children Czech history, Czech language and to love Czech books, something she could do only in a Czech school. She hoped that her mother would recognise that she could not jettison all her hard work and heartfelt desires because of some vague concerns and a move that was quite unnecessary.

But as time went by, it slowly began to dawn on Hana that her mother's concerns weren't exaggerated. Elsa Helerová was not the only one toying with the idea of emigrating. Hana could no longer ignore the fact that Czechoslovakia had become a hub for Jewish refugees, just as it was for the first wave of Jewish and, indeed, non-Jewish emigrants from Nazi Germany. She could see how anxious they were and how eager to move on as far as possible; she could feel their fears and their desire to put an ocean between themselves and their persecutors.

The wait for visas dragged on for ever and rumours abounded about quotas on the number of refugees being accepted overseas. Meanwhile, Elsa Helerová was still waiting for a reply from her brother and wondered whether to start looking for a tenant straight away or leave it until her passport and visa application had been approved.

Finally, in June, the long-awaited letter from Uncle Rudolf arrived. By then Hana had graduated and had been through another difficult conversation or rather, argument, with her mother.

'Now that you've graduated you should start studying English,' Elsa said. Hana had brought her certificate home, expecting well-deserved praise for graduating with distinction. But her mother was used to excellent results and had more important things to worry about, so she just glanced at the certificate and instead of praising her daughter, issued another order. Hana thought this attitude thoroughly unfair and cruel.

'But Mother, why should I study English? You were the one who decided I should go to teacher training college. You've always said that being a teacher was the right thing for me. And now you want to take me away? Is Jaroslav really so much of a thorn in your flesh?'

'I don't object to your Jaroslav, though I'm not particularly keen on him and I certainly don't think he's the right one for you,' Elsa replied, sounding conciliatory. 'The person I object to is that loudmouth Hitler in Berlin who's throwing his weight around everywhere.'

'Are you saying the four years have been a waste of effort?'

'Education is never wasted.'

'But with my Czech education I could never become a teacher in England.'

'You'll learn English. You can start right now.'

'I'm not going to England.'

'Oh yes you are.' Now Elsa raised her voice. 'What would you do here without us?'

'I'll get married.'

'I see, so has your brave soldier proposed yet?' She paused. 'No, he hasn't and he never will. He's looking for a bride with a dowry and you, my girl, are not getting one.'

Hana turned on her heels and ran from the kitchen, mortified. The really terrible thing was that her mother was right. Jaroslav had never uttered the word marriage. Their meetings were becoming more and more rare because of his many obligations at the barracks and all those military exercises he had to take part in. He had also said that the situation was serious and Hana sometimes wondered if that was a hint that moving to England might be best for her. Once she actually asked him if he wanted her to go but Jaroslav evaded a direct answer and insisted that, just like her mother, he wanted only the best for her.

But Hana knew exactly what was best for her. It was staying here with Jaroslav and believing they would live happily ever after.

The thin white envelope arrived from Rudolf in England bearing a single, exotic-looking postage stamp and lots of postmarks, square and round, one corner bent and all crumpled as if it had to fight to be delivered. Impatiently, Elsa tore open the shorter side of the envelope and pulled out a folded letter and started to read it.

The tone of her brother's letter frightened her. *I'm glad you've finally taken the decision,* he wrote. *Sell the house quickly, you will need the money. You must hurry, before it is too late. A lot of people have fled from Hitler to England and the locals are beginning to complain, calling for the influx of immigrants to be curbed. So you must not hesitate and come, and bring our parents along. You can't leave them behind, they will soon be dependent on our help ... A handful of other countries are still accepting refugees – the United States, Canada, maybe also the Dominican Republic – but the wisest thing would be to go to Palestine... That's something I'm also considering.*

Her brother's letter left Elsa bewildered. He was telling her to hurry up and sell the house. But that would take time. The original idea had been for her to let it, and have the tenants send the rent to her interim home until things got back to normal – surely that was bound to happen sooner or later – so that they had somewhere to return to. Her brother was advising her to come to England but he wasn't feeling welcome there either. Why did he mention all those other places? Was it just meant as another option or an oblique hint that she ought to apply for visas for one of those countries? He was telling her to bring their parents along, yet in the next sentence he said they weren't getting any younger... as if he didn't know that they would never leave Nový Jičín. He was obviously extremely worried about them.

She reread the letter but was none the wiser. It had clearly been scribbled in haste, his writing was more crabbed and unruly than in his previous letters, a sign of her brother's anxiety.

The next day she left Hana in charge of the shop and set out for Nový Jičín to deliver her brother's message to her parents. She anticipated a negative response and wasn't surprised that they wouldn't hear of emigrating.

'But you should go and join Rudolf as soon as you can,' her father said, and her mother nodded in agreement. 'Don't waste time on unnecessary matters. If you like, we can get power of attorney and sell the house for you so you can travel as soon as you have all the paperwork. I'll send on the money later.'

Elsa had expected her parents to be reluctant to leave the country where they were born and had lived all their lives but it surprised her that not only did they make no attempt to talk her out of leaving herself but told her to speed up her departure.

'Thank you, but that won't be necessary,' she said. 'Who knows how long I'll have to wait for the visas. And besides, I haven't found a buyer yet. I don't think we'll be able to leave before the autumn.'

'Please think about it,' her father insisted. 'If you need money for the journey, I can give you some.'

Everything became clear once she saw a white swastika daubed on the wall opposite her parents' house as she was leaving. She looked at her father who walked down the stairs with her. He nodded. 'The town is covered with these graffiti. You know how many Germans live here and now they've all gone crazy and want to join the Reich. Last night they marched down the streets, shouting and chanting. It was horrible.' He gulped. 'Your mother was in tears.'

His last words frightened Elsa more than anything else. She had seen her mother wail on many occasions, raise her arms to heaven and mumble prayers. She had heard her sob and tear histrionically at her hair and clothes. But she had never seen her cry.

Suddenly Elsa saw her father with new eyes. They hadn't been very close while she was growing up. An invisible but insurmountable wall stood between them, made of customs and a traditional upbringing. It left little space for relaxed conversation, let alone a caress or a hug. Father was Father, the breadwinner, a man who knew how to provide for his wife and children. A man who made it possible for his wife to enjoy life, while whining and complaining about life's problems. But never before did he have to see his wife shed tears of helplessness and fear without being able to comfort her.

Bruno Weis used to go to the office every morning and return in the evening to take his seat at the head of the table and eat the kosher meals prepared by his wife Greta, then spend the rest of the evening immersed in his books. He rarely spoke to his children and when he did, it was only to admonish them or remind them of some duty they had neglected. He recited his forefathers' prayers and observed the age-old customs because that was what his parents, neighbours and friends had done. The only life he knew was one wearing a yarmulke and he couldn't, or maybe didn't want to, imagine anything else.

Since she was a little girl Elsa knew that her father would always be there for her and make her feel safe.

But she hadn't realised that her father really loved her until she got married and followed her husband in renouncing their faith. Unlike his mother, he never uttered a word of reproach, didn't make any thunderous threats and his silence suggested that, while he had his own opinions, he respected Elsa's right to a free choice. He hadn't burdened her soul with reproaches, which for her was greater proof of paternal love than anything words could say.

And now he stood beside her looking utterly lost. He no longer understood the world in which he had spent seventy years of his life, no longer recognised the town whose streets he had walked every day, and was living in fear of his neighbours who no longer looked him in the eye or, what was worse, gave him contemptuous looks as if he were a dog begging for food, without smiling at him or even acknowledging his presence.

'Maybe you should come with us after all,' said Elsa.

Her father shook his head. 'Don't worry about us. What can they do to the old? We will live out our days here somehow. But your girls have no future here.' He looked at her bag. 'You haven't forgotten the pastries your mother has packed for you?'

Elsa looked back from the end of the street where she used to play as a little girl. Even though it was summer, the writings on the walls sent a chill down her spine.

In the summer of 1938 Elsa Helerová's visits to the Karáseks' home became more frequent. She pretended that she went there to have a chat or to ask Ludmila for advice but while they talked she would sweep the floor or tidy up as her friend could no longer get up from her armchair.

Once a week a cleaner would come and a washerwoman, Mrs Zítková, would collect the laundry. For a small payment, she did the washing for the more affluent housewives who didn't want to ruin their hands in the washtub. She would bring back the laundry fragrant, in meticulously ironed and folded stacks, and every time Ludmila paid the worn-out washerwoman, she thought with some envy how she would love to be able to bend her back over a washboard. She gave a little sigh and thanked Zítková for her work, and never complained that the sheets scratched her skin because the woman used too much starch.

As her illness progressed, Ludmila found it too hard to walk up and down the steep stairs in the mornings and evenings and took up permanent residence in the kitchen. She slept on a sofa and spent the day slowly shuffling to and fro. Most of the time she sat in her comfy armchair, looking out onto the narrow street, listening to the burbling of the nearby river and the rustling of the leaves in the canopies of the trees. Karel had brought the armchair out of the living room which they had used only occasionally, to receive special visitors. To save money, the room was never heated and the cold became so firmly lodged there that it was impossible to keep it warm in the winter months. As a result, their visitors never stayed too long and left chilled to the bone.

During the summer of 1938 Elsa started to bring Hana along with her when she visited the Karáseks and by the end of the summer she often sent just her daughter to help Ludmila out.

Hana didn't like going to the Karáseks. She didn't mind helping the sick Ludmila around the house, it didn't make much difference if she was stacking up goods in the stationer's or sweeping Mrs Karásková's kitchen floor. She was now a qualified teacher but she didn't apply for a job in a school. Elsa didn't want her to get a job before their planned departure for England, and Hana was fine with that as she wanted to be free to see more of Jaroslav.

During their increasingly rare meetings Jaroslav had grown more and more distant. Hana ascribed his bad temper to his worries. She knew that things weren't easy for him and all he ever talked about was how likely he was to be redeployed soon. He didn't know where and Hana didn't want to commit herself to a job so she would be able to follow him.

She was rather discomfited when he said that he might not be able to see her for a while and that, in light of the political tensions and the imminent threat of war, he might not always be able to let her know his whereabouts. But she consoled herself that as a future wife of a professional soldier she had to get used to such inconveniences.

Nevertheless, on the most recent occasion when they

met, she plucked up the courage to ask him straight out: 'Do you really intend to marry me, or are you just stringing me along? My mother says you're only after my dowry. Please tell me the truth. If you don't want me, I'll go to England with my mother and sister and you'll be rid of me.'

'Of course I want to marry you,' Jaroslav blurted out. How could he have said no, even if he had wanted to. And especially right after she implied that he wasn't being straight with her. She had the nerve to suggest that he was leading her on – how outrageous! He had always regarded himself as an honest man and wanted others to see him that way. How dare she doubt him? He was shaking with anger but controlled himself. 'This is not a good time to discuss the wedding. Can't you see what difficult times we live in? We can't think only of ourselves. But don't worry, I'll look after you – I promise.'

Hana never suspected that on that very evening, while he was taking the train back to the barracks in Hranice, Jaroslav decided that the best solution would be never to see Hana again.

On her visits to the Karáseks – if the hours spent cleaning and cooking could be described as visits – there were two things that frightened Hana. One was Ludmila's illness and the other Karel's hostile looks.

Hana was young and healthy and the sight of an increasingly decrepit Ludmila Karásková scared her. It was not so much that she was concerned about the sick woman but more that she dreaded the passage of time and what it might mean for her own future. Ludmila Karásková represented an unpleasant confrontation with how people could end up. A reminder that ageing, sickness, infirmity, and despair were all part of life. Ludmila's speech was becoming more and more slurred and hard to understand as the muscles in her mouth no longer obeyed her and words sometimes refused to pass her lips and stuck in her throat. The indistinct sounds she emitted sounded more like sobbing or barking and Hana didn't know how to respond.

Was she supposed to pretend that she understood, or should she ask Ludmila to try again and subject herself to another excruciating wait for the old woman to get the words out? At moments like these Hana hated Mrs Karásková for putting her in this awkward position.

Karel Karásek was more adept at making sense of what his mother was saying but he spent most of his time in his workshop. That was just as well since Hana couldn't stand his way of talking. Karel was a pussyfooting creature, even more sparing with words than his mother, and regarded Hana as an intruder, some louse-ridden feral cat trying to wheedle her way into their hearts.

In fact, she had no idea how close to the truth she was. Had she overheard some of Karel Karásek's evening chats with his mother she would never again have crossed the threshold of their house.

'Why do you keep inviting that Helerová woman and her daughter, Mother?' Karel would ask sometimes, no longer able to contain himself. 'I know you need help, but we can afford to pay someone.'

'I li...ke them. El...sa is a fr...iend.'

Karel sat down by his mother's side and took her hand. 'I know, Mother. But they have such strange eyes. The old woman always looks at me as if she knew something awful about me and the young one never even looks my way.'

'She's... not... an... old wo-man.' Ludmila lifted her heavy hand and stroked her son's head. Sometimes he's like a small child, she thought. I shouldn't have complained to Elsa about Karel taking his time getting married. Who knows what she thinks of him now? 'I... need the com... pa... ny.'

'Yes, exactly. If we hire home help, she will come every day and you won't be alone.'

'No, I... don't... want... a stran... ger.' Not yet, she thought.

But how much longer can you manage without a stranger's help, her son wondered. He knew there was no point tormenting his mother by saying it out loud. Deep down they both knew that sooner or later the dreaded moment would come, whether they liked it or not.

'They... will... leave... for... England soon... anyway,' Ludmila said after a brief pause.

The sooner the better, thought Karel, getting up with a sigh, and quietly slipped downstairs, back to the safety of his workshop and his clocks.

Chapter Fourteen

1938

A small crowd parted to let through men in white coats carrying a stretcher and closed again. People outside the circle stood on their tiptoes craning their necks to see over the umbrellas and shared their observations and speculations with other bystanders.

'He's a goner.'

'They've come too late.'

'Did you see him fall?'

'He clutched at his heart and that was that.'

'How could it happen? I knew him. A really nice man. He didn't deserve to die like that.'

Ivana Zítková thought the last comment particularly silly and uncalled for. Yes, Mr Erban, the teacher, had been a nice man. He had taught her Czech and history and as far as she could remember, never raised his voice at his pupils, not even when he caught them reading a book under the desk or whispering to one another when they were bored by the lectures he delivered in his monotonous mumble. But since when did it matter whether someone was good or evil? Did anyone really believe that life was fair?

She turned round and headed back to the delicatessen to deliver a package she had collected for her employer, Mrs Pašková, and to prepare another tray of open sandwiches. Her boss cast a meaningful glance at her watch. As if she didn't know that it was impossible to make it to the post office and back in less than forty minutes, not even if there was no queue at the counter and nothing as extraordinary happened as seeing a man walk towards you, suddenly let his umbrella drop, stagger to one side and drop to the ground like a felled tree. A man in a dark blue jacket waded through the puddles to the nearest shop to phone for a doctor, but Ivana could tell straight away that there was no point. The teacher's eyes rolled upwards, his jaw dropped and his head stayed tilted at an unnatural angle, just like that of her younger brother who had died of diphtheria six years ago. No, life wasn't fair.

If life had been dealt out according to merit, she wouldn't have to be on her feet in the scullery day in, day out preparing ham sandwiches with an egg and gherkin garnish for spoilt ladies who were able to enjoy them just because they were born under a lucky star. Who is it up there that decides whether someone is born into luxury or into poverty? Who was it that had decreed that Ivana should be making sandwiches her parents could never taste because they couldn't afford to lounge at a table in a café sipping fruit juice, or maybe a wine spritzer, a delicate china coffee cup in their hand and their little finger raised in that posh way, and choosing one of the treats on offer at the delicatessen that employed their daughter?

But she was supposed to be grateful to have found a good job! Did anyone seriously think she could be grateful for the privilege of serving customers who thought they were better than her just because their wallets were well-lined? Admittedly, preparing sandwiches and serving coffee was preferable to washing other people's laundry, as her poor mother had to do, but Ivana would much rather have continued her studies than been stuck in this place. If she had got that chance, she could have found a job where she wouldn't have sore feet from standing up all day, and the corners of her mouth wouldn't get tired of forcing the complimentary smile that her customer received with the pastries and snacks.

Fairness! What would be fair would be if it was Hana Helerová standing here in her place. That girl had never wanted to study, always said she hated school, but her mummy was keen on her darling daughter getting an education. Of course she was. The woman had more sense than both her daughters put together.

What Ivana would have given for a chance to attend the lycée, or at least the teacher training college... And yet Hana had the cheek to complain. Every now and then she would drop by the delicatessen, order a cream puff, her favourite, and wait for Ivana to tidy up the pantry and wipe the tables clean. Ivana's boss would give her the special smile she reserved for her best customers and ask to be remembered to Hana's mother, and before leaving the shop she'd whisper to Ivana that she should come earlier the following day and mop the floor before opening.

Then Ivana would walk home with Hana the way they used to when they were still best friends. Except that they were friends no longer. Not that Hana had noticed. But for Ivana, things were not the same from the minute she had to give up school, and their friendship received the final blow when Jaroslav Horáček took Hana on their first date.

Ivana could have sworn that it was her smiles that had attracted Jaroslav's attention to begin with. That it was her hips that had enchanted him, her easy-going manner that had encouraged him to chat them both up. Initially the young man in uniform divided his attention equally between the two girls, giving the same radiant smile to Ivana and Hana, and directing his flattering remarks at both of them, but after a few weeks Ivana noticed that it was to Hana that he addressed his questions more often, Hana whose arm he took more frequently and who he'd walk all the way home. And she knew exactly what was behind it.

It was the house in the Square that was to blame. The house with a first-floor flat, a stationer's and a tobacconist's on the ground floor. It wasn't Hana's allure but her wealth that had tipped the scales of happiness in her favour. Ivana clenched her jaws bitterly at the thought and she nearly choked with envy. In moments like these she almost wished she could squeeze Hana's slender neck and squeeze and squeeze it until... No, not really. But if Hana had vanished off the face of the earth, Ivana would certainly not have missed her.

Ivana picked up a tray and carried it from the pantry into the shop. She looked out of the window. The unceasing rain of the past few days, turning to drizzle by midday, had picked up again. The crowd had dispersed and the street was almost deserted.

What a strange day. The overcast sky weighed down on the town, advancing like an enemy army awaiting the order to attack. The delicatessen was normally busy on a Saturday morning but today only one table was occupied. The boss frowned at Ivana as if it were her fault that people didn't feel like venturing out into the rain. She switched on the radio but when she found only news and no music she turned it off again, annoyed.

Who would want to listen to the endless list of the concessions the Czechoslovak government was making to appease the mutinous Sudetenland?

Her boss shut the cash register and said to Ivana under her breath: 'I'll be right back. Can you manage on your own?'

Here we go again, Ivana thought. The boss knows that today won't be a busy day so off she goes to take a nap. Well, she can afford to. 'Of course, Mrs Pašková.' She forced the corners of her mouth upwards into a smile. 'Don't you worry.'

She took a clean tea-towel and went over to the tables to

give them another wipe. She had to find something to do to pass the next three hours.

The bell above the door of the shop tinkled its annoying tune. Ivana looked round but, seeing a figure in uniform, she started and turned back, bending above a tabletop to clean a non-existent stain. She needed a while to regain composure and calm her nerves.

The delicatessen was a place where ladies would gather for a bite to eat and mothers would stop by on their afternoon walk with their offspring to buy them ice cream or cake and enjoy a moment's respite from their chattering. Men would come less often, mostly when escorting a lady – they preferred a mug of beer in one of the town's many pubs or restaurants to a milkshake or cup of coffee with cream. Ivana said hello and put on a courteous professional smile – she took great care not to let Jaroslav think that she was unnerved by his presence.

'You've come to hide from the rain?'

'Guess again.'

Was it just her imagination or was Jaroslav flirting with her? 'Do you have a date with Hana here?'

Now Jaroslav shifted from one foot to another as if finding it awkward to hear Hana's name. Well, well, well! What might be going on here? Could there be trouble in paradise? Hana had not mentioned anything of the sort, even though the two girls had met only a couple of days earlier. Quite the contrary – Hana claimed that her mother was forcing her to leave for England with the rest of the family, but she wasn't prepared to go anywhere because she wanted to stay here with Jaroslav. But she did let slip that they hadn't seen much of each other lately as he was on some military exercise with his unit and not due back for another month at least. Interesting...

'So Miss Helerová hasn't left for England yet? The last time I saw her – I happened to run into her once this summer – she mentioned they were planning to leave after the holidays.'

Now that was strange. Very strange. Ivana went back to the counter, leaning on it with her elbows. 'She was supposed to leave but her sister's passport isn't ready yet. Hana didn't want to travel alone.' That was what Hana had told her mother who insisted that she should go ahead on her own. As a matter of fact, Hana had no intention of going. But she didn't want to break the news to her mother until the actual departure date. That's when she was going to move in with Jaroslav. Could she have failed to mention this to him? Or could one of them be lying?

'I've come back to make sure everything is all right,' said Jaroslav, quickly changing the subject. 'It's been raining so hard the river has burst its banks and the street where my parents live is often flooded.'

'Oh really?' Ivana raised her eyebrows feigning surprise. In fact, she knew perfectly well where Jaroslav's parents lived, having often deliberately walked that way with her former friend Hana, in the hope of running into him "accidentally on purpose". And then, one day, they did meet him but soon afterwards Jaroslav started to take Hana out for walks along the river after dark. 'I hope everything is all right.'

'Yes, the flood water passed us by this time,' Jaroslav said with a smile. 'I have to be back at the barracks tonight but it occurred to me that it's been a long time since I've seen my pretty friend. I couldn't resist and decided to stop by on my way to the station.'

Ivana's first thought was that he really wanted to find out if the Helers were still in town, but she blushed nevertheless. 'Can I get you something?' she asked quickly.

Jaroslav ordered an open sandwich, planted his elbows on the counter and started telling Ivana about the flood which, fortunately, hadn't reached further than their bottom step. Unlike the last time, when it got as far as the kitchen and they'd had to take the water out in buckets. There were no buckets left for him so he'd carried the water in a china cup but, instead of praising him, his mum took the cup away and slapped him across the face to boot because the china cup was part of her inheritance from her grandma, but how was he to know that, seeing as he'd been only three years old. Ivana laughed, completely forgetting that Jaroslav belonged to Hana, formerly her best, but now her former, friend. But she fancied Jaroslav so she didn't care in the least and agreed that the next time he came to Meziříčí she would let him take her for a walk by the river and would laugh at his stories.

As Jaroslav listened to her laughter, so full of joy and much more carefree than Hana's had been in the old days when she still used to laugh, he told himself that it was really Hana's fault that he was now standing at the delicatessen counter with Ivana, because Hana never smiled anymore and all she did was burden him with her worries and expect him to solve her problems for her, as if he didn't have enough to worry about as it was. So selfish of her.

He took the side streets on his way to the station to make sure he didn't run into her, and resolved to come back to Meziříčí only after Hana had left town.

But Hana didn't leave for England that September, nor did she leave later. While she still had the strength, she often wondered how different not just her own life but also that of her sister Rosa and her mother Elsa might have turned out if they had sold the house, packed their bags and boarded a train. If she hadn't met Jaroslav and fallen in love with him and had done the sensible thing instead.

Four years later, as Elsa Helerová and her parents perched above a freshly-dug ditch half-filled with bodies of those who had stood in the same spot before them, she shut her eyes firmly and thought that it was fate that had set her this test. But in actual fact it was Hana who had altered their fate by deciding, in the late summer of 1938, to do everything she could to delay their departure for England until the latest possible date. It was Hana who didn't do what her mother had asked her to do.

All their passports and visas had been issued except for one – Rosa's. Her papers had been delayed because she was under-age and her application was supposed to have both parents' consent attached to it.

'But her father is dead,' Elsa muttered as she opened a drawer and removed a sweet box made of tin in which she stored important documents. There, among the house deeds, her trading licence, marriage licence, and the family's birth certificates, was her husband Ervin's death certificate. 'Everyone knows me in this town, and everyone knows that I'm a widow, but these blessed bureaucrats won't do anything without their piece of paper,' she grumbled, stuffing the certificate into an envelope. 'Drop this letter off at the post office for me on your way to the Karáseks,' she called to Hana. 'I'm not going out just for one piece of paper! I'm busy as it is – some people interested in buying the house are coming to have a look.'

No sooner did the word get out that the house in the Square was on sale, a number of people showed interest. Who wouldn't be interested in a well-kept house with a stationer's and a tobacconist's on the ground floor, and a nice flat above? The problem was that everyone guessed the reason the widow Helerová was selling the house and that she was in a hurry to sell, and their offers were well below its real value. Truth be told, Elsa was desperate. She was terrified, just like thousands of other people who had by then realised that Europe – especially a small country like Czechoslovakia – was no longer a safe place to be. But she wasn't yet desperate enough to let herself be fleeced by those intent on exploiting her difficult situation and she clung to the hope that someone would come up with a reasonable offer. It could well have been Mr and Mrs Drozd, who were due to come at three o'clock this afternoon.

Hana took the envelope and stuffed it into the pocket of her light jacket.

'Don't put it there. Take a handbag. If you lose it, we're not going anywhere.'

If Elsa Helerová hadn't said this, it would never have crossed Hana's mind to do what she did. She would most likely have trotted off to the post office, bought a stamp and dispatched the letter. A few days later Rosa would have received her papers, and since the Drozds turned out to be decent people and after some haggling accepted Elsa's price, the Helers would have left for England that September.

Hana duly headed to the post office, but even as she was running down the stairs she already knew that she wasn't going to send the letter. In fact, she hadn't even brought it with her, having tucked it instead between the pages of *War and Peace*. It would be safe there. Elsa would never pick up a fat volume like that, and Rosa kept reading and re-reading her *Gabra and Málinka* novels.

It had been a long three weeks since Hana last saw Jaroslav – he must have been on a military exercise somewhere – but the last time they met, he had said explicitly that he was serious about her and would take care of her. Before she heard him utter these words, she had nearly been swayed by her mother's snide remarks about Jaroslav and was beginning to adjust mentally to the idea of setting out on the long journey. But now she knew she had to stay. Because her future was here, with Jaroslav.

Of course, she would send off the letter with the final bit of paperwork for her sister's passport. She would do it later. But not just yet.

For the first time in ages she felt almost happy. She had gained the time she so badly needed.

Chapter Fifteen

September 1938 - February 1939

Come September, Hana was in despair about Jaroslav's silence and the growing signals that after Austria, Hitler would next set his sights on Czechoslovakia. On several occasions she was tempted to trot off to the post office and send the letter with Rosa's certificate after all.

At night Hana's sleep was disturbed by nightmares as Sudetenland was gripped by unrest, with Henlein's supporters looting shops that had Czech and especially Jewish owners. The radio and newspapers carried reports of shootings, some of them fatal. It was frightening how much rage was unleashed by every hate-filled speech of Hitler's broadcast on German radio.

Eventually the army was ordered in and the looting was brought to a stop. Hana was relieved but couldn't stop worrying about Jaroslav. She was sure his unit must have been sent to the Sudetenland. Why else would he have been out of touch for so long? She had no news from him so she tried writing to him a couple of times at his barracks but never received a reply. That was to be expected. After all, he had advised her during their brief meetings in early summer not to write to him, that it would be pointless because he wouldn't be able to reply anyway. Hana wondered what else she could do to find out how he was.

She imagined him on the Western front, guarding fortifications he claimed to be impenetrable, with her photo in his breast pocket.

She was right in one respect. Jaroslav did indeed carry a photo in his breast pocket, except it was not hers but Ivana's. The army was combat-ready and he had to spend most of his time in the barracks and on manoeuvres, yet he still managed to find time to visit his new girlfriend. He would wait for her on the tree-lined road in Krásno, watch her through the delicatessen shop window and give the Square a wide berth to on his walks through town to make sure he didn't run into Hana.

When President Beneš declared general mobilisation, Hana realised that the war her mother wanted to protect her from was imminent. And that she had exposed her loved ones to danger. Mobilisation was the first step to war. And war meant shortages, fear, poverty and death.

She went to the room she shared with Rosa, and to the bookshelf where she kept Tolstoy's big volume that had failed to teach mankind any lessons, since those who read the classics are smart enough to understand the pointlessness of war without reading depictions of its cruelty, while those in need of a lesson would never reach for such a profound book anyway.

She found the letter, put it in her pocket and said, poking her head into the kitchen: 'I've promised to stop by Mrs Karásková.' Before her mother could ask why, she added: 'I'll be right back.' Then she raced to the post office as if she could catch up on the month by which she had delayed posting the letter. Maybe it's not yet too late, she kept telling herself, maybe Mother and Rosa can still get away in time. As for herself, she had no idea what she would do. It was now two months since she had last heard from Jaroslav.

Rosa's papers arrived in mid-October. But by then the situation had changed completely and Elsa Helerová had given up hope of leaving for England. She cancelled the removals company she had hired to transport her most valuable pieces of furniture and some bare necessities, tore up the list of things to pack, which she had spent ages drawing up, and returned the carefully cleaned suitcases to the attic. After the Munich Agreement was signed, Germany annexed the Sudetenland and the town of Nový Jičín, now known as Neutitschein, where Elsa and her parents had been born, was incorporated into the German Reich.

That was when Bruno and Gerta Weis fully realised how insignificant they were.

Three quarters of the population of Nový Jičín declared themselves German nationals. Bruno and Gerta Weis also spoke German at home and had sent their children to German schools. But they were Jewish and it wasn't only the reports from their son and other German refugees but also historical experience, ingrained in their genes and passed on from generation to generation, that made them pack the most valued possessions that they had inherited from their parents and grandparents and acquired in the course of their lives, and move in with their daughter in Meziříčí. They didn't wait for the German army to invade their town and for furious crowds chanting hostile slogans to march past their windows.

After her parents' furniture was unloaded in Meziříčí, Elsa stored it temporarily in the back yard of her house, covering it with sheets. Over the following week Karel Karásek helped the removals men carry the most valuable items up to his attic. This was the least Ludmila Karásková felt she could do to repay the Helers for their kindness. Parts of the bed in which Elsa had been born, and her brother Rudolf before her, were stowed under the Karáseks' attic window, the wardrobes with their bentwood doors were left in the middle of the room and the Thonet chairs were placed against the walls, all in the hope that one day everything would be loaded onto a removals truck again and taken, along with Mr and Mrs Weis and their possessions, back to Novy Jičín.

Bruno's armchair and Greta's two sets of dishes, one for milk and one for meat, found a new home in Helers' flat on the Square above the stationer's. Elsa's heart sank when she saw the growing piles of stuff. Soon there wouldn't be any room to move in the house. 'But Mutti,' she protested as her mother started to open yet another box: 'Where am I supposed to put all this? I have enough dishes as it is.'

'Hitler has driven me out of my house and kitchen so the least I can ask now is that you don't make me break the rules of kosher cooking,' Greta Weisová declared. 'From now on I'm in charge of the cooking.' She opened a cupboard, knelt down with a sigh, removed all of Elsa's pots and pans and started arranging her utensils on the shelves. Rather than watch this, Elsa went to show the removals men where to put the beds.

'Take them to the living room,' she said. 'We don't need a sitting room, we usually sit in the kitchen anyway.' Her father's armchair with its dark blue upholstery and armrests, said to have been custom-made for his grandfather, also found a place there under the window and Bruno Weis would sit there reading, raising his head from time to time and gazing in the direction where he guessed his town was.

The very same November day that Arnošt Langer's wife and her daughter arrived in Meziříčí found Bruno Weis sitting in his blue armchair. In the good old days when the Weis and Langer families had been neighbours, the two men would pass each other on the stairs, exchange respectful greetings, chat about the weather and ask to be remembered to their spouses. But while Mrs Langerová and her daughter were staying with the Helers, their discussions revolved around a single subject: what lay in store for Arnošt Langer and his son Max, taken away by gendarmes soon after Neutitschein's own *Kristallnacht*. The gendarmes claimed they did it to protect them from the enraged crowds swarming through the streets, looting Jewish shops and pillaging the synagogue.

'They have taken away all the men,' the stout Mrs Langerová sobbed, while her terrified, skinny daughter huddled on the sofa, dabbing at her eyes with a grubby handkerchief. 'I told them my Otto wasn't yet eighteen, but they didn't believe me. They yelled at me and threatened they would take us as well. When I looked out of the window, I saw them being piled onto a lorry. It was almost full.'

'Mrs Langerová,' Elsa cautioned her, 'you must take care not to speak German here in Meziříčí. The locals don't like it – especially these days.'

By now Mrs Langerová, too, had burst into tears. 'Czech, Czech! I can't even speak the language properly.'

Mrs Langerová and her daughter were the first of many overnight guests who found shelter at the Helers. Hana and Rosa had to vacate their room and share their mother's bedroom, and the left-hand side of the marital bed. This was particularly hard for the reclusive Rosa. 'I don't understand why they all pick us to move in with,' she complained. 'This house will soon turn into a dormitory.' And she continued, lowering her voice. 'Did you notice how Mrs Langerová's belly wobbles when she cries?'

'Rosa!' Hana reprimanded her, but she couldn't help laughing. Mrs Langerová was so fat that every single part of her wobbled.

After the annexation of the Sudetenland Elsa Helerová had definitely given up on the idea of moving to England. Secretly, she was quite relieved that the circumstances took the decision for her and that her place was now in this house, where she could provide at least temporary shelter to the unfortunates who had lost their homes. She empathised with them, understanding that she would have found herself in the same situation in England.

'Hitler got what he wanted so maybe now he'll leave us alone,' she said when her father tried to persuade her not to give up and keep trying to leave with her girls.

'You forget,' he said, 'that if you throw a begging dog a slice of salami, it won't leave you alone until it gets another and another.'

Elsa was reluctant to admit that her father was right. 'But tell me, where would you live if I sold the house and went to join Rudolf in England? At least I can be of some use here. Just look at these poor souls with nowhere to go. I'm sure the Langers aren't the only ones.'

Mr Langer and his son were released three weeks later on condition that they left German territory. All they were given for the journey was ten Reichmarks and the advice never to come back. They came to Meziříčí and Elsa Helerová helped them find a room to rent above the local tailor's workshop. The Langers would have preferred to move somewhere further away, like America, but they were penniless since they had to leave all their possessions behind in the Sudetenland. The Langers were followed by many others.

Few people ever came to the watchmaker's, two or three a day perhaps, to ask about a watch that needed fixing or to buy a new one. There was quite a lot of repair work as those were days when nothing was thrown out. People had more patience and appreciated the fact that everything needed time – relationships as well as things. They wouldn't file for divorce after a first row or waste money on buying something new the minute it stopped working properly. Craftspeople took care to make things durable, and many objects outlasted their makers, staying in the same family for generations.

Karel Karásek loved his work. Few of the clocks he handled were the same. Each new repair job was a challenge, a puzzle to be solved.

He enjoyed the peace and quiet of his ground-floor workshop. The only music he listened to was the gentle tune of the clockworks, the swinging of the pendulums and the chiming of clocks hanging on the walls. In his workshop he felt safe. He had no trouble answering his customers' questions and words of appreciation for a job well done flattered him. It made him feel that he wasn't quite the dolt his mother and those arrogant Heler women took him for.

Admittedly, sometimes he did feel rather ill at ease, especially in the company of women, but there were reasons for his lack of confidence. He had been raised by his mother and hardly remembered his father. He had no idea how a man ought to behave with a woman, didn't know where to draw the line between polite behaviour and presumptuousness. He was wary of offending women by staring at them, so he preferred not to look at them. He didn't know what men and women chatted about so he chose to say nothing. He didn't want women to think that his smile was too forward, so he frowned instead. And they had the cheek to call him an oaf! The devil alone could work out what went on in women's heads.

But he wasn't happy about the situation, as he didn't want to spend the rest of his life alone. He liked women and was particularly fascinated by their hands. They were full of life – slim, with slender fingers and delicate palms. He liked to imagine what it might be like to touch them.

The hands he especially longed to touch belonged to Ivana Zítková. What might it be like to let his hands wander up her arms all the way to her shoulders, bury his fingers in her long hair, slide them down to her blouse buttons, place the palms of his hands on her soft breasts and be close enough to inhale the sweet, sugary fragrance that Ivana gave off. Before falling asleep he allowed his fantasies to take him further, much further, and then he felt ashamed, as if he had actually defiled an innocent girl.

Sometimes, when Mrs Zítková's lower back was more painful than usual, it fell to Ivana to deliver the piles of ironed laundry to customers after she finished at the delicatessen. And since the washerwoman was no longer in the first flush of youth, evening deliveries gradually became Ivana's chore. Unlike Ivana, Karel Karásek was very happy about this. On Tuesdays when she was due to come, he would be waiting in his workshop impatiently, hoping to have a moment with her alone. He beamed with joy when she praised the work of his skilful fingers and she was the only person he allowed to touch the clocks on display. She was the only one for whom he was prepared to leave his workbench, open the glass door on the tall pendulum clock and show her how to wind up the clockwork by means of the weights suspended from metal chains, while breathing in her sweet fragrance from close up.

Then he would pay her for the laundry, adding some small change as tip and promise himself that on the next occasion he would pluck up the courage and ask Ivana to the cinema or even for an early evening walk in town. Lately, there was often a smile on Ivana's face but it had never occurred to Karel that it was not meant for him and that she was smiling not in anticipation of her tip but because outside, around the corner, Jaroslav was waiting for her as dusk fell. Ivana was excited about meeting him because by now, in January 1939, he was no longer Hana's Jaroslav but hers. The only problem was that her former best friend didn't know it yet.

'When I get married, I'll buy a clock like this one,' said Ivana, carefully closing the glass door and placing the key in Karel's open palm.

He was disconcerted by her touch: it felt almost intimate. 'And when's that going to be?' he blurted out, stunned that he found the courage to ask such a question.

She smiled. 'If it were up to me, I wouldn't mind getting

married straight away. But my Jaroslav is in the army...' She left the rest of the sentence hanging in the air and gave a deep sigh.

Karel Karásek stood there dumbfounded and couldn't believe his ears. He was expecting to hear something quite different. 'But I don't have anyone to marry' or 'Who would marry a girl like me', to which he would have responded 'Actually, I might', and then they would go to the pictures together and the rest would be the stuff of fairy tales. They would get married and Ivana would make a wonderful wife, he was sure of that, she would also be good at taking care of his mother. He had it all nicely worked out, but now he was standing in the middle of his shop in confusion, staring at the young woman who had been in his fantasies for many a night, and the only response he managed was a tactless: 'Jaroslav Horáček? But isn't he going out with Hana Helerová?'

That didn't unnerve Ivana. For a long time now she had been waiting for an opportunity to share the news that she and Jaroslav were a couple, with someone she could count on to relay it to the right address – that is, Hana. 'But Mr Karásek, that's long in the past. He and Hana broke up when she decided to leave for England.' Ivana picked up her money from the workbench, put it in her purse, popped the extra change into her pocket, buttoned up her coat all the way to the neck and said, flashing him a last, radiant smile: 'See you next week, Mr Karásek.'

'Bye now,' said Karel, returning to his workbench as if nothing had happened. He sat there for a further two hours without fixing any more watches.

Hana Helerová continued to put together her trousseau. She made two sets of bed linen, hemmed some towels and dishcloths, knitted a throw for a double bed and another for the kitchen sofa. As the pile of pillowcases for cushions both round and rectangular grew in her wardrobe, Hana kept going, patiently crocheting fine curtains and doilies and refusing to give up hope that the moment would soon come when Jaroslav was available for more than the odd fleeting, almost chance, encounter.

'We're living in difficult times,' he would repeat, as if she didn't know it. 'We must be patient. Don't worry, it'll all work out in the end.' And he would vanish for long weeks at a time.

In the evenings she transmuted her hopes, musings and anxieties into delicate doily patterns. She knew she couldn't complain and besides, she had no one to complain to. And she also knew full well that compared to the problems other people had, her unhappiness paled into insignificance.

The whole world was in motion. Not a week went by without yet another family from the area annexed by Germany arriving in Meziříčí. The Tintners, the Haases, the Kleins, the Honigwasches... They stayed with relatives or in rented rooms that the town authorities and various charities helped them find. The brunt was borne by the Jewish community, but Elsa Helerová, who wasn't a member, also tried to make herself useful. Jewish refugees found temporary shelter in the Helers' house. Elsa's mother Greta cooked kosher meals and in the evenings they found comfort discussing the *Daf Yomi*, the relevant page in the Torah for a particular day, with Bruno Weis.

Elsa Helerová had neither the time nor the inclination to concern herself with her older daughter's love troubles, but neither would Hana have wanted to confide in her. She remembered that her mother had never been keen on Jaroslav and had no desire to hear her say 'I told you so.'

The delicate Rosa felt for her sister and to her fifteen-year-old mind Hana's situation seemed tragic. She was less concerned about what the people who spent a few days staying with them were going through. She felt that their predicament was like illnesses or traffic accidents, something that affected only strangers, rather than something that could happen to her or her loved ones. Hana's grief, by contrast, pained Rosa, but she didn't know how to comfort her.

Hana had seen Jaroslav only four times since the summer. Their encounters were brief and marred by Jaroslav's restlessness and irritability.

In late February she ran into him on her way from the dressmaker's. She dashed towards him on wings of joy and would have thrown her arms around his neck if she hadn't been too shy. 'When did you come back?'

'Earlier today, but I'm here just for the afternoon. I would have sent word, but I didn't know how to, as your mother is not exactly happy about our relationship.'

'I see. When's your next day off?'

'I'm on duty all the time,' he explained impatiently and defensively. 'And when I do come home, I have to help my parents out, they're not so young anymore, you know.' Hana nodded. 'So many soldiers have been withdrawn from the Sudetenland, you can't imagine how much work the demobilisation involves. To say nothing of the need to secure the new border.'

Hana understood Jaroslav's problems, but she wasn't minded to discuss the difficult situation of the army. 'Maybe you could send me a postcard from time to time, just so I know that you're all right?'

'I can't write to you, I've told you already, remember?'

'Why are you cross? I'm just worried about you.'

'Don't you worry about me, you should worry about yourself.'

'How do you mean that?' asked Hana, tears welling up in her eyes. 'You said I didn't need to worry, that you'll take care of me.'

Well, yes, I did say that, Jaroslav felt like yelling. I said it when I thought you were about to get the hell out of here.

Have you really not clocked yet that it's over between us?
'Sure, of course,' he said. 'I will.'

'Forgive me,' said Hana. 'I know how tired you are and here I am, bothering you with my silly moaning. It's just that I love you and care about you.' She pressed her forehead into the lapel of Jaroslav's coat.

Casting an embarrassed glance around the street, he stroked her hair. 'I know. But I have to catch my train now.' After a moment's hesitation he said. 'I might have Sunday off in two weeks' time. Let's meet at five at our spot by the river. Do you think you'll be able to make it?'

'I'm sure I will,' Hana nodded. 'I'll think of something.'

Jaroslav nodded without a word and promised himself that he would use this time to figure out how to end the protracted relationship with Hana for good, however painful it might be.

But man proposes and something else – be it events, coincidence or malicious fate – disposes. In Jaroslav's case it was the events unfolding at the far end of the country, in Slovakia and Transcarpathia, that necessitated the presence of the Czechoslovak army. This time Jaroslav really wasn't to blame for finding himself in the thick of events that stopped him from keeping the appointment with Hana that she was so eagerly anticipating and which he had justifiably dreaded.

Hana had told her mother that she had to see Mrs Karásková but she kept her visit at the sick woman's house as brief as possible before hurrying to the shady spot under the trees where she and Jaroslav used to meet when they still were a real couple. After waiting in vain for more than half an hour she realised Jaroslav wasn't coming. Chilled to the bone and terrified by the unusually alarming noises around the dark river she returned home disappointed and went back to crocheting curtains in a new pattern Grandma Greta had taught her.

Chapter Sixteen

March 1939

Rain-sodden snowflakes fell from the sky, turning the streets into beds of squelching slush. A damp chill gripped the town, swamping it just like the German soldiers as they slowly marched down the streets of Krásno and crossed the bridge leading to the town centre. The Square, where vendors used to sell vegetables from their gardens and fruit from their orchards on market days, where townspeople stopped to taste home-made honey, check the poultry with an experienced hand and inspect the wares of the expert craftsmen, was now filled with military vehicles and ugly motorbikes with angular sidecars. Taciturn soldiers in rainproof coats sat in parked cars looking as if they planned to stay there forever.

People stood quietly on pavements lining the Square, pressing their backs into the walls of the houses. Maybe they hoped that the walls would protect them from the rough weather as well as the evil reality. For a while they looked on in silence, as if they couldn't believe the news on the radio and had to validate their misfortune with their own eyes, before returning to their homes in humiliation, their heads bowed under the burden of thoughts, hats jammed into their foreheads, drenched to the bone and filled with dread of the future.

The Helers didn't need to leave the house, as the horrible spectacle was unfolding right under their windows. Elsa and her parents were horrified. They sat helplessly amidst all the furniture, crammed into a room whose windows faced the other way. Perhaps they subconsciously wanted to keep as far away as possible from the Square, or maybe they just didn't want their tears to scare the girls even more.

Rosa resumed her childhood habit of sneaking into a corner behind the wardrobe and huddling there with her collection of postcards, her thin fingers picking over pictures of sunlit places where she longed to be at that moment. Only Hana stayed in the kitchen. She perched herself on the wide windowsill and watched as the Square filled with military lorries and motorbikes. Further vehicles crammed full of soldiers just passed through on their way to the local barracks.

A car screeched to a stop in front of the town hall and two figures in long military coats and flat caps leapt out. From the distance Hana could see them looking around for a welcoming committee, but not a single councillor had shown up. A lone flag with a swastika the wrong way around hung limply above the entrance. The men walked up the wide steps and disappeared into the building.

The direction of the wind changed, making the soggy snowflakes stick to the outside layer of the double-glazed window and blocking Hana's view. She slid off the windowsill and went to the bedroom. She crouched down by her sister's side, leaning against the wall. Silently she watched Rosa browsing through the postcards.

'This is where we could have been,' said Rosa, showing her a picture of Buckingham Palace that Uncle Rudolf had sent.

'I think you'll find that place is already occupied – by the King,' Hana tried to joke but Rosa didn't even smile.

'I was really hoping I'd see the sea,' Rosa went on without looking at Hana. 'That was one of the reasons I wanted to go to England so much. I was looking forward to crossing the English Channel in one of those big boats.' She raised her dark eyes to her sister and looked at her in a way that gave Hana a lump in her throat. 'You wanted to stay here because of Jaroslav, didn't you?'

There was no hint of a reproach in Rosa's question, but Hana certainly heard one. For an instant it flashed through her mind that Rosa knew about the certificate that had stayed hidden in the fat book for a month and was blaming her. She was tempted to start explaining why she had acted the way she had but Rosa continued. 'I heard the army will be disbanded now. That means Jaroslav will be able to marry.' She paused without taking her eyes off Hana. 'Does that mean that once you marry him you will no longer be a Jew?'

'What on earth makes you think that?'

'This afternoon Mummy said to Mutti Greta that it might be the best way out. Because the Germans hate the Jews and being married to a gentile would keep you safe.'

'Keep me safe? Safe from what?'

Rosa's eyes were still fixed on Hana, as if she didn't need to blink. 'I don't know. There is nowhere to flee now, they won't let us out anymore.' She drew her knees up and pushed herself deeper into the corner between the wall and the wardrobe. 'I don't think I will ever see the sea now.'

Hana reached out to her and patted her leg with a faked light-heartedness. 'Don't be silly, we're not proper Jews. You know how Mutti Greta keeps complaining that we wouldn't know how to behave in a synagogue if we happened to find ourselves in one.' She rose to her feet and gave Rosa a hand to help her get up.

A very similar conversation was taking place next door. Elsa's parents were trying to persuade her to make one last attempt to leave the country. But it was all in vain. Elsa was more scared of travelling through the Nazi-occupied country than of the uncertain future looming on the horizon if she didn't leave.

'I can't deprive my children of their home. And I absolutely can't leave you behind,' she repeated. 'If Ervin were still alive, I would be scared for him, but surely they won't harm women and old people. We pose no danger to them.'

'But they will take all our possessions away,' her father tried to persuade her. 'Haven't you heard the stories from the Langers and others who fled from the Sudetenland? How will you get by? They won't let you keep the shop, that's for sure. And who knows what will happen to the house? Just take the girls and leave. You must try. You have the documents. Maybe you can still do it.'

But Elsa had made up her mind. And, just as over the years she had got used to widowhood, she wiped her tears away and set her mind to planning how best to survive the difficult times ahead. Planning always helped to calm her down.

'Hana must marry that Horáček man of hers as soon as possible. And I will talk to Skácel, the tobacconist, and see if he would buy the stationer's from me, for appearances' sake. I will forgive some of his debts and lower his rent.'

'Things are not as simple as you imagine, my dear girl. Once you've signed the shop over to him, you'll never get it back.'

'I'm not stupid. I'll ask a lawyer to draw up papers stating that I'm the real owner...'

Her father shook his head. 'Listen to my advice, Elsa...'

All of them had trouble falling asleep that night. Bruno and Greta Weis were quietly discussing how to make Elsa leave. Elsa was wondering how to persuade the tobacconist to go along with a fictitious purchase without ripping her off. Hana was picturing Jaroslav's face when she told him that her mother approved of their relationship. And Rosa was lying on her back trying to keep her eyes open because, as soon as her eyelids fell, lorries would swarm out of darkness with endless rows of soldiers jumping out of them.

The very next day Elsa went to consult a lawyer, Dr Lewy. Like Elsa and Ervin, Karel Lewy had renounced the Jewish faith, which gave Elsa some hope that he might understand her situation. She was sure that he, too, must feel trapped in limbo, not belonging anywhere. Jews no longer saw him as one of their number while everyone else took his Jewishness for granted. 'Which lawyer will you hire?' the locals would ask, and the answer would always be unambiguous: 'The Jewish one.' Until recently this wasn't particularly significant. In fact, being Jewish was regarded as a recommendation for a lawyer since Jews were generally known to be good at business and law. But lately the term had acquired a different, ominous subtext, and people uttered it in hushed tones, as if ashamed of using the word.

Elsa Helerová returned home with mixed feelings. Dr Lewy thought it would be a good idea for Hana to marry an Aryan. 'From what I know about the new German legislation I assume that a mixed marriage won't erase your daughter's Jewish origins but it might offer her a degree of protection,' he said. 'In fact, that's exactly what my brother is also hoping for.' As for the sale of the shop, Dr Lewy promised he would help Elsa, but only after emphasising that in the circumstances there was no guarantee that her tenant wouldn't cheat her. 'You have to think twice before handing your property over to someone, Mrs Helerová. You'll have to choose someone you can really trust.'

And there was the rub. Elsa Helerová knew she couldn't trust Skácel but neither could she think of anyone else she could sign the shop over to without it being too obvious. She knew that the Karáseks would agree to do it, but the new owner – even if only a straw man – had to actually run the shop. And that was something she couldn't expect of Karel Karásek. Maybe she ought to see Mr Berger, the furrier, and ask his advice. Berger was an experienced man who had been through a lot and always managed to cope. Perhaps he might suggest a solution.

She tightened the scarf on her head and started walking back to the Square, lost in thought. She avoided looking anywhere but straight ahead, as the sight of armed soldiers in the streets alarmed her. They might pretend to be the liberators, even give food handouts to the poor, but everyone was aware that the food actually came from the storerooms of the Czech army barracks.

The Square was almost empty. Elsa turned towards the furrier's but after a few steps she noticed that the windows were covered with heavy black shutters and a gendarme was standing outside the door. A Czech gendarme. She hesitated for a moment, then plucked up the courage to approach him.

'Has there been a burglary?' she asked, realising how silly her question sounded. Who would be foolish enough to try thieving when the town was teeming with uniforms?

The gendarme raised his eyebrows. He must have been thinking the same thing. Then he looked around, shook his head slightly and said quietly: 'You'd better go home, lady. Mr Berger has hanged himself.'

She didn't need to ask why. The gendarme knew why, she knew why, the whole town knew why. Mr Josef Berger, a respected citizen of Meziříčí, was a Jew. He knew that Hitler hated the Jews, had heard reports of arrests, persecution and humiliation of his co-religionists and of synagogues burned down during the *Kristallnacht,* and refused to bow to the inevitable. After lunch he returned to his shop early and took his own life. He decided to do it his own way, a decision which his widow Rudolfína, frantic with despair, regarded as a sign of weakness at the time but would come to regard as clear-sightedness a few years later when she stared death in the face herself, in the Łódź ghetto. But for Elsa that wasn't a solution. She was not alone in the world – she was responsible for her two daughters. She had brought them into this world, had always wanted only the best for them, and she would continue to take care of them now. She had to.

She turned on her heels and hurried home across the Square. At the front door she bumped into the tobacconist. She would have a conversation with him as soon as possible and come to some arrangement, but she wasn't feeling up to it now. She said hello and wanted to go inside, but Skácel positioned himself in the door so awkwardly that her way was blocked.

'Excuse me,' she said, trying to enter the building.

Skácel didn't move and Elsa realised that he was blocking her way deliberately.

'Please let me through,' she said, trying to squeeze past him.

Skácel gave a laugh and moved to make it even more difficult for her to pass. Elsa stopped, baffled. 'What kind of joke is this? Please let me through, I'm going home.'

Skácel burst out laughing as if she had said something very witty, before stepping aside. 'Do come in, my good woman. You won't be throwing your weight around here for much longer. Soon enough Hitler will clip the wings of people like you.'

Elsa stood there aghast. 'What do you mean? I've always treated you fairly.'

'Oh, is that what you call fair? You've been fleecing me with your exorbitant rent. Typical. A stingy Jewess.'

Elsa hurried towards the stairs.

'It's over, Helerová,' she heard behind her back. 'Why don't you follow the example of your pal Berger?'

Once inside, she slammed the door shut and leaned back against it. Her knees were shaking, and her temples throbbing with rage. She had never liked Skácel but didn't expect such an outpouring of hatred. He had always talked to her in a polite way before.

Then it dawned on her. As of yesterday, she had become a second-class citizen. A dreadful thought crossed her mind. Was this how everyone would treat her and her daughters from now on?

Rosa poked her head into the hallway. 'We have a visitor, Mummy.' Eyeing her mother suspiciously, she asked: 'Is something wrong?'

Elsa shook her head. 'I'm just out of breath, I went up the stairs too fast.'

'You must have heard the news of Mr Berger?' said Rosa, taking her mother's coat and hanging it up.

'So you've heard already?' Elsa couldn't believe how fast news travelled around town.

'The gentleman here to see you told us. He says he's come about the shop.'

Here we go, thought Elsa. The vultures are circling.

The man who rose from the chair to greet her seemed familiar, but Elsa couldn't place him.

'Good afternoon, boss,' said the visitor and only then did she recognise Alois Urbánek, the former boy from Ervin's stationer's. He was no longer the slender youth he had been, his features had grown coarser since she last saw him six years ago but he still put too much grease on his dark hair. He stood there scrunching the hem of his hat in his hands, looking awkward.

'Take a seat,' she said and hesitated, not sure how to address her visitor, 'Mr Urbánek,' she continued after a pause, when she realised that her long silence was impolite. 'What has brought you here... after all these years?'

Alois Urbánek sat down on the edge of the chair and fixed her with the gaze she couldn't stand in the old days. 'I've heard that you're moving abroad. And that you might be letting your shop. I've been thinking... I know I didn't treat you well after the boss died, and I'm sorry about that. You needed me and all I was thinking of was money. It must have been a difficult time for you. But I've learnt my lesson, believe you me. I work at the factory, the job isn't bad and they're happy with me, but my place is in the shop, Mrs Helerová. I've always been good at selling things, Mr Heler used to praise me, so I've been thinking, in case you're looking for someone to let the shop to, I could send you the rent every month or however often you'd like me to. I know you think that I'm trying to exploit your situation again but please believe me, the only reason I've acted so quickly was to make sure nobody got here before me.'

Elsa remained silent.

'This isn't a bad idea, Elsa, don't you think?' her father chipped in.

But Elsa shook her head. 'You are wrong, Mr Urbánek, we are not planning to leave.'

Elsa's father gave a deep sigh and bowed his head.

'I'm sorry, I didn't realise, I thought...' the former shop assistant stuttered. He rose to his feet and made for the door.

'Wait a minute,' Elsa held him up. 'I might have a proposition for you.'

Alois Urbánek stopped and looked at her in anticipation.

'Wouldn't you like to buy the shop from me?'

'But Mrs Helerová,' said Urbánek with a sad smile, 'where on earth would I find so much money? I have a wife and two children, and hardly any savings.'

'Rosa,' said Elsa turning to her daughter, 'go down to the shop and give Hana a hand.' After Rosa reluctantly left the room, Elsa turned to the former shop hand. 'Take a seat and let me explain.'

And so, while people walking down the main square cast furtive glances as the coffin with the body of poor Mr Berger was being carried out of the furrier's and Skácel the tobacconist couldn't wipe a smile off his face because he'd finally given the Heler woman an earful, Elsa and Alois Urbánek agreed to a fictitious sale of the shop.

The next day the two of them went to see Dr Lewy who provided not only advice but also practical assistance. He recommended backdating the contract a few years, to the time after Ervin Heler's death. 'It will be less conspicuous that way.'

'But surely that can't be done just like that?' Elsa objected. 'It's all been in my name all this time: the trading licence, the tax returns...'

'Leave that side of things to me, Mrs Helerová. And I'm sure I don't need to stress that you should keep this to yourselves.' Lewy looked at the young man at Elsa's side. 'With a bit of luck these terrible times will blow over one day, and you will get back what is yours.'

Alois Urbánek understood and nodded.

Chapter Seventeen

March 1939 - December 1939

As it turned out, Elsa showed great foresight in taking these steps. Only a week later a decree was issued that prohibited Jews from selling or leasing factories or workshops, public houses, restaurants as well as shops, large or small. Everyone knew this was just the beginning.

By then Alois Urbánek had started working in the stationer's and Elsa had to admit that her late husband had been right. The young man seemed to be made for business. The customers – especially female ones – were delighted with the new shop assistant.

'You've got yourself a wonderful new assistant, Mrs Helerová,' the women said as they left the shop carrying not just the wrapping paper they had come for but also waxed paper bags, paper baskets and a tiny notebook, which no good housewife could manage without, as the new assistant assured them.

'Mr Urbánek has always been a part of the shop,' Elsa would say vaguely, so that if necessary, she could later say: 'Why, I told you the shop belongs to Mr Urbánek.'

Although she would never have said so aloud, she regretted having fired Urbánek some years ago. Had she come to an agreement with him then, she would have saved herself a great deal of trouble. Maybe her hair wouldn't have turned grey so fast and the worry lines at the root of her nose might not have been so deep. She might have been able to spend more time with her daughters and instead of just teaching them things, she could have listened to them and learned more about their likes and dislikes, their hopes and fears.

She gave a deep sigh. Let bygones be bygones. She had only done what she thought was right, back then, when Ervin suddenly left them, but also now that she had made a deal with Urbánek. There was nothing more she could do to save the family property. Now she had her daughters to take care of.

Her parents tried to persuade her to let the girls join their uncle Rudolf in England but that would have meant Rosa dropping out of middle school, only a few months before graduating. She obviously had to finish school: what would become of her without any education? These troubles wouldn't go on forever, surely. Sooner or later things would settle down. They always did.

As for Hana, Elsa couldn't manage without her. She often sent her to drop in on Mrs Karásková in her stead. Hana was helping to keep the Karáseks' home tidy, doing some cooking and occasionally kept the sick woman company. No, the girls would stay here where they were born.

Dr Lewy had said that marrying an Aryan wouldn't be a bad solution. Rosa was too young to get married, but Hana was clearly itching to tie the knot. She'd been collecting her trousseau for months now and her sighing was getting unbearable. So why not let her marry that soldier of hers?

In the evening, after Hana had gone to Mrs Karásková's and Rosa sat at the kitchen table struggling with an essay, Elsa went into what had been the sitting room and was now the bedroom of her parents Bruno and Greta Weis, pulled up a chair to face her father's armchair and shared her ideas with him. If she had expected advice, she certainly didn't receive any. Her father Bruno just nodded and implored her for the hundredth time to take the girls and go to England to join Rudolf. Mutti Greta prayed quietly. Elsa would have to decide on her own.

She returned to the kitchen, sat down opposite Rosa and watched her painstakingly compose her essay. Hana came in just as Rosa was writing the last word and triumphantly shutting her exercise book.

'Hana,' said Elsa, relieving her daughter of an empty saucepan in which she'd sent some potato soup to the Karáseks, 'do you think your Jaroslav would like to come for lunch this Sunday?'

How was Hana to tell her mother that she had no idea where Jaroslav was? The Czechoslovak army ceased to exist once the Protectorate of Bohemia and Moravia had been declared. Most professional soldiers had turned down the offer to join the Government Army – as the Protectorate's military force was known – and left it one by one. Hana could only guess what Jaroslav had chosen to do but as he hadn't been in touch since their last chance meeting, she concluded that he had yet to return to Meziříčí.

She decided to write him a note and deliver it to his parents' house. The couple had kept their relationship secret so she had never visited the little house by the river and had never met Jaroslav's parents.

But everything would be different now that her mother had changed her mind, she thought. They would no longer need to worry about being seen by someone who might give their secret away.

She knocked on the door of the one-storey house and looked around as she waited. The river had risen in the past few days, rushing downstream over the boulders that normally jutted out of the water, and the bare trees on its bank looked like skeletons reaching their gaunt arms out as if begging for a piece of bread. A misty chill hung in the air, settling in tiny drops on everything – the muddy path, the frozen clumps of grass, the patches of damp on the walls of the house, as well as Hana's warm coat.

Hana knocked again, this time more firmly, and before she had time to pull her hand back, the door opened. The first thing that crossed Hana's mind was that the tiny woman in a woollen cardigan couldn't possibly be Jaroslav's mother. She looked too frail and petite.

'Can I help you, young lady?' the woman flashed her the same kind of smile Jaroslav used to have for her, and Hana instantly felt more at ease.

'Hello, Mrs Horáčková. My name is Hana Helerová. I've brought a message for Jaroslav, would you be so kind and give it to him when he comes back?' she asked, taking the letter out of her pocket.

Mrs Horáčková looked at the envelope but didn't take it. 'Why, he's at home, Miss Hana. I'll get him for you and you can give him the letter yourself.' She took a few steps to a door on the right and called: 'Jaroslav, you have a visitor.' She smiled at Hana and disappeared inside the house.

Jaroslav peered out of the hallway and pulled a surprised face. 'Hana....' he said, quickly closing the door behind him. Hana beamed at him, slipped the letter back into her pocket and cast a quick glance at her shoes to check that she wasn't bringing any mud into the hallway. But Jaroslav didn't invite her in. Instead he took his coat off the hook on the wall of the narrow hallway, put it on hastily without doing up the buttons, grabbed Hana by her elbow and started dragging her away.

'Wait a minute,' said Hana, wresting herself free. 'Why do you have to drag me like that? Aren't you pleased to see me, not even a little bit?'

Jaroslav looked around and once he made sure they couldn't be seen from the windows of his house, he stopped and let go of Hana. 'What are you doing here?'

'I've come to ask you for lunch at our house. My mother has invited you for lunch, do you understand?' She smiled at him as if he were an uncomprehending child and tried to stop him from dragging her away. 'We don't have to hide anymore. My mother said we can get married.'

'Married?' Jaroslav repeated in disbelief.

'Yes, she even said that the wedding should be as soon as possible.' She hesitated, not sure whether to continue and give the impression that she wanted to marry Jaroslav out of self-interest. 'Apparently it's a good thing that you're not Jewish.'

Jaroslav suddenly looked tired. 'You're not getting it, are you?' he asked quietly.

'I'm not getting what?'

'That it's not your mother who's the problem.'

Hana threw up her arms in surprise. 'Well...' then she let her arms drop.

He sighed. 'The problem is that *you are Jewish.*'

Hana took a deep breath. 'Yes, and that's precisely why my mother said that when we get married...'

'But we're not going to get married. Precisely because you're Jewish. What planet are you on? Haven't you noticed the mess you're in? Hitler hates the Jews! I told you to leave the country.'

'You told me no such thing.'

'Please don't drag me into this now. I didn't try to talk you out of it either.'

'You said you would marry me, that you'd take care of me.'

'Only because I thought you'd have the sense to clear off to England. You and that mother of yours. First I'm not good enough for her and now suddenly I'm a great match!' He looked around as if he was worried that he might be overheard. 'You must know about the anti-Jewish laws now in force in Germany. If they are introduced here, which they will be, things will look bad for you.'

Hana pressed her hands to her ears. She could no longer hold back her tears. She now understood why they had seen so little of each other lately. Why their meetings had been so fleeting and what was behind Jaroslav's unease, which he kept putting down to the times being difficult. She finally admitted to herself what she had long suspected. Jaroslav didn't want her. It was as simple as that.

She turned around and hurried away. In her heart of hearts she still hoped that he would call out to her and ask her to come back, give her a hug and ask for her forgiveness. Maybe he would say she'd been too heavy-handed and given him a fright. But no call came and by the time she reached the bridge and looked back, the street was deserted.

She dried her tears and hurried home, staring at the pavement so that the passers-by wouldn't see her red eyes and guess what had happened. She passed the door of the stationer's where she saw her mother serving a soldier in a German uniform, ran up the stairs and locked herself in her room. She sat down on her bed hoping that a good cry would relieve her humiliation, disappointment and hopelessness.

Even though her meetings with Jaroslav had become rare, he still was a part of her life. When he wasn't around, she would talk to him in her head, imagining what she would say to him when they met. She would confide all her worries to him and he would comfort her. He would say that she shouldn't worry and that he would take care of her.

Now she knew these were all lies. She waited for her tears to wash away the sense of powerlessness and emptiness that threatened to overwhelm her, but the tears wouldn't come.

Two tears, she thought. Just the two tears that seeped into the sleeve of her coat. That was all Jaroslav was worth. She went over to the pile of bed linen and tablecloths she had assembled, shoved it all into the wardrobe and then furiously kicked her trousseau into its farthest corner.

That evening she told her mother that Jaroslav wasn't coming for lunch because they had had a disagreement. And that it was over.

'Is there no way...? This is not a good time for petty quarrels,' Elsa ventured.

Hana looked her mother straight in the eye. 'You were right, Mother, he was never going to marry me.'

She couldn't bring herself to be completely frank with her mother and admit that Jaroslav didn't want her because she was Jewish. It would have been just as humiliating as admitting that he had left her because she had bad breath or dirty fingernails.

Elsa just shrugged and stopped asking questions. She had never liked this Horáček fellow anyway and was willing to tolerate him only because she thought he could save her daughter from any discrimination that she might experience in the future.

Luckily, people aren't to know what lies in store for them. Elsa, Hana or Rosa didn't know either and that was the only reason they could go to bed night after night and get up in the morning hoping that the new day would be no worse than the previous one. But that happened very rarely. The Helers were spared the arrests that occurred in the first few days after the Germans marched in, but they couldn't escape the impact of the regulations the new authorities introduced soon after the Protectorate was declared. In June the Nuremberg Laws came into force.

'I'm well aware of being Jewish and don't need any official decrees to show it,' Elsa commented on the introduction of the new laws one day while visiting Mrs Karásková. 'And even if I did want to remarry, I would certainly not pick a loud-mouthed Kraut and would never let my daughters marry one either.'

Mrs Karásková did nothing but nod. She knew that Elsa was trying to drown her worries by shouting and didn't want to frighten her friend even more. In addition, she found it increasingly difficult to speak and you had to be used to her halting way of talking to understand her.

In September Germany invaded Poland. Hana and Rosa had to move into their mother's bedroom once again as the Helers often shared their house with overnight visitors. And they were not the only ones, as the girls soon discovered – the refugees also found shelter with other families, sent there by Anna, the wife of the leader of the Jewish community in Meziříčí and sometimes also by Dr Lewy.

Mutti Greta took charge of the Helers' kitchen while Elsa divided her time between the shop and looking after the refugees. Hana and Rosa listened in horror to their accounts of the frightful events in Poland. They weren't to know that the wind that was starting to blow would soon turn into a ferocious whirlwind that would sweep them along. Poland seemed so far away.

The refugees were mostly young people who would stay for a night or two before setting out in the dark to continue their journey into the unknown, never to come back.

Elsa was often so exhausted she had no strength left for her late afternoon visits to Ludmila Karasková's house. Instead, she would send Hana more and more often. Hana would tidy up and help Ludmila do things Karel couldn't or wouldn't do. It wasn't so much the sick woman's slurred speech that prevented Hana from having meaningful conversations with her but rather their completely incompatible characters, interests, experiences, and not least the generation gap. She couldn't talk to the old woman about their occasional overnight visitors who stopped by on their journey south, so instead, to live up to her role of a good companion, she offered to read to her from the newspaper.

'I'd pre... fer a no... vel ...' Ludmila said. 'With a hap – py en – ding.'

And so Hana, tormented by betrayal, picked up the *Evenings under the Lamp* paperbacks and read her romantic stories of love overcoming all obstacles. She was usually gone before Karel Karásek came home from his workshop.

One evening she heard heavy steps on the stairs and thought the Karáseks had a visitor. She wasn't expecting Karel. Normally he crept around as silently as a ghost and didn't come home until his mother was alone. Hana knew he wasn't keen on visitors – her in particular – and guessed that this was why he avoided her. The kitchen door opened and Hana raised her head from the book. Karel squeezed through the door sideways, carrying a pile of freshly pressed laundry in his arms.

'Poor Miss Ivana,' he said, putting the laundry down on the table. 'She does bring the washing in a handcart, but in this...'

Hana looked up and reached for her coat. 'Ivana Zítková? I'll be off then. I haven't seen her for ages, I might still catch up with her.'

Karel cleared his throat awkwardly. 'Oh, so you're still friends?'

'Why shouldn't we be friends? We went to school together.'

'Erm, I just thought...' he glanced at his mother and stopped in his tracks.

'You thought what?'

'Oh, nothing.' Karel turned his back on her and took some tea-towels from the pile of laundry and put them in a cupboard.

Hana looked at Mrs Karásková but the old woman averted her gaze.

'Has something happened?'

Karel didn't reply.

'Why can't you tell me what's happening? Do you think that just because you can't stand me, no one else can either?'

Karel turned to face her, planted his hands on the table and took a deep breath. 'Well then. I just thought you might not be best pleased that your friend is marrying

Horáček.' He picked up the bed linen and left the room, slamming the door.

'Does he really hate me so much?' said Hana, her eyes stinging with anger, grief, betrayal and humiliation. She caught Mrs Karasková's pitying look and realised he had told the truth.

She stormed out of the kitchen without saying goodbye, ran down the stairs, slipped on her shoes and coat and left the house. She reached the end of the street just in time to catch a glimpse of two figures pulling a handcart across the bridge.

Hana Helerová stood on the corner of Bridge Street clutching the lapels of her unbuttoned coat and watching her best friend Ivana Zítková let go of the handcart's handles, gather some snow from the bridge railing and throw a snowball at the man by her side. In the light of the streetlamp she saw the man turn around, give a laugh, shake the snow off his coat, put his arm around the girl's shoulders and grab the handcart with his free hand. By the time she caught a glimpse of the familiar profile she knew Karel Karásek wasn't lying.

However humiliating the Nuremberg Laws may have been, they hadn't affected the Helers very much before September 1939. But after the invasion of Poland, after war officially broke out, the pace of events quickened. One anti-Jewish decree was issued after another. First they were forbidden from going to cinemas and theatres. Next, when separate areas had to be set aside for them in public houses and restaurants, Elsa declared that they would never set foot in those establishments. Hana thought that was quite an unnecessary remark, since, owing to Elsa's proverbial thriftiness, they never went to restaurants anyway.

The next restriction was a ban on going out after eight o'clock in the evening. Elsa stubbornly broke it, keeping up her early evening visits to the Karáseks, but this lasted only until she was waylaid by the tobacconist who threatened to inform on her. Skácel's threats had to be taken seriously. Elsa knew he was just waiting for an opportunity to get rid of his mounting debt. He'd owed her back rent since March and instead of blaming difficult times as before, he would now just bombard her with vile curses.

Things started to get really tough in November. All Jewish businesses were assigned a *Treuhänder*, a custodian. Everyone knew where this person's loyalties lay. The custodian's main job was to prepare Jewish businesses for Aryanisation, being taken over by non-Jews. This was the moment Skácel had been waiting for. Before even the decree became widely known, the tobacconist expressed his interest in being appointed custodian to the stationer's owned by the Jewess Helerová.

To his immense surprise he learned that the shop didn't belong to Elsa Helerová but to Urbánek, the man who had recently started working there. 'Helerová sold her shop to Alois Urbánek right after the Jew Heler died,' he was told at the property office.

'That's impossible,' Skácel shouted angrily. 'Urbánek has been working there for less than six months. He'd never shown his face there before.'

'The documents show he's been the owner since 1933. But we can double-check that, of course.'

Dr Lewy had done a thorough job. The check confirmed that the widow Helerová hadn't owned the shop for the past six years. When Skácel received the definitive confirmation from the authorities, he dived into the first pub and got quite drunk even though it was well before lunchtime. In this inebriated state he staggered into the stationer's, stopped at the counter and yelled at the astonished Urbánek: 'I will get that stinking Jewess out of here, just you wait. And you'll go with her. Don't think you've won. Once I've figured out how you did that, you'll end up in the slammer – all of you!'

Elsa Helerová didn't dare to stick her nose out of the storeroom and hoped that the yelling couldn't be heard up in the flat. Meanwhile, Urbánek came out from behind the counter, grabbed the drunken Skácel and pushed him out of the side door and into the tobacconist's across the corridor. There he pressed him against the wall and whispered right into his face: 'Don't go shouting too loudly or someone will hear you and one day you'll be found hanged! Don't you know what happens to traitors?'

The whispered threat must have left its mark on Skácel despite his drunken state, as from then on he limited himself to shooting hateful looks at Urbánek and Helerová. He probably had no idea that Alois Urbánek was even more terrified by his own words and that he didn't sleep a wink for two nights, stunned by his own bravery. He relaxed only when he realised that Skácel was genuinely scared of him. And although he was sorely tempted, he resisted the urge to brag to his wife about his heroic deed, because he had an inkling that rather than justly deserved praise, her response would have been an undeserved reproach.

Chapter Eighteen

1940-1941

How often Elsa Helerová wished she could turn the clock back. 1940 saw further decrees curbing the rights of Jewish citizens of the Protectorate, regardless of whether their Jewishness was as important to them as much as it was to Elsa's parents – who accepted their difficult situation as the age-old tragic lot of their people – or whether they had never given it any thought, like Hana and Rosa. Until recently, they hadn't regarded their origin as anything more than a kind of common hereditary trait, like the colour of one's eyes or a predisposition to putting on weight that may run in the family. Elsa now knew that she had made a mistake that could no longer be put right.

It was dreadful to be made to pay for a form, personally delivered by the chairman of the Jewish Religious Community, which required her to list all her property. But it was even worse to see how embarrassing it was for someone who used to be a lawyer to charge her for the form, which he had to hand in at the local council.

She was frightened when in March the German authorities issued another decree, giving Jews just two weeks to hand over all items made of gold, silver, platinum, precious stones and pearls. Elsa didn't own any jewellery and she refused to give up her wedding ring, a memento of her late husband. Overcoming her vertigo, she climbed up a steep ladder to their attic, squeezed through a narrow opening and managed to hide the ring in a knothole in a beam so well that it was never found again.

As the summer drew to a close, an order was issued for an inventory of all Jewish property to be drawn up, and Elsa's anxiety grew to the point that she could barely breathe. But she was even more saddened by the resignation in her parents' faces and the unspoken question in her daughters' eyes. What next? their eyes were asking. Luckily, Elsa didn't know the answer.

Next the Jews were banned from holding jobs in public service and Hana couldn't start teaching at the local primary school. As a matter of fact, she had never wanted to be a teacher but she needed a job and so she started working at the local tapestry works, an even less attractive proposition. They badly needed the money as the takings from the shop, although Alois Urbánek was dutifully handing them over to Elsa in secret, were not enough to sustain a family of five. As Jews, Elsa's parents were not entitled to any pension or benefits, and Rosa was employed in the stationer's only for the sake of appearances, because Elsa was still plagued by groundless fears about her daughter's health.

Dr Lewy helped Hana find a job a few weeks before the Gestapo came to arrest him for anti-German activities. One morning three men rang the bell at the lawyer's house and dragged him out as he was, in his home clothes and slippers. Before he was shoved into a waiting car, his mother Berta managed to take his light summer jacket off the hanger and pick up a worn pair of shoes he used to wear to tend to the roses in his garden. She stuffed everything into a canvas shopper, ran to the car and squeezed it through the door at the last minute. Then she watched the car start and turn at the end of the road towards Vsetín. That was the last she saw of her son.

Rather than bothering the courts in the Reich with the case of some Jew from Meziříčí, Mr Karel Lewy, until recently one of the town's most respected citizens, wearing his home trousers, a light jacket and worn-out gardening shoes, was sent straight to Auschwitz in Poland, where he died of exhaustion two months later.

For several weeks after his arrest the Helers were in great anguish, in case the Gestapo discovered while interrogating Lewy that he had helped Elsa with the fake sale of the stationer's and that the Helers were giving shelter to Jews who had managed to escape from Poland.

One day in September 1941 Hana was again sitting by Mutti Greta, her head bowed over her handiwork. This time, however, she wasn't busy embroidering monograms for her trousseau. She was sewing yellow Stars of David, with the word *Jude* in black lettering, on their coats, blouses and pullovers.

'If you had done as we told you and left in time, you wouldn't have to walk around town branded like cattle,' said Mutti Greta with tears in her eyes, and it didn't escape Hana's attention that her mother just shook her head and left the kitchen.

'Do a proper job,' Mutti Greta reprimanded Hana. 'Can't you see a corner is coming unstuck there? You don't want people to bad-mouth us for looking dishevelled, on top of everything else.'

The first time Hana ventured out wearing a jacket with a Star of David sewn above her heart, she was grateful that the Czechs had stuck to their peculiar custom of starting work at six in the morning. Introduced under Austro-Hungary by the insomniac ruler Franz Josef, the custom had been sensibly abandoned as irritating and unhealthy by other successor states after the break-up of the empire, but now it enabled Hana to walk down the still-dark streets almost without being noticed. Her fellow workers at the tapestry works avoided looking at the Star of David and pretended to pay no attention to it, and this pretence actually became a reality after a while. Hana noticed that the women chatted to her more often than before, and that some who had previously ignored her would now strike up a conversation. She realised they did it to indicate their disapproval of the degrading badge and to show their solidarity.

This knowledge made it easier for her to walk home. Most people pretended not to see the symbol sewn onto her coat, some passers-by guiltily averted their gaze, while others nodded their greeting, even if Hana didn't recall having met them before.

The authorities now started to assign people to forced labour. Hana's mother Elsa, registered as a housewife and, like her parents, not employed, was therefore classified as a person who was not useful, as she made no contribution to the common good of the Reich and its victory. She was therefore assigned to a brigade of six persons.

Together with five other unfortunates she was made to sweep the town pavements, scrub off anti-German graffiti that would sometimes appear on the walls of side streets, and in winter, wearing lace-up boots, thick stockings and her warmest coat embellished only with the Star of David, she had to clear away snow with a wooden shovel.

The names of Greta and Bruno Weis were added to a reserve list of some hundred people capable of auxiliary work. As a result, during their final months in Meziříčí, Elsa worried that her parents, now in their seventies, might also be forced to go out into the streets with a broom in their hands.

It was a November evening. A cold wind ruffled Hana's hair, blasted up her sleeves, sent a chill down her skirt and made her fingers turn blue as she gripped a shopping bag. She walked fast. She didn't like going out after dark because of the blackout; she could hardly see where the pavement ended, or a step jutted out, or if there was a gaping hole in the pavement. But this time it wasn't the potholes that bothered her as much as the rude remarks from a bunch of cocky young brats. Branded as she was with the Star of David on her dark coat that shone into the night, she felt she was at their mercy. Four ten- to twelve-year-old lads latched on to her on the bridge and followed her, shouting abuse and chanting half-witted slogans. As she was nearing the Square Hana started to run but the boys were faster. They caught up with her in front of the stationer's and surrounded her. 'Filthy Jew!' shouted one. A boy in a peaked cap got hold of a corner of Hana's coat and smelled it. 'Yuck, she really does stink.' Hana swung her bag at him and tried to push through to the front door. Just at that moment the door of the shop swung open and Alois Urbánek shot out. 'Get lost, you scoundrels,' he shouted. 'You do it again and I'll find you!'

The boys ran off, and once at a safe distance, they slowed down and one of them shouted bravely over his shoulder: 'Jew lover!' They all laughed and bounded down Bridge Street.

Urbánek held the house door open for Hana and when he noticed that she was holding back tears, he comforted her: 'Don't give them a second thought, Miss Hana. They're just little kids. They don't know what they're saying.'

'They get it from the radio,' Hana said. The Helers no longer had a radio, this being one of the things Jews were lately not allowed to own, but from the days before they had to hand it in, Hana remembered the inflammatory broadcasts describing the Jews as a homeless people who have been eating their host country out of house and home, scrounging off the work of others and exploiting the kindness of those who worked hard. Such people didn't deserve any privileges and that was why they didn't receive ration cards for fruit, fish, poultry or meat. Hana couldn't even remember when she had last tasted sugar and at night she dreamt of bread with honey. But as a Jew she wasn't entitled to anything sweet.

'Thank you, Mr Urbánek. I don't want you to get into trouble because of me. What if these boys tell someone that you stood up for me?'

'They won't. And I'm sure their parents wouldn't pat them on the back for behaving like this either,' said Urbánek, trying to reassure her, although he wasn't at all certain of it himself. 'But you shouldn't be out so late. They wouldn't have dared to pounce at you in daytime.'

Hana lowered her eyes. 'Surely you know that we...' and she paused, hoping that Urbánek would guess whom she meant, 'are allowed to go shopping only between four and six in the afternoon. And by then it's dark.' She shook her half-empty bag. 'And to top it all, nearly all the produce is gone by the evening.'

Alois Urbánek glanced at her limp bag. 'Oh, I've almost forgotten, I have some apples for you. I'll bring them when I've locked up.'

'Shush, not so loud,' said Hana, looking around apprehensively in case someone overheard them. Jews were forbidden apples and other fruit. 'Thank you,' she whispered and ran up the stairs.

Urbánek went out into the Square again to draw down the shutters. As he fastened the hook of a long metal rod in the eye of the shutter, he remembered the time he used to stack boxes in the factory, dreaming of the day he would be back at the little stationer's in the Square. Now he was actually running it, yet he often caught himself thinking that he might be better off back in the storeroom at the factory, loading heavy boxes onto lorries.

The third step from the top on the staircase that led from the ground floor to the first in the Karáseks' house was darker and less worn than the rest. In 1938, as they carried the Weis family furniture up to the attic, one of the removals men lost his grip on a strap that held a heavy wardrobe. It slid off and dropped with its full weight onto the wooden step, chipping off a piece. The poor removals man quickly regained his composure and propped up the wardrobe with his shoulder. After that he couldn't even lift a chair and had to be off work for a whole week, which didn't make his wife happy at all, as all he did was swear and curse while he nursed his bruised shoulder with rum and cold compresses.

Karel Karásek declared he'd always known that the Heler women would bring them bad luck. Elsa Helerová should pay for the damage. But after a frosty stare from his mother he found a carpenter who made a new step. It didn't matter that the colour was slightly different. But the new wood groaned desperately every time someone stepped on it. It even creaked under the feet of Karel Karásek, whose tread was as soft as a cat's, and would sometimes let out a moan in the middle of the night – perhaps just to keep in practice.

It must have been the creaking of the newish step that gave Hana Helerová away one evening as she was leaving after a visit to Ludmila Karásková. Karel appeared in the door that connected his workshop with the residential part of the house, cleared his throat and proceeded to spill out what had kept him awake for some time now.

'Miss Helerová,' he said. 'Can you come in here for a minute?'

Hana sighed. She couldn't stand Karel's circumspect way of speaking, his hunched shoulders and eerily quiet steps. His hushed voice always gave her goosebumps. This new brusque and condescending tone didn't augur well.

Karel stepped aside and, once she was inside the shop, closed the door softly behind her. Hana guessed that he didn't want his mother Ludmila, up on the first floor, to hear their conversation. 'I must ask you and your mother to stop coming to our house.'

Hana didn't need to ask why. Associating with Jews was prohibited and Karel was worried that a neighbour might report them. She also knew that he found it easier to tell her than her mother. But she had no intention of making the awkward situation easier for him.

She pulled a surprised face. 'But why? I promised Mrs Karásková I would come and wash her hair on Saturday.'

Karel Karásek's face turned red. He expected that Hana would understand and leave at once, and hoped that neither she nor her mother would ever show their face in their house again. He wasn't ready to offer explanations. 'Isn't it quite obvious?' His voice crackled with agitation. Karel noticed a spiteful glint in Hana's eyes. 'You are exposing us to danger. You know very well that it's dangerous for us to associate with people like you.' Although he spoke in a whisper, it sounded like shouting. 'I don't want to end up in prison because of you. I'm no friend of yours.'

'You certainly aren't,' said Hana, turning on her heels and heading out into the dark. There were only a few minutes left till eight, the Jews' curfew, so she quickened her pace. Elsa was waiting for her at home. 'I was worried something had happened to you,' she said in a trembling voice as she took Hana's coat to hang it up. 'Make sure you don't stay so long at the Karáseks' the next time.'

'There won't be a next time,' said Hana. 'Can you imagine, that moron Karásek said we shouldn't...'

'Just a minute.' Her mother stopped her and whispered, 'Not in front of Rosa.'

'Why is Karásek a moron?' Rosa called from the kitchen.

'We say Mr Karásek,' Elsa shouted at her. 'And don't listen to grown-ups talking. If you're done with the dishes, go and read to Grandma. You promised you would, didn't you?'

'But I am a grown-up, Mother. I'm nearly eighteen.'

Elsa just raised her eyebrows and gave Rosa a stern look.

With a sigh the girl disappeared into her grandparents' room.

'But she really isn't a child anymore,' said Hana. 'She ought to know what's going on.'

'I don't want to burden her with unnecessary worries, she's too frail.'

Hana rolled her eyes. 'Rosa isn't frail at all. She's a normal girl. She may have been a bit strange when she was little, but I'm sure she wasn't the only child who liked to be alone. And I can't even remember the last time she was sick.'

'Touch wood,' Elsa reprimanded her. 'But that's not why I've sent her away,' she said, motioning Hana to sit down at the table. She lowered her voice. 'I've heard that all the Jews are going to be relocated somewhere.'

Hana raised her hand to her mouth: 'Oh my God.'

Elsa continued. 'Mr Mantel, who is in my work brigade, said it may be better for us. At least we'll be amongst our own. He thinks we'll have our own shops, doctors, offices, a whole Jewish town. And every family will have its own flat. I'm not so sure. I don't like the sound of it, but I can't think of any way to get out of it. But apparently those Jews who are in mixed marriages will be allowed to stay and I've wondered if you knew anyone ... who would marry you. And Rosa...'

'Are you serious?'

'Well, it could be just for the sake of appearances... What about your Horáček fellow?'

'Mother! Not Horáček or anyone else. And as far as I know, many mixed marriages are in the middle of a divorce now. We have lost everything. No one will risk losing their possessions just to stop some Jewish woman being relocated.'

At the thought of Jaroslav Horáček a lump formed in her throat. She didn't feel like telling her mother that Jaroslav had married Ivana Zítková some time ago. She used to be her best friend but she hadn't even let Hana know. Maybe she didn't want to be seen with a Jew but it was more likely that Jaroslav's former girlfriend made her uncomfortable. Hana learned about it by chance from a common friend in the tapestry works. Now that two years had gone by, she couldn't understand what she had seen in Jaroslav. If she had any feelings left for him these were of loathing and contempt.

'I was thinking that maybe Karel Karásek... just for his mother's sake.'

'Karásek! That coward told me today he doesn't want us to visit them anymore. He's scared that someone might report him for associating with Jews.'

'He might be right,' Elsa said after a pause. 'Why attract unnecessary attention. But I still think he could relent if I asked his mother.'

'I wouldn't be too sure, Mother. And maybe it's premature to worry about relocation anyway. Maybe it's not going to happen.'

'You're right,' said Elsa with a forced smile. 'It's probably just a false alarm. People do say all sorts of things...' But deep in her heart she knew that relocation to a place specially designated for Jews was inevitable.

Each time the Germans issued a fresh decree, there were whispers about it in advance, but people refused to believe it, thinking it was just a rumour because it sounded so outlandish and humiliating. But the rumours proved to be true in the end, every time. Elsa Helerová heard that in some cities the relocations had already begun. Josef Mantel also told her the name of the place where Jewish families were being taken. It was somewhere north of Prague, a town called Terezín.

Saying the name of the place, Mr Mantel looked around to check if the gendarme overseeing their work was nearby.

The uniformed man was sheltering from the wind in a courtyard, leaning against a wall, smoking and passing the time by chatting to passers-by. 'Except, Mrs Helerová,' Mantel whispered, 'not all the Jews stay in Terezín. They couldn't fit all of them in there anyway. Rumour has it that trains crammed full of people have been leaving from there, headed east.'

'Where are they taken?'

'That's the thing. Nobody knows. But nobody wants to go. They fear it's a place from which they might not come back when the war is over.'

Nobody knows. These words echoed round Elsa's head as she stroked Hana's hair, repeating, 'Don't worry, people say all sorts of things.' And she swore to herself that she would do everything she could to make sure her daughters wouldn't leave on those mysterious trains.

Chapter Nineteen

September 1942

In 1917, when Elsa Weisová married Ervin Heler, she wanted to have lots of children. Growing up with only one brother who was much older, she had a lonely childhood with a distant father who spent his days in his office and evenings poring over a book, and a solicitous mother who cared more about her daughter's clean cuffs than her wishes and desires. She never doubted that her parents loved her, but she couldn't help feeling that her childhood would have been happier and more fulfilled if there had been more children in the family.

Elsa's first pregnancy ended in its eighth week. The reason was quite trivial: she tripped while walking in the street and although she didn't even fall – she managed to steady herself by leaning against the wall of a house – after a few steps she felt some tugging in her stomach and by the time she got back home she was no longer pregnant.

With her second pregnancy she started to bleed after a month for no apparent reason. Elsa suffered from nausea, cramps and a general weakness that stopped her from getting out of bed, and the midwife told Ervin behind closed doors that Elsa might as well get out of bed and miscarry because she was going to lose the baby one way or another, so she'd be better off getting it over with and sparing herself the suffering. Before she left, she added that some women just weren't meant to be mothers.

Elsa didn't get out of bed. For one thing, she wasn't able

to because of the vertigo and vomiting that started every time she tried to sit up, and for another, Mutti Greta had forbidden it. The Weises had come for one of their regular visits, during which they usually sat on a sofa for a while, exchanged a few words with their daughter, and Bruno Weis also spoke with his son-in-law, for courtesy's sake, before returning to Nový Jičín. But on this occasion, instead of leaving, Mutti Greta took charge of looking after her daughter and her household. Throughout Elsa's pregnancy she applied cold compresses to her forehead, massaged her sore back, brewed herbal infusions, mashed potatoes and cooked nutritious mushy meals, fed her, washed her, emptied the washing bowl and the night pot. This was a period of pain and suffering not only for Elsa but also for Ervin, with whom Mutti Greta didn't speak once all this time. She wouldn't even look at him, let alone share a table with him.

Contractions started after exactly forty weeks of pregnancy and went on for a horrific three days and nights during which Mutti Greta reproached herself for not letting her daughter miscarry, and Elsa swore to herself that if she survived this labour, she would never put herself through another pregnancy. Should this child be stillborn, she would remain childless for the rest of her life.

At the end of the third day, with the assistance of a doctor who had to be summoned and by means of his forceps, a perfectly healthy little girl was born. She weighed nearly four kilograms and was given the name Hana. Ervin chose this name because that's what his first love was called, although he had told Elsa that it was the name of his beloved paternal grandmother. Mutti Greta was delighted that even though the little girl's parents had renounced their faith, at least she was given the Czech version of a Jewish name, that of the mother of the prophet Samuel. Nevertheless, she never forgave Ervin, but that was the least of Elsa's worries at the time. She lay exhausted in her blood-stained bed waiting for the afterbirth to come out, convinced that she wouldn't live to see the following morning.

But she survived and to everyone's surprise she recovered from the long labour so quickly that Mutti Greta was able to return to her husband Bruno and her kosher household, which may have made Ervin even happier than the birth of his dark-haired daughter.

Elsa resolved that Hana was going to be an only child. Ervin consented, alarmed by the proximity of death and the hostility of his mother-in-law and for four years they managed to fulfil their marital duties without conceiving. But then one day Elsa found she was pregnant again and was plunged into despair. She didn't confide in anyone, not even Ervin, so as not to burden her husband's conscience unnecessarily, and did everything she could to miscarry. When running up and down the stairs didn't work, she tried jumping off the kitchen table. She soaked her legs in hot water up to her knees and took baths in water that was so hot she was red as a beetroot for two days. She drank herb potions and ate spicy food, lugged heavy bags, and when none of this worked she began to pummel away at her stomach furiously, weeping and wailing out loud.

Eventually she bowed to the inevitable and in February 1924, after a relatively trouble-free pregnancy, she gave birth to a little girl weighing just two and a half kilograms.

People say that all children are born with blue eyes, but this baby's eyes were black and enormous and gazed at Elsa with reproach. You see, her daughter's eyes seemed to say, it's because of you that I'm so tiny and thin. It's because of you that I'm so weak that I whine like a kitten because I don't have enough strength to cry. It's all because you didn't want me to come into this world.

Anxiety about her daughter, who was named Rosa, haunted Elsa every day of her life. Because of her delicate disposition, Elsa made the little girl swallow cod liver oil. In winter she swaddled her in coats, hats and scarves and she flew into a panic at her slightest sneeze. She stayed up every night while Rosa went through the childhood diseases and every time the little girl, exhausted by her mother's unrelenting attention, crawled into a dark corner for a moment of peace and quiet, Elsa would panic and ascribe her daughter's peculiar behaviour to some mental disorder that she must have inflicted on her by her behaviour while she had been pregnant with her.

Ervin's premature death saved Rosa from irreversible damage as a result of her mother's excessive care. Elsa had to turn her attention to the family's basic needs and entrusted Rosa to the care of her older sister Hana, whose perspective wasn't clouded by guilt and who could clearly see that Rosa was an ordinary child, who eventually grew into a pretty young woman with large brown eyes and a gentle smile.

For a full eighteen years Elsa had fretted about her younger daughter, tending to her as her most precious treasure and that was why, as soon as the Helers were told to report, along with all the other Meziříčí residents of Jewish origin, for a transport on September 14, she was determined not to let Rosa go with them; in fact, she had everything planned out in advance.

The day before they left for the unknown Elsa filled two ordinary shopping bags with Rosa's clothes and even though it was a warm day, she made her put on several layers of clothing. Baffled, Rosa obeyed her mother. She was used to doing as she was told and her mother wouldn't answer her questions anyway. Tight-lipped, she walked down the stairs quickly and resolutely, urging Rosa to hurry.

'But I really can't walk any faster,' Rosa objected, wiping her brow with the back of her hand. 'I'm all wrapped up like a snowman. Where are we going anyway?'

'You'll see,' Elsa replied laconically, taking the path that skirted the Square. Every now and then she looked around as if they were doing something forbidden, and after a final glance over her shoulder she pulled her daughter into a side street. By then Rosa had guessed that they were headed for the Karáseks' house. 'But Mother, the Karáseks...'

'Shush,' Elsa stopped her and opened the door to the watchmaker's. Without so much as a glance at Karel Karásek, who made as if to rise, ready to oblige a customer – but when he recognised Elsa Helerová, opened and closed his mouth silently like a carp and sat down again – she dragged Rosa through the side door into the hallway and then up the stairs. Once there, she opened the kitchen door and spoke to the figure seated in the armchair by the window. 'Ludmila, I've come to say farewell. We're leaving tomorrow, and Rosa is staying with you, as we agreed.'

The gaunt figure slumped in the armchair, wearing a thick woollen sweater with a blanket thrown over her knees, forced a smile and raised her hand slightly, saying barely intelligibly: 'All right.'

'Mummy...' Rosa started to cry and seized her mother's hand. 'But I want to come with you, please don't leave me here.'

Elsa shook her off. 'You're staying here. We'll be back, don't worry.'

'But I didn't even say goodbye to Hana or Mutti Greta and Grandpa.'

Elsa held her tight. 'I will give them your love, and remember not to ...' She wanted to say she had to make sure not to be seen by anyone, but was interrupted by the door slamming and Karel's out-of-breath voice.

'You can't come in here, Mrs Helerová. Please understand that you're putting us in danger!' He fell silent when he saw Elsa give Rosa a final firm hug, plant a kiss on her forehead, whisper thank you to Ludmila Karásková, turn around and run down the stairs.

Rosa was left standing in the middle of the kitchen, wrapped in two pairs of stockings, three sweaters and a winter coat, tears rolling down her cheeks and shoulders shaking with sobs. Two shopping bags sat on the table. Ludmila Karásková was slumped to one side of the armchair and her son shifted from one foot to the other, not sure whether to run after Elsa Helerová to stop her, or grab Rosa and push her out of the door.

Finally, he turned to his mother. 'Come on, Mother, we can't do this. She can't stay here. They'll shoot us all.'

He fell silent, as if it had only just dawned on him that this could really happen. Rosa sobbed and wiped her nose. Both of them looked at the helpless Ludmila.

'And so?' Ludmila Karásková said slowly.

For as long as they lived, neither Karel nor Rosa forgot these words even if each of them interpreted them differently.

I'm sick, was what Karel took his mother's words to mean, I'll be dead soon anyway and you're good for nothing. What is the point of fearing for your life if you're not really alive?

I might be sick, Rosa heard, but no one is going to tell me how to live or who I may be friends with.

Rosa cleared her nose, wriggled out of her coat and shed the layers of sweaters, then approached the sick woman and wiped the saliva dribbling from the corner of her mouth. Karel Karásek came up to her from the other side, and together they raised Ludmila into a sitting position, propping her up with a pillow behind her back. Then they sat down at the table facing the armchair.

'I'll have to cancel the home help,' Karel said after a while, turning to Rosa. 'Mrs Zítková has been coming every day to help around the house,' he explained slowly. 'But it would look suspicious if I fired her straight away. We'll wait for a month or two. Until then, Miss Helerová, you'll have to hide in the attic.'

'My name is Rosa,' said the girl; she wiped off her tears and blew her nose. 'And I want to go home.'

Except that, by that point, Rosa had no 'home' left. Over in the Square, in the house she was born and had lived the entire eighteen years of her life, her mother was making final preparations for departure. She, too, was crying. She was crying because she had just abandoned her daughter and didn't know whether she would ever see her again. She was crying because her parents were upset that she didn't tell them what she was planning to do and gave them no opportunity to say farewell to Rosa. They couldn't understand that Elsa had no choice, since the parting would have turned into a heartrending scene and Rosa would quite certainly have refused to leave the house.

She was crying because she could tell from Hana's gaze and her dumbfounded silence that her older daughter blamed her for putting Rosa first again.

'Hana, dear,' she said, stroking her daughter's hand, 'I would dearly like to leave you here as well, but I couldn't find anyone who would hide you.' She gave a sigh. 'The Urbáneks have young children and they've done so much for us already. I even went to see that friend of yours, Ivana Zítková, but she said she was expecting a baby.'

'Mother!' Hana sat down next to an open suitcase. 'I don't want to stay here.' And Ivana's house was the last place I would stay, she wanted to add, but stopped herself in time. Did her mother really have no idea that Ivana was now Mrs Horáčková? Surely she couldn't expect Hana to find refuge with the family of the man who had rejected her?

'She owes it to you, as she's married Horáček,' Elsa said angrily. 'He led you on for so long with all his promises, it would be only right and proper that he should take care of you.'

So her mother knew. Of course, everyone was aware of Hana's humiliation. 'He never promised me anything,' said Hana softly, folding her skirt as tightly as possible so that it would fit into the suitcase.

'Leave this one behind,' said her mother, setting the skirt aside. 'Take the thick woollen one instead. And two pairs of warm stockings.'

Unlike Josef Mantel, Elsa Helerová entertained no hopes that life would be more bearable in Jewish towns just because they would be amongst 'their own'. Polish Jews, mostly young people who had managed to sneak out of Poland, told her about the atrocities that took place when Jewish families were herded into ghettoes, about the miserable conditions in which they had to eke out their lives, the hunger, the spreading diseases, executions and escalating German brutality.

The reports were so horrific that Elsa was reluctant to believe them, but she was nevertheless determined to do everything she could to keep out of harm's way. Or at least, seemingly out of harm's way. If the Germans found Rosa at the Karáseks, they would all be shot. That was why she didn't tell her parents or Hana where she had taken Rosa, although, of course, they guessed. And she was full of regret that she didn't manage to save Hana from the transport.

Young women are always in the greatest danger, she thought, removing Hana's silk blouse from her suitcase and packing a cotton vest instead. The girl seems to think we're going on holiday.

Elsa entrusted the few precious things the Helers and Weises still possessed to Alois Urbánek, even though the instructions she received along with the summons to the transport threatened harsh penalties for anyone who gave anything away as a gift, let alone sold anything. Any possessions that didn't fit into one's luggage, including houses, money and furniture, would pass into the ownership of the German Reich. But how could Elsa allow some newly-arrived Nazi wife to eat from the china service she had received as a wedding gift, to wind up the gilded grandfather clock or look at the oil painting of a shadowy forest, even if Elsa had never believed it really was the work of the renowned artist Julius Mařák, as Ervin used to claim? The only thing she did take was money, which she rolled up and sewed into the hem of her coat despite being unsure if it would be of any use where they were going.

On their last night in the house on the Square in Meziříčí, instead of discussing the tragic lot of the Jewish people, Greta and Bruno Weis argued whether it was worth risking taking some tobacco, which was among the forbidden items. Mutti Greta opposed the idea on principle but Bruno insisted. He said tobacco stopped his hands shaking and once his wife fell asleep he scrambled out of bed, took a pair of manicure scissors, cut a hole in his coat lining and stuffed his treasured tobacco in the sleeves.

While Bruno Weis struggled in the dark with his coat lining and Elsa wondered in her bedroom if she should have packed a bigger cooking pot, Hana was lying on her bed curled up in a foetal position reflecting on the fact that she was twenty-three years old. Her schoolfriends were now married, cooking dinners for their children, looking after their households and joining their husbands in bed at night. She had none of that, and may never have. She didn't want to leave Meziříčí, but in her heart of hearts she hoped that where they were going to the next day, somewhere among all the Stars of David, there might be one that was meant for her.

On the night of 14 September 1942, Rosa Helerová stood at the attic window of the Karáseks' house, straining her eyes to penetrate the darkness and the mist of her tears to catch a glimpse of the figures walking across the bridge towards the railway station. But the night was pitch black and the windows were blacked-out, so she couldn't see anything at all, and although she pricked up her ears, the roaring river and her own sobbing drowned out the heavy shuffling steps and sighs of those headed for eternity.

Chapter Twenty

The roll call for the transport wasn't until the next evening and no one had started looking for Rosa yet, but Karel Karásek couldn't wait for the girl to move up to the attic. With every one of his senses he was acutely aware of her presence. Her scent, carried on the air, seemed to be seeping into the upholstery and the plaster on the walls, and he feared that it would immediately give her away if anyone entered the house. In his imagination Rosa's soft voice bounced off the walls, echoing off the windows and burning his skin.

He allowed Rosa to eat dinner with them and help him feed Ludmila, who could no longer do anything for herself, but after she cleared the dishes away and was about to put the kettle on to wash up, he urged her almost indignantly: 'Get a move on, hurry up. What if someone comes?'

Rosa, who didn't know that no one except for the cleaner ever came to the Karáseks', gave an apologetic smile and started to gather up her clothes. The kitchen was warm, and she had arrived wearing several layers which she'd gradually peeled off in the course of the afternoon, so it took her a while to collect everything. Meanwhile, Karel picked up her two bags and waited for her impatiently by the door.

'Bed... lin... en...' Ludmila Karásková stammered out.

Karel was already halfway out of the door.

'She wants us to take bedlinen,' Rosa reminded him.

He turned around reluctantly. 'That would be too

conspicuous. If someone went up to the attic and saw fresh linen on the beds, they would know straight away that someone was hiding there.'

'You really think of everything,' said Rosa and Karel thought he detected a touch of admiration in her voice. 'But more to the point, they would find me, wouldn't they?'

Didn't I say it was dangerous? Karel felt like shouting. You should never have come here! But he managed to control himself just in time. 'We'll have to find you a hiding place,' he said, trying to sound as if he had thought it all through carefully. 'Like inside a wardrobe or under a bed. There's plenty of junk up there.'

He was right. The attic was crammed full of the furniture Rosa's grandparents had brought from Nový Jičín, which they had nowhere else to store. It ended up in the Karáseks' attic, all in a jumble, just as the exhausted removals men had left it. While Rosa was putting the bedding on a duvet she found hanging on a line that ran across the attic, Karel started to assemble the bed. He was good with his hands, figuring out which bit went where and piecing them together, even though the clock wheels and springs he handled in his ground-floor workshop were on a different scale altogether. By the time night fell he had the bed assembled and with Rosa's help pushed it under a window against the southern gable wall.

'The window is high up, but you shouldn't take any chances so don't go anywhere near it. And don't walk around too much, the floor here is made of wood and the sound of footsteps echoes all the way down to the ground floor. But above all: you mustn't turn the light on. On no account.'

He walked to the trapdoor and looked around. 'Come and give me a hand. Let's move these wardrobes to the middle, to block the view. If the worst comes to the worst, you should throw the bedding onto the line, squeeze through the window and jump across to the house next door. It's quite high but their roof is flat so...' He glanced at her. 'As I've said, if the worst comes to the worst...' Rosa climbed onto the bed, carefully poked her head out of the window and peered into the dark abyss below. As far as she was concerned, things couldn't get worse than that.

Rosa spent two months in the attic. In the early days she was terrified every time she heard a door slam or the stairs squeak, expecting the Gestapo to come and its men in uniforms to drag her down the stairs by the hair, the way they did when they came to arrest Eva Fuchsová. Someone had grassed on the woman for ripping the Star of David off her jacket and going to the shops outside the hours permitted to Jews, to find food for her family, as most groceries sold out by the time they were allowed to go shopping.

Mrs Fuchsová never returned home. Rumour had it that she had been sent to a concentration camp, but Rosa was sure that she and the Karáseks would be shot straight away.

In the mornings, while Mrs Zítková was cleaning the house, Rosa stayed in bed, since the temperature in the attic wasn't much higher than outside and the roof offered shelter only from the wind and the rain. While some light came in through the window above the bed, Rosa would wrap herself in Ludmila's heavy winter coat and huddle under two duvets, reading romances and old journals that had accumulated in the chests and bedside tables over the years. After discovering some knitting needles in one of the wardrobes, she filled an entire drawer with socks knitted from wool she got by unpicking old jumpers. She was looking forward to giving them to the Karáseks as a surprise Christmas gift, and to her mother, Hana and grandparents at Christmas next year. As she sat there knitting she thought of Mutti Greta, who had taught her how to make the heels, sighing indignantly over Rosa's messy handiwork and holding up Hana's perfect creations as a model.

After dusk Rosa would nod off or just lie on her back, watching the clouds and stars in the window above her bed and dreaming of life after the war.

Mrs Zítková usually left the house before noon and rushed back home to her wash trough. The piles of laundry were no longer as high as they had been before the war, as her customers were forced to economise in these difficult times, but that didn't make Mrs Zítková happy. It was difficult for a washerwoman to feed a bunch of children and a sickly husband, and she had no one to help her. Her eldest daughter Ivana was now married and living with her husband and their baby son in the little house by the river that belonged to her in-laws.

Rosa couldn't wait for the door to close behind the cleaning woman. After a few minutes, Karel would cautiously double lock the front door, go upstairs and knock on the trapdoor from below to let Rosa know that the coast was clear. Rosa would hesitate for a while until she was sure Karel had gone back to the ground floor, as she was embarrassed to carry a full chamber pot down from the attic. Then she would gingerly climb down the steep steps, taking care not to spill the contents of the china vessel.

After getting this hygiene chore out of the way she would go to the kitchen to join Mrs Karásková. She would have been happy to help around the house but couldn't do too much in case the cleaning woman suspected her presence, so at least she looked after the sick woman. Even though it was all new to her, in a few days she was able to perform all the tasks as well as a qualified nurse would.

Unlike Hana, Rosa became attached to Ludmila. She didn't mind the odours that, despite all the care, the sick woman gave off, she didn't find it hard to talk to her and make out her slurred speech, to read her romances about impoverished girls and wealthy suitors, feed her, change her clothes, prop her up on the pillows to prevent bedsores forming, and if despite all her efforts red blotches did appear on the patient's skin, she didn't mind putting ointment on them and massaging them gently. Bedsores were likely to result in a painful death, and to stop them developing Ludmila had to be turned from one side to the other several times during the night. Rosa was keen to make life easier for Karel and offered to sleep in the same room as his mother and get up whenever necessary, but he insisted that she return to the attic for the night.

He was scared that soldiers might burst in and search the house, fretted that Rosa might not manage to return to her hiding place before the cleaner arrived in the morning, or that they might overlook some detail that would give her away. As if it wasn't enough that long after Rosa went up to the attic, wherever Karel moved he felt her scent lingering in the air. Every night he turned off the lights, threw the windows open and waited for it to dissipate. But he could still smell it as he fell asleep, when he woke up in the middle of the night, and first thing in the morning.

One day in the middle of November Karel Karásek was sitting in his workshop, trying to manoeuvre a pin into place with tweezers. He had nearly completed the task when he suddenly heard a strange noise from the kitchen, located right above the workshop. First something fell on the floor – Mrs Zítková must have dropped a broom, he thought – then, for an excruciatingly long time, he heard some shuffling as if someone kept moving a chair up and down the floor. He sat up angrily and the pin slipped out of the pincers. Dammit, Zítková must be making this racket on purpose.

On purpose! He threw the pincers down, leapt out of his chair and the magnifying glass fell out of his eye. He sprinted out of his workshop and climbed the stairs faster than usual. By then he heard heavy steps from the second floor and saw Mrs Zítková carrying a basket of freshly washed laundry. 'Do you know you have mice up in the attic?' she snapped at him aggressively, putting the basket down on the floor.

'Mice?' Karel repeated.

'Or rats maybe, I could clearly hear them scuttling up and down. I'm not hanging the laundry up there, no sirree. I'll just hang these few pieces to dry on a line here in the kitchen, if you don't mind.'

'No, of course I don't,' said Karel softly as he opened the kitchen door. Ludmila was sitting in her armchair but her walking stick, which was usually propped up within her reach so she could summon Karel by knocking on the floor if she needed him, was lying on the floor and the chair on which he had placed the items she might need had been moved aside. She gave him a reproachful look. How could he have failed to understand that she was summoning him?

'I got such a fright I nearly wet myself,' continued Zítková, evidently so rattled by the presence of rodents in the house that she forgot there were things one didn't speak of in decent company.

'I'll put some traps out straight away.' Karel left the kitchen, closed the door and nervously shifted from one foot to the other. This wasn't a good time to go looking for the mousetraps, which he kept in the pantry. On the other side of the door he could hear Mrs Zítková's muffled complaints and since it didn't look as though the cleaning woman would return to the rodent-infested attic any time soon, he ran up to the second floor and climbed the steep steps. He lifted the trapdoor and looked around. Everything was quiet. The attic seemed totally deserted.

'Rosa?' Karel whispered but no reply came. He climbed up, closed the trapdoor and repeated, this time a little more loudly. 'Rosa, say something. It's me, Karel.'

Then he noticed some bedding scattered on the floor and

the window above the empty bed. It was open. He remembered the advice he had given Rosa when she moved in and a sense of panic spread through his whole body, starting from his feet, rooted to the wooden floor. Reeling, he staggered over to the bed, put both his hands on the window frame and tried to summon up the courage to lift himself up and look out.

What would he see there? Rosa, bruised from falling onto the flat roof of the neighbour's house? How would he bring her down from there without being noticed? He couldn't leave her lying there all afternoon. What if she was injured? Would he be strong enough to pull her up? And what if it was worse than that? What if Rosa hadn't managed to cling to the roof and had tumbled down into the neighbour's courtyard or into the street? She couldn't possibly have survived a fall from there. What could he have been thinking of when he gave her that stupid piece of advice? Why hadn't he kept quiet instead?

He stood up on the bed and looked out. The roof was empty. That could mean only one thing...

'I couldn't pull myself up,' a voice said behind his back. 'I don't have the strength.' It was Rosa, huddling at the bottom of a wardrobe, her eyes red from crying.

Karel Karásek couldn't remember when he'd last felt so relieved. He collapsed onto all fours by the wardrobe and clutched Rosa to his chest. He had no idea when it had happened but, all of a sudden, he couldn't imagine his days without Rosa. Nor did he want to.

'That woman saw me,' said Rosa and Karel drifted from the clouds back to earth. 'She stood by the trapdoor and looked straight at me.' Rosa tried to dry her tears with the back of her hand. 'She's not going to report me, is she?'

Karel did his best to reassure the shaken and constantly apologetic Rosa that Mrs Zítková would definitely not report her, but he wasn't convinced of it himself. The punishment for hiding Jews was execution by firing squad and that also applied to anyone who knew of others who were hiding Jews and failed to report it. Mrs Zítková wasn't a snitch but she did have a big family. What if she decided that charity began at home?

These were the thoughts that raced through Karel Karásek's head as he returned to the kitchen. Although the door was closed, he could hear Mrs Zítková's plaintive voice, which was strange in and of itself, because the hard-working woman didn't usually say much, as if unwilling to waste the energy she needed for other things. He stopped outside the door, took a deep breath and resolutely pressed down the handle. There was no way around it, he would have to have a word with Mrs Zítková and explain that they had no choice and had to take Rosa in. Maybe he could appeal to the cleaner's maternal instincts.

The laundry had been messily hung on a line above the stove and Zítková was just folding her apron into her threadbare bag. 'I don't mind spiders, even snakes I'm not scared of, but the one thing I can't abide is mice. Yuck,' she shuddered. 'Now they're in the attic and before you know it, you'll have them in the pantry and all over the house.' She turned to Karel. 'I've just been telling your mother that I wouldn't be surprised if you also had rats in the basement. Your house is close to the river, the cellars are damp and that's what these creatures like. I'm sure they're scurrying around the ground floor too. No, no, Mr Karásek, I can't clean a house like that. Please don't be cross with me, I just can't. I'm really scared of vermin. I'll keep doing your laundry, don't worry, but you'll have to find someone else to do your cleaning.' She closed her bag resolutely as if she couldn't wait to get out of the door. 'You'll pay me the next time I bring the laundry,' she said and, made for the door and was suddenly gone.

Karel Karásek's only hope was that Mrs Zítková would stick to her story that all she had seen was mice, at least until this horrible war was over.

The socks Rosa knitted over the long days in the cold attic and later, after Mrs Zítková stopped coming, in the evenings in the Karáseks' kitchen, didn't end up as presents at Christmas, 1943. They ended up at the bottom of a drawer in the bedroom, which by then Rosa was sharing with Karel Karásek.

Just as Ludmila Karásková assumed back in the days when she was still able to plan ahead and had something to live for, once you have two young people living in close proximity and cut off from the outside world, sooner or later they will either form an attachment or start to hate one another. Luckily for Rosa and Karel, the former proved to be the case.

Rosa liked the deliberate way in which Karel approached every decision, something that many other people – including his own mother – mistook for hesitancy. She was impressed with the silence enveloping him and his calm tone of voice gave her a sense of security. Karel was fourteen years her senior and in her eyes that made him fourteen years wiser, more experienced and worldly-wise. She looked up to him with such reverence that she initially didn't even dare to address him by his first name.

How could Karel resist a pretty girl whose dark eyes gazed at him with undisguised admiration, whose scent he found beguiling and who was so easily within reach?

Since he loved Rosa and was very happy with her, it came as a surprise that his body hadn't forgotten the desire Ivana Zítková aroused in him. Ivana was a married woman now, the mother of a one-year-old boy, yet whenever she came to his workshop and placed on the counter the pile of laundry her mother had washed, Karel couldn't help but feel that she wouldn't mind all that much if he took her by the hand, drew her to himself and showed her how much he wanted her.

He wasn't wrong. Ivana's dream of marrying the man she wanted came true, but she hadn't anticipated the extent Jaroslav Horáček would be changed and broken by having to leave the army. The genial man he had once been turned into a grumpy nit-picker who, instead of complimenting Ivana on her looks and telling her how lucky he was to have found her, just grumbled about his fate and about the soup being too thin.

So, once a week, Ivana basked in admiring glances, even if they came from another man. And then one day, when Karel Karásek plucked up the courage to take her hand and show her how to wind up an antique grandfather clock, she didn't shrink back. On the contrary, she edged closer, pressing her shoulder to his arm. Karel Karásek, who by then was no stranger to sex, knew instantly that he was only one step away from having his dream fulfilled and he didn't hesitate. He quickly locked the door to the workshop and skilfully manoeuvred the beauty of his dreams to a sofa, discreetly hidden behind a screen.

It may have been a one-off and the fifteen minutes in the locked workshop might have been something of a disappointment to both of them, but the implications for both parties were far-reaching. Karel could never rid himself of a guilty conscience towards his Rosa and Ivana was never quite sure who had fathered her blue-eyed daughter Ida.

Despite Karel's initial feeble protests, soon after Mrs Zítková's beat a retreat Rosa moved down from the attic and took charge of the household. It helped her pass the long days she was condemned to spend locked inside the house and left her less time to wonder why nobody had heard from her mother since she left for Terezín. Rosa knew that her mother couldn't write to the Karáseks so as not to expose them, but she couldn't understand why she hadn't written to Mr Urbánek at least, and it made her very worried.

Karel Karásek stopped by the stationer's a few times and once he was alone with Urbánek, he would ask 'Any news of the Helers? Have they been in touch?'

Alois Urbánek shook his head. 'No they haven't, I think it's really strange. Mrs Helerová promised she'd let me have her new address so I could send them something from time to time...' He hesitated. Why say more than necessary?

In fact, he had promised Elsa Helerová he'd send her the rent for the shop every month. That was before he knew that as soon as the Helers left, a German officer stationed at the local barracks would move into their flat with his family, get rid of Grandpa Bruno's armchair and Grandma Greta's kosher pots and pans, hang the curtains from Hana's trousseau on the windows, sleep in the bedlinen bearing Hana's monogram and demand rent for both shops to boot. The turnover wasn't high enough for Urbánek to pay both the officer and Mrs Helerová, but he would have tried to help in some way at least...

Karel didn't tell Rosa that Elsa Helerová had promised to send Alois Urbánek her address so as not to add to her worries. He saw only one explanation – Rosa's family hadn't stayed in Terezín and it was forbidden to write from wherever they had been taken. Even though there hadn't been much love lost between them, he hoped, for Rosa's sake, that they would all be together again after the war.

Rosa sat by Ludmila's armchair and kept her company through all those days when the sick woman could barely communicate with the world of the living while the world of the dead, which she longed to join more eagerly every day, was not yet ready to accept her.

In the last few weeks of her life Ludmila Karásková could no longer tell day from night and wasn't able to swallow any of the food or drink Rosa patiently spoon-fed her. She would gasp for air and found respite only in short bursts of sleep that resembled oblivion, from which she would be roused, after a while, by a lack of oxygen.

Karel kept the shop open for just two hours a day and took turns with Rosa at his mother's bedside. Neither of them said it out aloud but their only wish was for Ludmila's suffering to end.

This finally happened at noon of the shortest day of 1943. Ludmila woke up, took one last look at Rosa who was tasting the garlic soup she'd made following a recipe from Ludmila's old family cookery book, and at Karel who was sitting in the armchair by her bed, before her gaze moved over to the window.

Snowflakes were drifting from the sky, floating, undulating through the air, landing on the window one after the other as dusk slowly enveloped the room. Ludmila closed her eyes again but the white snowflakes began to swirl before her eyes, turning into a whirlwind of snow and then an avalanche that lifted Ludmila Karásková high, let her take a deep breath for the first time in ages, and with her final exhalation carried her out of this world.

His mother's death didn't bring Karel Karásek the relief he had hoped for, awakening in him instead the most severe pangs of conscience. How could he have wished for something as irrevocable and definitive as his mother's death? Had he really wanted his mother's suffering to end or had he just been selfishly concerned about himself and his own peace of mind?

Apart from his guilt, he was also beset by practical concerns. As long as his mother was alive, they were entitled to rations for two adults. Ludmila had been eating very little in the past few months which meant there was enough food for all three of them. How would they manage now, on a single person's rations?

For a moment it even occurred to him that they should keep his mother's death secret from the world and the authorities. He could bury her in the cellar or in the small backyard and wait until the war ended to give her a dignified funeral. Rosa was horrified at this idea and declared she'd rather starve than let the remains of her beloved Ludmila be buried somewhere in the corner of a backyard like the carcass of some pet. Karel agreed. He also couldn't sleep well with the knowledge that his mother hadn't found peace after death, and worse still, he would have been haunted by the fear of the consequences he would certainly have to face if such a spine-chilling deception had come to light.

And so Ludmila Karásková was given a modest funeral and Karel and Rosa were left to their own devices. At first they found it strange to have the house to themselves, not to have to take the presence of a third person into consideration, to be able to touch and kiss, even make love, without being constantly on guard because Ludmila might need turning over, be given a drink, or have her sore back propped up by a pillow.

But within a few weeks they got used to being alone and learned to recognise the sounds from outside. Rosa no longer had to make a frenzied dash for the attic every time someone's hurried footsteps passed by the front door and Karel was no longer afraid to leave her at home alone, certain that she would be as still as a mouse and wouldn't go anywhere near a window.

As Christmas of 1944 approached, Rosa took up her knitting needles again. This time she wasn't making socks. She still had a drawer full of them, in a range of colours and sizes, and she clung tenuously to the hope that one day they would be worn by those they were meant for. Now she was knitting tiny jumpers, hats and booties for a baby which, according to her calculations, was due in the middle of next year. She put a brave face on it and tried not to cry at the thought that she would have to give birth alone, assisted only by Karel who was even less experienced in these matters than she was, and that, should she survive the labour, she would have to look after the baby on her own, even though she'd never held a baby in her arms and had never even looked after a kitten.

Karel also kept his concerns to himself. 'The war will be over by the spring,' he said to reassure both Rosa and himself. 'Before the baby is born, the Krauts will be gone and we'll even manage to get married. And old Zítková can be our wedding witness!'

Rosa laughed but it didn't escape her that Karel didn't dare promise that her most ardent wish would come true: that her mother, Hana and her grandparents came back home at last.

In early 1945 the Eastern Front moved closer to the border of the Protectorate and the Germans started bringing young men drafted to do forced labour to neighbouring villages and made them dig anti-tank trenches. When Karel heard the news, he panicked that he might also be called up and Rosa would be left locked in the house on her own without any help, but he calmed down when he learned that only teenage boys were being drafted. Soon he had reason to be frightened again, when flyers were posted in shop windows all around town, telling people where to seek shelter in case of an air raid, and what supplies to take with them.

For Rosa, going to a shelter was out of the question. Karel desperately scoured the damp cellars of his house, trying to work out which corner was the safest, then he lugged some heavy horsehair mattresses from the attic down to the part of the cellar where the well used to be and where walls seemed the most solid.

Had any of the bombs that came raining down on

Meziříčí in early April hit the roof of their house, it wouldn't have survived, and neither would Rosa, Karel and their unborn child. It wouldn't have helped Rosa to go down into the deep cellar, it would have been no use to huddle up into the mattress-lined walls. All that would have been left of the house would have been a burnt-out crater, like those that remained of the houses just two hundred metres from the Square.

None of their inhabitants survived and lived to see Soviet troops approach Meziříčí from the south and east in early May. The battle for the town didn't last long, but it cost the lives of dozens of soldiers in the final days of the war and almost completely destroyed the bridge connecting Meziříčí with Krásno.

And then suddenly it was all over. On the evening of 6 April, a heavily pregnant Rosa crossed the threshold for the first time in nearly three years and, arm-in-arm with Karel Karásek she trudged up the narrow street, then turned right and came into the Square. Once there she stopped in front of the house where she had grown up. She looked up at the windows covered in curtains crocheted by her sister Hana's nimble fingers. The stationer's shop window was shuttered with heavy bars and the front door of the house was locked.

'We'll come back tomorrow and get the keys from Mr Urbánek. We have to clean up the flat before Mother, Hana, Grandma and Grandpa come back,' said Rosa and Karel nodded, stroking her hand.

However much Rosa wanted to wait for her family's return, she gave in to Karel's insistence and they were married in early June. Karel didn't want his first child to be born out of wedlock and they took their vows at the local council.

I was born one week later and my parents gave me the name Mira, which is supposed to mean gentle, amiable and miraculous. I am certainly not gentle, but I always do my best to be amiable. As for miracles, they have accompanied me from the day I was born to this very day. My entry into this world was a miracle, I survived the typhoid epidemic by a miracle, and I hope that further miracles will help make my dreams come true.

A month went by but the clean flat with the view of the Square remained empty. Neither Elsa nor Hana, neither Greta nor Bruno came back. And neither did the Hirsches, the Bačas, the Kleins or the Perls. None of the people who had left the station in Meziříčí on that transport in September 1942 had so far come back.

PART THREE
I, Hana
1942-1963

CHAPTER TWENTY-ONE

My head is filled with fog. Sometimes it is impenetrably thick, so thick that it won't let a single thought shine through. This is the state I regard as happiness. But then the mist melts away and the images come back to haunt me. They beset me from every direction, there is no escaping them. Anxiety constricts my chest and my lungs gasp painfully for air.

Fear seizes my whole body and I stumble.

Figures begin to emerge from the mist. They are bright, much brighter than the world around me. They speak to me, yell at me, reproach me for being still here and remaining silent. But I can't talk about the dead. I want to put them to rest, at least in my memories.

How could I possibly talk about them anyway? Nobody would believe me. No one knows how much suffering a person can endure. That is what I tell them. I beg them, again and again, to leave me alone, or drag me off to join them in their world of shadows. But they won't. Not yet.

All I want from life is for it to release me from its clutches. Why does it insist on clinging to me so, when I have seen how readily it abandoned those who clung to it at all costs, those who had someone in this world that they cared about? And who cared about them. I have no one like that. At least, these were the thoughts that were going through my head as I stepped off the train and onto the platform at Meziříčí railway station.

Summer 1945

It was high summer when I returned to my hometown. I had been perched on the wooden seat by the open window of the passenger train, eyes wide open, my luggage in my lap. I was holding on to my black canvas bag, pressing it to my body. Not because I was worried that someone might steal it. It held nothing of importance to me. A jumper and some underwear. I'd stuck the piece of paper meant to serve as my temporary ID into my pocket, next to my most prized possession, a slice of bread. I'd stuffed some more slices into the pockets of my cotton dress and the buttoned up black jacket that was two sizes too big for me, and patted the pockets from time to time to check they were still there. The countryside hurtled past the window, but I didn't take it in. The only thing I was aware of was the rhythmic sound of the wheels of the train taking me away. The jolting of the carriage and the rumble of the tracks took my thoughts back dangerously close to the days I never wanted to revisit but whose horrors held me firmly in their grip, choking me. I felt I was sinking back in time. The interior of the carriage went dark, a sweetish smell tickled my nostrils and a lump formed in my throat. I gasped for air and clutched at my throat to push away the invisible hands trying to throttle me. I must have cried out because every eye in the carriage turned towards me in disapproval and a woman sitting near the aisle moved further away and lifted the little girl sitting between us into her lap.

The staring eyes of my fellow travellers brought me back to the present. The train was packed but the seat next to me remained empty. I edged closer to the window to make more room. Nobody took the seat. People were reluctant to sit close to a gaunt female in baggy clothes and men's ankle boots, bundled up in her coat in the middle of the summer. Perhaps they guessed where I was coming from, perhaps they caught a glimpse of the pain wracking me and didn't want to be tainted by it. The war was over after all, and the country was striding towards a bright future.

I looked around. The man in the sweat-stained blue shirt on the seat opposite looked away and gazed out of the window, while the others stared at the floor. I knew I wasn't a pretty sight. I pulled the headscarf covering my scant white hair further down my forehead, reached for a piece of bread, stuck a bit of crust into my toothless mouth and let it slowly dissolve on my palate. The sweet-and-salty taste of the bread banished the ugly thoughts for a while and allowed me to sink back into a timeless mist.

The train squealed to a halt and people started pushing for the door. I raised my head in confusion.

'Meziříčí,' said the man opposite, sighing with relief when I moved over to the aisle, and stretched his legs out comfortably.

My body had grown stiff from several hours' sitting and my legs wouldn't obey me. I grabbed the door handle and tried to reach the step looming far down. My left knee buckled and I landed on my right foot from up high. There was a sharp, shooting pain in my swollen ankle. I tried to reach for the handle with my other hand and let the canvas bag drop onto the platform. Gingerly I lowered myself to the ground and bent down to pick up my bag, but the blood rushed to my head, I saw black and fell onto all fours. I didn't have the strength to get up so I crawled to the nearest bench and somehow scrambled up onto it. My muscles were shivering and I felt dizzy.

'Look at her, she must be drunk,' remarked a young man with a cigarette dangling from the corner of his mouth to his companion in high heels who looked around and gave an amused laugh. She might have been twenty-six – my age. She's someone they would have sent to the left, I thought, reaching into my pocket for another crust of bread.

I stayed on the bench even after the dizzy spell subsided and my legs stopped trembling. I was in no hurry and wanted to keep the tiny flicker of hope alive for at least a little longer, the hope that our house in the Square was still standing, that I would climb the stone stairs to the first floor, enter our flat, breathe in its familiar smell, walk through the hallway to the kitchen and find my family sitting around the table. My mother Elsa, Grandma Greta, Grandpa Bruno and my little sister Rosa. That was my most ardent wish, but I knew it was a vain hope and the minute I entered our flat, the dream of a home would vanish forever, because the journey I had embarked on in the night of 14 September 1942 was a journey to hell.

September 1942

That evening the train left not from the station but from a siding at the far end of the park where it had been shunted.

It was already dark as we came down the stairs of our house, loaded with backpacks, suitcases and blankets rolled into bundles. My legs were shaking with fear and I felt like crying but I tried not to show it. Mother locked the door and put the key in her pocket, ready to hand it over by the train to the officer responsible, as instructed in the summons to the transport.

We paused on the bridge for a short rest. I put down the heavy suitcase, propped my rucksack against the stone balustrade and looked back at the Square.

I could barely see anything. The night was very dark and all the lights had been turned off so the town shouldn't make an easy target for the air raids. Deep below, the river flowed impassively in its rocky bed and the motionless silhouettes of the houses looked hostile, as if the town couldn't wait to be rid of us so it no longer had to watch our daily humiliations. The town, just like its inhabitants, had turned a blind eye to us.

It made people uncomfortable to witness the humiliation of their friends and acquaintances, of neighbours who had, until recently, lived in the same street, worked in the same factory and done their shopping in the same stores. Now they were forbidden even to exchange a greeting with a Jew, let alone stop to pass the time of day.

Maybe they were glad to see us go. Maybe relieved. Now they would no longer have to avoid us, to lower their eyes and pretend they didn't see us. But above all they would no longer be reminded of what might happen to them, too, and worry that it could be their turn one day.

Somewhere in one of those darkened houses, whose contours I was guessing at rather than actually making out, was my sister Rosa. I didn't know whether to be glad that she wasn't leaving with us. Back then I think I rather resented my mother for the decision she had taken. I thought it was wrong to leave my sister alone with strangers. Now I know that my mother did the right thing. I will never know whether it was foresight, or if she had some information she chose not to share with us.

Grandma Greta and Grandpa Bruno were weary, bent double and still out of breath, but we had to press on. The time to report by the train was fast approaching. We picked up our luggage again and trudged along the cobbled street.

In the avenue of trees in Krásno we met a family with two young children. Their steps echoed in the night just like ours, bouncing off the walls of the dark houses and massive tree trunks. The younger child was asleep in its pram and the other one was whimpering, holding on to his mother's hand. We acknowledged each other with a nod and continued to walk together. We hadn't met the young family before but knew that all those making their way along the streets at this hour were Jews headed for the transport, since the rest of the town was under curfew.

Half an hour later we staggered to the siding. People with suitcases and rucksacks on their backs were queueing before men with sheets of paper. They handed over their house keys, presented their papers, and in exchange for their jewellery received a card with a number to hang around their neck. We joined the end of the fast-moving queue. 'Rosa Helerová?' asked the record-keeper, without raising his eyes from the list.

'Rosa left for England three years ago to join her uncle,' said mother feigning surprise and awaited the next question. But it never came. The record-keeper crossed out Rosa's name without a word, scribbled something next to it, handed each of us a card on a string of hemp, and pointed to the open doors of the waiting train. 'Get on.'

We sighed with relief. Expecting tough questioning and checking, we had meticulously rehearsed everything in advance at home. We made up details of Rosa's departure and memorised fictitious dates and reasons. Now it seemed that, with a bit of luck, Rosa might not be missed by anyone.

We picked up our bags and approached a group of people trying to get into the carriage. Since the train had stopped outside the station, the first wooden step was so high that it was nearly impossible to climb up without help. Someone above reached out a hand to me, Mother gave my hips a push and once I was up, she passed me our bags. Then we joined forces to pull Grandma and Grandpa into the carriage. We even managed to find them seats. Mother and I sat down on our bag that held our bedlinen. That was the first time I glanced at my card. My number was 79.

The train didn't go directly to Terezín as we expected but took us to an assembly point in Ostrava first. For several days, while we waited for further transports bringing Jews from the whole district to arrive, we were put up in an old school building. That was where Grandma Greta fell ill. Her eyes burned with fever and she was freezing all the time even though she lay huddled under a blanket.

'She'll be fine in a day or two,' said a doctor my mother managed to locate among the deportees, shrugging his shoulders. 'It's just a cold.' There was nothing more he could do. Even if he'd had any medication, he would have been reluctant to squander it on some stranger's common cold.

But how can you recover from a cold lying on a freezing tiled floor in a draughty room with windows and doors permanently open? In a dormitory packed with people talking, arguing, constantly going to and fro, and trying to soothe children bored by the long waiting and bewildered by the adults' strange behaviour?

'We'll soon be in Terezín, Mutti,' Mother reassured Grandma in the hope that it would be more peaceful and quiet there, while I wondered how my sick Grandma would manage the long walk back to the train. And how we would carry all our luggage if we had to support her as well.

Over the four days we spent at the marshalling point Grandma Greta developed a hacking cough. On the eve of our departure we divided the contents of her rucksack between us and the following night we trooped through the empty streets of Ostrava towards the transport to Terezín, supporting her on both sides. Grandpa Bruno strapped the bag with bedlinen to his rucksack and carried it on his chest, thus freeing both his hands so he could also carry Grandma's suitcase. He'd done a test walk up and down the corridor, deliberately raising his knees high and kicking the bag to make it bounce in a funny way. We all pretended that it was hilarious. But in reality the strap was cutting into his shoulders and the bag was making it difficult for him to walk. But we couldn't rely on anyone else to help.

Grandma was not the only sick person around and everyone had their own family to look after, their own problems and their own anxieties.

I thought the journey from Ostrava to Terezín would never end. Nobody got on or off the train, and yet we were constantly shunted onto side-tracks and made to wait. Trains carrying soldiers and munitions to the Eastern Front had priority and we didn't reach our final destination until the evening. Exhausted, we got off the train and heaved the heaviest pieces of luggage onto a lorry while soldiers in SS uniforms barked at us. Then, in a long line, Indian file, we set out on the three-kilometre march from Bohušovice to Terezín.

None of us had believed that life in Terezín – the city that, as Nazi propaganda would have it, Hitler had gifted to the Jews as a place to sit out the war in peace – would be better than at home. But we may have harboured a tiny sliver of hope that at least we would be amongst our own and that the Star of David blazing on our chests wouldn't feel quite so degrading.

But none of us was prepared for what lay in store for us in Terezín.

As soon as we reached the ghetto courtyard, bellowing SS-men relieved us of our last remaining valuables, separated the men from the women and escorted the terrified new arrivals in small groups to their temporary quarters.

At the time of our arrival the Terezín ghetto was hugely overcrowded. Women's and men's dormitories were filled to the rafters, and people were squeezed into corridors, cellars and attics. Grandma Greta, Mother and I, along with the other women from our transport, were herded into the attic of a tall brick tenement. Grandma, drained by fever, her excruciating cough and the long journey, had to be supported on either side. We walked slowly, having to make frequent stops, and as a result, by the time we finally made it to the attic, all the mattresses were taken and not an inch of free space remained. We found a spot on the mezzanine but a man in uniform and a flat cap pushed us through the attic door, yanked the mattress from under the woman nearest to the door and shoved it towards us. Next, yelling as he wielded his stick, he made the older residents push their mattresses closer together, and in this way he managed to cram a further dozen new arrivals into the attic.

We ended up right under a light well. We helped Grandma to stretch out on the mattress and sat down by her side. The woman on the mattress next to us shifted aside to make more room for us. She had a beautiful profile and long slender fingers.

'Don't worry, tomorrow it will be less crowded here.' She raised her hand and showed us a thin strip of paper.

We didn't know what it meant. 'Are they moving you somewhere else?' Mother asked.

The woman shrugged. She might have been my mother's age but she didn't have a single grey hair. 'I'm on tomorrow's transport east.' She waved her hand as if standing on a stage. 'Almost everyone gets sent away.'

'The east? Where in the east?'

'I don't know but all that matters is that I will be with my family. My husband and son got the summons, but I didn't, so I asked to be put on the same transport. I couldn't let them go on their own.'

Mother surveyed the overcrowded attic. 'Do you think it will be better there than here?'

Our neighbour remained silent for a while and then replied, with a touch of defiance in her voice: 'A ghetto is a ghetto. Can it get any worse than this?'

That very afternoon Grandma Greta and Grandpa Bruno also received a strip of paper. My mother couldn't abandon her sick Mutti Greta and asked to be sent on the same transport east. A ghetto is a ghetto, she said, echoing the words of the beautiful lady.

So why did she stop me from asking to be included in the transport? Why did she keep telling me that I should try to stay in Terezín for as long as possible?

The beautiful lady with slender fingers was a music teacher. She had given up her concert career to raise her son and started giving music lessons at home. The next day, as I walked my family to their transport, I saw her report to the assembly point alongside her husband and son, who can't have been more than fifteen. She was just as terrified as Mother, Grandma and Grandpa and the hundreds of others assembled at the departure point they called 'the sluice'.

That was where I embraced my nearest and dearest for the last time and watched as, weighed down by luggage – now somewhat reduced thanks to the items that had been confiscated – they slowly headed back to Bohušovice, where they would board another train and continue their journey. Rumour in the ghetto had it that people were forced to travel in wooden cattle trucks that once took their bovine passengers to slaughter. And that the wagons were crammed to bursting point. I found that hard to believe, but the image became indelibly seared in my memory.

I watched Grandma Greta, leaning heavily on Grandpa Bruno and Mother. I saw my mother look back from the gate for one last time but I don't know if she managed to catch a glimpse of me. I didn't move until the gate was shut.

'When all this is over, we'll meet again at home.' These were Mother's last words to me.

My mother had always told the truth, even if it was sometimes hard to stomach. But that time in Terezín she was lying. And we both knew it.

From then on, I was on my own.

CHAPTER TWENTY-TWO

Meziříčí, summer 1945

I straightened my feeble legs, stood up carefully and slowly left the station.

It was as if I was stepping into the painting that used to hang above the sofa in our living room. I recognised everything that I saw around me. The streets and the houses, the trees and the sky above. As I breathed in the familiar smell, I could feel the sun beating down on my face and the summer breeze lifting the corner of my headscarf. Sounds assaulted me on all sides. Car engines, the clicking of heels, subdued conversations, birdsong, and the rustling of leaves in the trees. Everything seemed familiar, yet completely strange. Because I was no longer part of the picture.

The town hadn't changed. Only I had changed.

I trudged along the streets, my eyes fixed on the pavement. Every now and then I stopped to rest and look around this strange town where I was born twenty-six years ago. People skirted around me, some indifferent, others irritated. They must have wondered who this weird woman was, dawdling in the middle of the pavement, getting in their way. In the old days I would have found that upsetting. Now I didn't care.

I tugged the headscarf further down my forehead and forced myself to take another step. Just place one foot in front of the other. Take one more step and don't think of what comes next. This had been my credo for all of the past three years.

I reached the delicatessen where I used to stop for a cream puff and a chat with Ivana before the war, before she became Mrs Horáčková. I used to be very fond of her. She had been a bubbly girl who felt she should seize with both hands all that life had to offer. And that was precisely what she did.

But now I had no wish to think of what had happened before... When was it? In a past life? And who did it happen to?

I needed a rest. Outside the delicatessen there were two tables with red-and-white chequered tablecloths and some wooden chairs. An elderly lady was sitting at one of them with a little boy who was kicking his legs about happily and licking his ice cream. I sat down at the other table, rested my sore feet and put my bag on the other chair.

'Can I help you?'

It took me a while to realise that a woman in an apron was talking to me. I looked up. Mašková or Pašková her name was. The owner of the delicatessen. She knew my mother and had always asked to be remembered to her. *Give my regards to your mother, Hana...*

The woman still bore the same courteous expression, but the tone of her voice had changed. She positioned herself so that the other customers at the outside tables and inside the shop couldn't see us and hissed: 'If you're not having anything, please leave.'

I was exhausted and by now accustomed to being sent away. I continued to stare at the table. Mašková or Pašková grabbed my bag and dumped it in my lap. 'Please go. You can't sit here. You're driving my customers away.'

'Water,' I said.

'Water? We don't serve water here. Only lemonade. Would you like some lemonade?'

I nodded and Mašková or Pašková turned on her heels, annoyed, and slipped into her shop. The little boy at the next table had spilt ice cream on his shirt and his grandmother was cleaning it up with a handkerchief. Then she spat on it and wiped the boy's face. I got up and continued walking to the Square.

I walked past a pub that was reeking of cigarette smoke, beer and urine and was full of regulars even now, early in the afternoon, then I turned right, crossed the road by the pharmacy and headed to the river. For the past two hundred years, a stone statue of St Valentine had stood on his plinth at the foot of the bridge, looking over his shoulder. He must have been waiting for my return and now wondered if it really was me, surprised to see me walk so slowly, hesitantly, and on my own.

Across the river the town came into view. It hadn't changed at all. The trees, the Karáseks' tall house, as bland and cold as their owners, the castle walls with their flaking plaster. The bridge itself was the only reminder of the recent war. On one side it was missing a chunk of pavement and the balustrade. As if a huge whale had bitten into it, ripping a piece out of it before diving back into the sea. The wound had been temporarily dressed with wooden planks and some boards had been prepared for plastering over the cracks.

The bridge is just a few dozen metres from the Square. I hobbled up the hill with leaden steps. It had never seemed so steep before. And then, all of a sudden, there it was. Our house. It was standing there as if nothing had happened. I took a few more steps and looked up at the first floor. I even recognised the curtains, why, they were the ones I had myself crocheted in a pattern Grandma Greta had taught me. One window was slightly open. What could that mean? For a brief moment I believed a miracle had happened.

I pressed down the handle of the front door but it was locked. I walked past the sparkling clean shop window with its display of summer wares and went to the stationer's. It was empty, only the bell above the door made a tinkling noise, summoning the shop assistant.

I knew it wouldn't be my mother who'd appear behind the counter, but even so, when I saw Mr Urbánek, I got a lump in my throat and my knees started to shake. I planted my elbows on the counter, put my forehead against the wooden board and burst into tears. I wept aloud, sobbing and moaning, gasping for air and stuttering incoherently. Mr Urbánek was saying something but I couldn't take it in. Suddenly a chair materialised behind me, Mr Urbánek detached my hands from the counter and made me sit down. I was trembling all over, but my sobbing was now silent. I wiped my wet cheeks on my jacket sleeve.

'Are you all right, madam? Do you want me to call someone?'

I sniffled and raised my head. Mr Urbánek's face turned from curiosity to shock and, finally, sympathy. 'Miss Hana...' he said, and tears welled up in his eyes as he looked at me. Perhaps I could have fooled myself that he was weeping for joy at seeing me, but I knew that these were tears of grief and horror. Horror at the way I looked.

Although by then I had put on twelve kilos, I was still fifteen kilos below my weight before the war. At the time I didn't know that I would never put that weight back on. I just can't help it. Even if I had any appetite, which I don't, my stomach can't take very much. Whenever I feel weak, I stick a piece of bread into my mouth, roll it around my tongue and swallow it very slowly. It does me good and also helps to calm me down. I always keep some bread handy – in my pockets, in drawers, even under my pillow.

By now my hair had stopped falling out but it grew back totally white, with some bald patches. The doctor had said it would get thicker again but would probably stay white forever. As if it made any difference.

What would have made some difference was if I were able to move my fingers again.

The joints in my fingers were swollen much more than in my legs and arms. But Mr Urbánek couldn't have seen that and that is why I think that what terrified him most was my toothless mouth, my gaunt cheeks, and my eyes. My eyes had seen so much that they had sunk deep, deep inside their sockets and were buried under the heavy lids.

'Miss Hana...'

Yes, there was once a time when I was Miss Hana. But then I became a Star of David, transport number 79, a resident of Terezín and finally a six-figure number in Auschwitz.

Terezín, September 1942

I was now all alone in Terezín, among thousands of strangers. Many of the new arrivals were soon sent on to the east in the crowded wooden cattle trucks that in those days left the overpopulated ghetto daily, carrying away most of the Jews of Meziříčí. At least that's what I think, because in all the time I spent in the Terezín ghetto I never came across anyone from my hometown.

I returned to the attic and took possession of my mattress just in time, before more women arrived on the afternoon transport and another battle for every free spot ensued. I was sitting in a crowded room trying to erase from my mind the image of the cattle truck taking my family into the unknown, while at the same time reproaching myself for not accompanying them on their journey, at least in my thoughts.

The place next to me was taken by a young woman with

a little girl, aged about six. The girl was wearing a pair of spectacles with a plaster over one of the lenses. I moved my mattress closer to theirs to create a more comfortable double bed and offered them some of my space. The woman flashed me a grateful smile, put the girl down between us and when the little one fell asleep, carefully removed her glasses and stowed them away in their case.

'We have to look after them, they're the only pair we have. They're getting too small for her but I don't know if I can get hold of another.' She stroked her sleeping daughter's head. 'The doctor said she has to wear the glasses for at least another year or she'll be cross-eyed for the rest of her life.'

'Your little girl is very pretty,' I said since I couldn't think of anything else to say and wanted to be friendly. It was true, after all, and besides, it was beginning to dawn on me that to survive in the ghetto I needed friends. Before I managed to ask what the little girl's name was the young woman lay down next to her, put one arm around her daughter's waist and fell asleep, worn out by the long journey.

That night nearly all the women in the attic were told to report for the next transport. My neighbour and her daughter were among them. 'What does it mean?' she asked me fearfully, holding the strip of paper in her hand.

'Terezín is overcrowded and most of the new arrivals are sent further east to build new settlements. Apparently, all of us will move there eventually,' I replied, repeating what I had heard the night before. The woman calmed down and my answer even seemed to cheer her up a little. 'Life here would be quite difficult,' she said, eyeing the leaky roof. 'And maybe I can get my Pavlínka another pair of glasses there.'

I wasn't so sure because I couldn't get out of my mind the question of why they were sending old people and families with young children to do the hard work, which the building of new cities undoubtedly involved, while keeping the younger people in Terezín. I was one of them, and the following day I started to work in a workshop repairing German uniforms.

I was moved from the attic to the women's dormitory in the former barracks. That was also when my new companion – constant fear – moved in with me. The fear of transports, of punishments, hunger, illness and loneliness. Thirty of us were crammed onto three-tier wooden bunks in a long narrow room, but having four walls around me was better than sleeping under the rafters. I knew I was really lucky not to be stuck in the attic with no room to move, the wind blowing in from every direction, and water dripping through the holes in the roof. The barracks, too, were cold, but by no means as freezing as the attics, wooden sheds, cellars and damp dungeons in the fortifications where those less fortunate than me had ended up.

I spent most of the day in the workshop, wearing all the clothes that I owned. My job was mending German uniforms and as I sat there holding the thick, scratchy material in my frozen fingers, I was glad to be inside rather than outdoors, digging trenches or breaking up mica, or in the enormous marquee in the square where engine parts were being packed and prepared for shipping to Germany. I thought of my mother and mentally thanked her for the foresight she showed when she packed our things. I hoped that she, Grandma and Grandpa found better living conditions wherever they were in the east, and that they weren't suffering from cold or hunger.

I was hungry practically all the time. Breakfast consisted of some liquid they called coffee, lunch was a bowl of soup or some kind of sauce with a few unpeeled potatoes, and for dinner we were given a piece of bread, sometimes with a little margarine.

But the hunger wasn't as bad as the grief and the loneliness.

The first time I went into the dormitory and found the bed I'd been assigned nobody took any notice of me. The room was half-empty because many of the women had relatives in the ghetto and used the evenings to spend time with their families. Some women were leaning against the bunk beds chatting, others lay resting in their bunks. There was no furniture in the room apart from the beds and suitcases. Not a single table, wardrobe, chair... nothing.

After some hesitation I pushed my little suitcase under the bottom bunk. I wanted to sit down but didn't know how. Mine was the middle bunk and my legs got in the way of the woman below me while I kept hitting my head on the planks above me. After squirming about for a while, I decided to lie down.

The upper bunk shook and a head leaned down from above. 'Hey you, when did you get here?'

It was a girl about my age so I wasn't surprised to be addressed in a familiar way. 'The day before yesterday,' I replied.

'I'm Jarka,' the girl said and stretched out a hand towards me. 'This isn't comfortable. Can I come down and join you? It'll be easier to talk.'

When I nodded, Jarka lowered herself from the upper bunk and swung down to mine. I moved over to the wall. I found it slightly uncomfortable to be so close to a stranger but at least I felt less lonely.

'Do you have anyone here?'

I shook my head and was about to say that the rest of my family had been sent on a transport east, but Jarka wasn't expecting an answer.

'I have a boyfriend here. He works in the Jewish self-administration, the technical department, so if you ever need anything...'

I didn't respond because back then I had no idea how vital connections of any kind were in Terezín. Only connections could help you secure better accommodation, lighter work, or extra food. Sometimes having the right connections could even save you from the transports.

'You should get yourself a boyfriend too,' said Jarka.

I was puzzled. I had no idea how to go about getting a boyfriend. I had been going out with Jaroslav but the way that came about was that we met, liked each other and then continued meeting, the idea being that we would eventually get married and spend the rest of our lives together. At least that's what I'd thought at the time.

I wanted to ask Jarka what she meant but she went on. 'You should hook up with someone who works in the self-administration or in the kitchen.' She smiled. 'I'm so glad I now have a friend here, I couldn't talk to Majerová who had this bunk before you.' She paused. 'Although I didn't wish the transport on her; that's something I wouldn't wish on anyone.'

I froze. 'Why is everyone so scared of the transports?'

This time Jarka remained silent for a while. 'Because none of the people who have gone have been in touch since. That's strange, don't you think?'

Yes, it was very strange indeed. We both sat there wondering what it might mean.

'Let me give you the low-down on the other women here,' said Jarka and I suddenly realised that the reason she was talking so much was to stop herself thinking.

By the time she climbed back into her bunk half an hour later, she had treated me to quite a few juicy comments and opinions on our roommates. And before I had time to decide whether Jarka was the right kind of friend for me, something dropped on my blanket. 'A little present for you,' I heard from the upper bunk.

I felt around with my hand and found a potato. A big potato. Yes, Jarka was a friend.

The potato was proof.

Chapter Twenty-Three

Meziříčí, summer 1945

'Miss Hana...'

Mr Urbánek was at a loss. He was saying something, his voice rising from joyful heights and sinking to compassionate depths and back again, but I found it hard to concentrate. I was exhausted and bombarded with memories wherever I looked. I was too scared to ask what had happened to Rosa because I was sure I knew the answer. We had left her in this town all alone. What was the chance of a young Jewish woman surviving here for a whole three years?

I was tired from travelling, unsettled by my encounter with the town, and the whole world was becoming one big blur. I closed my eyes and in the white darkness I heard the distant jingle of the bell above the shop door. When I opened my eyes again, I was all alone in the stationer's but that didn't bother me. I put a bit of bread into my mouth, rested my head on the counter again and sank into an apathetic slumber.

Someone shook me by the shoulders. Startled, I opened my eyes and turned around. It took me a while to work out where I was. There was Mr Urbánek and next to him stood Karel Karásek, somewhat thinner than I remembered him. He tried not to stare but his curiosity got the better of his manners. He inspected what was left of me. That, too, was something I had long got used to. With the back of my hand, I wiped away a drop of saliva from the corner of my mouth, fixed my eyes on the wall and waited to see would what happen.

After exchanging a few words, the two men turned to me but their voices weren't getting through to me through the thick fog. They came closer, unbearably close, and flanking me on both sides they reached their hands out to me. I supposed this was to help me get up, but I wrested myself free. I can't bear strangers touching me.

They shrank back in surprise.

Mr Urbánek again said something. I watched his lips move and tried my best to find my way out of the fog. 'We'll take you... home... Rosa... the Karáseks.'

'Rosa?'

'Yes. We'll take you to her.'

I didn't understand why I had to leave my house again, now that I had finally come home, but I followed the two men out into the street. They led me across the sunlit Square, marching alongside me like a military escort, and I tried to work out why on earth I was supposed to go to the Karáseks. Did I understand them right, that Rosa was there? But why didn't she come herself? Why wasn't she at home, in our house?

Thinking exhausted me even more than walking. I had to concentrate hard on every step I took and the fog in my head started to thicken up again. 'Rosa,' I kept repeating.

'Rosa.'

Next thing I knew we were standing on the doorstep I had reluctantly crossed so many times in the past while I was looking after my mother's friend, Mrs Karásková. As we entered the semi-darkness of the cold hallway I heard footsteps running down the stairs. Someone threw their arms around me, pressed their wet face into mine and sobbed into my shoulder. I had to lean against the wall. The familiar scent of vanilla enveloped me and my heartbeat resumed because at that moment it dawned on me that I wasn't, after all, alone in this world.

'Hana, Hanička... you're back. So that means Mother will

soon be back too, as well as...' The light came on in the hallway. Rosa took a proper look at me for the first time and burst into tears because she knew instantly that only the two of us were left.

I stepped back guiltily. I was the one who had brought this great grief upon her. Nobody said a word, only Rosa sobbed softly as she squeezed my hand. I shrank back quietly.

Terezín, Autumn 1942 - Autumn 1943

Life in Terezín followed firmly fixed rules. I soon discovered that this town, Hitler's 'gift to the Jews', may be run by a Jewish administration but the Nazi headquarters called all the shots.

The self-administration, run by a Council of Elders, was responsible for the day-to-day running of the ghetto, from job assignment through food distribution, healthcare and children's homes, to burying the dead. It was also in charge of compiling the lists for the transports to the east, which was why, Jarka said, it was useful to be on good terms with someone who worked there, preferably someone with influence, someone who could prevent one from being sent on a transport.

In Jarka's vocabulary, being 'on good terms' with someone meant sleeping with them, 'influence' meant the ability to obtain food or other things that could be 'traded', which in turn meant bribing and selling on the black market.

While all of us in Terezín were in the same boat, we weren't all equal. We were divided by language, age, beliefs, and upbringing. Officials higher up in the administration received bigger rations and were lodged together with their families. People assigned to hard labour and young children were also entitled to more food. Older people, not able to work, received rations that were correspondingly smaller, and were reduced to having to beg. They starved to death unless they had someone to look after them or were sent on a transport. Obtaining a good job was vital not only because of food but also to make oneself indispensable. Those assigned to important jobs enjoyed a degree of protection from the transports.

It took me only a few months to learn that no one in the ghetto could be sure what the next day would bring, not even members of *Ghettowache*, the Jewish police – who in their caps with black visors and white armbands for identification kept order in the ghetto and handed out the summons to the transports in the evenings – or the Council of Elders, not even the *Judenältester*, Jacob Edelstein himself, and his family.

My job in the uniform repair workshop didn't provide much protection from transports. You don't need any special skills to mend uniforms – show me a woman who doesn't know how to use a needle. As new people kept arriving in Terezín, the light in both the men's and the women's dormitories would often come on at night and a man from the *Ghettowache* would appear at the door handing out strips of paper with summons for the transport east.

At first I had clung to the foolish hope that I would receive one of these strips of paper and be allowed to join my family, but Jarka explained that while all the trains were headed east, they didn't all go to the same destination. 'You wouldn't find your family anyway,' she told me as she cut my hair to make it easier to comb out the lice. 'You're better off staying here, in a place that you know, than rushing off into the unknown.' After a short pause she added: 'Why would the people in the administration try to keep their families off the transports if things were better over there?'

My friendship with Jarka meant a great deal to me. The women in our dormitory were friendly but they were keen to spend every free moment with their families. They would visit their children in the children's homes, wash their husbands' clothes and were always on the lookout for extra food. They looked down their noses at Jarka and made snide remarks behind her back about the looseness of her morals, yet whenever they needed help, she was the first person they would run to. She could organise food, shoes and medications, and sometimes she even managed to get someone taken off a transport. The women rewarded her with whatever they had but then gossiped about her even more.

'You have to know the right people,' she said when I asked her how she did it. 'I've been telling you to hook up with someone.'

I would have liked to 'hook up with someone' as Jarka recommended, if for no other reason than to have somebody who cared about me, but it was easier said than done. I was stuck all day with other women in the workshop, repairing uniforms, and spent every free minute queueing up for food, and stayed in the dormitory in the evenings. Besides, I now understood that by 'someone' Jarka meant someone influential, who could provide me with protection.

Throughout September and October one transport after another left Terezín but then the exodus to the east stopped. From the little news that the newcomers brought into the ghetto we gathered that the Germans had run into trouble on the eastern front, and we began to allow ourselves to hope that that the transports wouldn't start again. And that the Germans would get a hiding, the war would end, and we would finally get out of this hellhole and return home. But in January rumours started to spread that thousands of people were about to be sent to the east.

Lights were again being switched on in our dormitory at night and someone from the *Ghettowache* would read out a list of names.

At the end of January my name was among them.

'I told you so,' commented Jarka, furiously snatching the strip of paper from my hand. What she meant was that I should have found a protector a long time ago, as well as a job that would have made me less dispensable. 'Leave this to me.'

The next day an official in the self-administration crossed out my name on the list and replaced it with another. I wanted to repay Jarka but didn't know how. She was unusually quiet and just shrugged her shoulders when I thanked her. After coming back from work she climbed up to her bunk and turned to face the wall.

I thought she was cross with me. To have me taken off the transport must have cost her more than she had wanted to give. I was lying on my back trying to warm up my feet, which had gone numb with cold, staring into the dark and listening to Jarka turning restlessly from side to side.

I didn't see Jarka the following day as she was on the night shift at the hospital. Although she had no medical training, she was working as a nurse.

'You don't need any training, all you need is connections,' she laughed when I asked her how she'd landed a job like that. 'I can pull some strings if you like, and we could work together.' I turned down her offer. I may have had more nursing experience than she did, thanks to having looked after Mrs Karásková, but I also had some idea of the responsibility this kind of job entailed. There was enough misfortune in Terezín without me adding to it.

That night the dormitory was in disarray. I climbed up to Jarka's bunk and perching next to her watched some of the women packing for the following day's transport. The one I should have been on.

'How did you manage to have me taken off?' I asked.

'It was easier than you might think,' she replied, and after a brief pause continued: 'Mrs Hanzelková is going instead of you. Her daughter was on the list and she volunteered to go so she could be with her.'

Mrs Hanzelková slept in our dormitory, close to the door. She usually returned shortly before eight, after visiting her daughter in the children's home. I remembered her well. One night she was delayed and a man from the *Ghettowache* caught her in the street after curfew, marched her to the police department where they took a statement, and she was disciplined. She came back upset and in tears. She was terrified they might put her on the next transport because of the incident. On that occasion she got off lightly.

I bent down to see what she was doing. She was standing by her bed, trying to cram the permitted thirty kilos into two suitcases.

'That bastard in the registry office has it all figured out,' said Jarka suddenly. 'He selects a few children for the transport and then just sits back waiting for their mothers to come rushing in and beg him to add their names to the list. He digs his heels in for a while but then he obliges them, for a bribe, of course, and puts the mother's name on the list instead of someone else who had greased his palm earlier to have their name taken off. He takes from both sides. And everyone is happy.' Jarka shook her head. 'The bastard. He knows full well that those children will never come back.'

'You can't be sure of that.'

She looked at me. 'I can.'

I didn't ask how she could be so certain, because if she was right it would have meant that what I had only guessed at until then was true. That I would never see those I loved again.

At that moment I hated Jarka.

The transport Jarka saved me from turned out to be the last one for a long time. During the spring and summer months no further trains headed east from the ghetto but the railroad siding from Bohušovice to Terezín, whose construction was completed by prisoners in June 1943, was a constant reminder that the transports could resume.

By now I had been living in the ghetto for almost a year and although I had lost some weight and felt constantly tired, at least I was alive and there was nothing to suggest that I was in imminent danger. I was young, I had a job, and was therefore entitled to an *Essenkarte*, which guaranteed three, if meagre, meals a day. I had learned the ways of the ghetto – and I even had a relationship.

Leo worked in the kitchen. He said he noticed me when I came up to the counter with a mess tin for my meal. He would sidle up to the dispensing point, measure out a generous helping of sauce and exchange a few words with me. I was happy about the bigger portions but felt uneasy at the same time, as the others grumbled when they saw that there was more in my bowl than in theirs. I didn't enjoy Leo's comments, which were quite crude for my taste and sometimes wondered if I should take offence. But hunger is hunger, so I would just flash him a smile and walk off.

But I couldn't resist bragging about it to Jarka. I was flattered that someone showed interest in me, even if he was just some uncouth cook in grubby overalls. 'I wouldn't be surprised if he tried it on with every woman he met,' I added.

'Well then, all the more reason for you to move fast, before someone else snaps him up,' was Jarka's advice and she meant it. A cook had access to food and that made him a good catch in Terezín.

Even if I had intended to follow her advice, which I didn't, I couldn't because I fell ill. The tiredness I had put down to the meagre rations and long hours of work developed into a permanent nausea and stomach pains. My skin was itchy, but I didn't suspect that the rash was a symptom of an illness because fleas, lice and bedbugs were our constant companions in the dormitories of Terezín. A few days later the supervisor at my workshop noticed that the whites of my eyes had turned yellowish. She flew into a rage and said I could infect everyone and told me to see a doctor. He sent me straight to hospital, where I was looked after well, no complaints about that, but a stay in the isolation ward hardly amounted to treatment.

Medicines were just as precious in the ghetto as food, and as I had lost my appetite, this was the first time in ages that I didn't feel hungry. In addition, my gums were bleeding, boils had started forming in my mouth and my teeth began to come loose. I lay in bed dozing, waking up only during ward rounds and when Jarka came to visit.

Being a nurse didn't give her access to the isolation ward, but Jarka wouldn't have been Jarka if she hadn't been able to find a way. She sat down on my bed and held my hand. 'Count yourself lucky you can spend time just resting here. The doctor said you'd recover from the hepatitis, but you're also suffering from lack of vitamins and that could spell trouble. You're lucky it was discovered early. We'll do something about it.'

I didn't consider myself lucky as I felt very poorly and couldn't begin to imagine how I might get hold of fruit or vegetables in Terezín. Apart from the apples Mr Urbánek had once given us back in Meziříčí I'd had no vitamins since the war began.

'Here,' she said, slipping something into my hand so that the other patients wouldn't see. 'It's from Leo.' It was a raw beetroot, a real treasure. Except that, even if I'd had an appetite, I wouldn't have managed to take a bite out of it.

'It's too hard. You keep it.' I handed the beetroot back

to Jarka, turned to face the wall and closed my eyes. I wanted to do nothing but sleep.

She put it in her pocket. 'Fine, I'll take it and make you some soup. And I will thank Leo for you.'

It was Jarka's soup, made of beetroot and potatoes supplied by Leo, that restored me to health. A few weeks later, when I was discharged from hospital, I didn't go back to the workshop but was reassigned to the garden where vegetables were grown for our German overlords, who lived in comfortable houses on the outskirts of Terezín.

When I asked Jarka if she had anything to do with my reassignment, she just shrugged her shoulders. 'You need vitamins, don't you? Just make sure you bring us a tomato every now and then.'

By 'us' she meant herself and Leo. I didn't like the idea that I was now in Leo's debt. He had risked a lot by sending me food. Had he been caught by the *Küchenwache,* he could have ended up in prison, in the small fortress. I sensed he was expecting more than just a thank you and that there was only one way of repaying him.

The rules that applied in Terezín were different from those I had been used to. I saw nothing reprehensible about Jarka's intimate relationship with an official in the self-administration, since it helped make her life in the ghetto easier in many ways. But I couldn't imagine doing something like that myself: allowing someone to touch me just because he had given me a bigger helping of soup and slipped me a beet or a potato from time to time. But in Terezín that was a compelling enough reason. The war was bound to end one day, and more food meant a greater chance of surviving and returning home.

I couldn't look for Leo during the day, so I stopped by the kitchen in the evening on my way from work. I was tired. My body had yet to recover from the long illness and the doctor in the isolation ward said that my liver had been

permanently damaged by hepatitis. As I had never done any
gardening before, I found a whole day's work in the garden
unusually hard. I knew that Jarka must have wanted to help
and thought that being in the fresh air and getting the odd
vegetable now and then would do me good but I was
hoping that I could get back to my old workshop before the
arrival of autumn and the cold weather.

All I wanted to do was say thank you to Leo and hurry
back to the dormitory, but when he saw me he waved to
indicate that I should wait while he talked to an older
colleague as he pointed to me. The greying man cast a
glance at me, gave a shrug, said something, and soon Leo
took off his grubby overalls and came dashing out.

'I don't want to keep you, I just wanted to say thank you,'
I said, looking around to make sure no one could hear me.
'You know why.'

'You're not keeping me.' Leo grabbed me by the hand
and dragged me down the street, which was teeming with
people returning from work.

'Where are we going?' I asked, panting, but let him pull
me along.

'Don't worry, we're not going far.'

He needn't have said that. Nothing was far in the ghetto.
Leo turned into the first street on the right, then into a
narrow passage leading to a courtyard, with stables opposite
a wooden gate. When I'd arrived in Terezín the ghetto was
at its most overpopulated and dozens of people were
crammed into these stables. Now they stood empty. Leo
had clearly checked the place out beforehand. He pushed
open a door and pulled me inside.

'Why are we...' I was going to ask why he'd brought me
there but of course I knew the answer.

Leo didn't waste any time on explanations. In one of the
low stables he pushed me down onto the earthen floor,
pressed his body hard against mine and started to hitch up

my skirt with one hand. It wasn't easy as the skirt was not only tight but I was lying on it.

'Come on, give us a hand,' he grunted impatiently.

I was terrified. I'd never been in this kind of situation before and though I understood that this was basically just a business transaction, I had nevertheless imagined that my first time would be different. But I didn't wish to be difficult and raised my hips and helped him hitch up my skirt. He pulled down my panties but when his hand reached between my legs, I couldn't take it anymore and flinched.

'Don't be silly,' he rebuked me and forced me down onto the floor. And so I gritted my teeth and waited. He kissed me on the mouth. That was something I was familiar with, so I calmed down a little. He felt around the floor for my cloth knapsack, pushed it under my buttocks, prised my legs apart with his knee and lay down on top of me. The pressure between my thighs increased, becoming a dull ache in my loins. I turned my head to one side, shut my eyes firmly and clawed the ground. He started to move inside me, slowly at first, then faster. I hoped his exertions wouldn't last too long and tried to hold back my tears, but I couldn't. His breathing was heavy and harsh above me, as if he were running up a hill, then with a brief shriek, he slumped down on me with all his weight.

I waited to see what would happen next. 'It'll be better next time, you'll see,' he whispered, panting. I didn't reply. I didn't care for any 'next time'.

Leo helped me to get up and dust off my skirt. I picked up my cotton panties and when he wasn't looking, used it to wipe off the liquid dripping down my thighs.

'We've got to go,' he said. 'It's nearly eight o'clock.'

I don't know how he could tell since everyone had their watch confiscated on arrival in Terezín, at the sluice. But I didn't want to be late, so I dried my tears with the back of my hand, stuffed my panties into my knapsack and followed him through the low stable door and out into the early summer evening. My legs were still shaking.

'Wait.' Leo stopped me in the dark passageway. I thought he wanted to kiss me goodbye but he slipped something soft into my hand, then turned around and took off with the words 'See you on Sunday'. I looked at the two dumplings in my hand, opened my knapsack, and put them next to my panties and two totally squashed tomatoes I had stolen for Leo and Jarka from the vegetable garden.

CHAPTER TWENTY-FOUR

Meziříčí, Summer 1945

The wooden table, the chair, the whitewashed sideboard, the sofa with its brightly-coloured crocheted cushions, and geraniums on the windowsill, the window slightly open – the Karáseks' kitchen looked exactly as I remembered it. Only the armchair where the sick old woman used to sit was no longer there.

Mr Urbánek went back to close the stationer's and to his family. I sat with Rosa and Karel Karásek at the kitchen table. Rosa was weeping quietly because I had just robbed her of the last glimmer of hope that some of our loved ones might return. I stared at the tablecloth, trying to work out how I had ended up here, while Karel looked as though he'd much rather be somewhere else.

By now Rosa had stopped asking me questions. She must have realised that I wouldn't answer any of her hows and whys. I did have some of the answers, as I already knew where the trains departing from Terezín were headed, but even if I'd been able to utter those words I would never have done so.

The silence in the kitchen grew too long and oppressive. The room around me was becoming blurred like a watercolour painting. I was tired and wanted to lie down, in the hope that at least in my sleep I could go back to being the Hana I used to be. Sometimes this worked but waking up would then be all the more difficult. I pushed my chair away and raised myself with difficulty, supporting myself on the table. 'Shouldn't we go home now?' I asked, turning to Rosa.

She gave me a startled look. 'Aren't you going to stay here with me?'

I had no idea what she was talking about. Why should I stay at the Karáseks'? And why did Rosa want to stay?

'Here?'

'For a few days at least.'

Karásek seemed to stir uneasily in his chair, but he said nothing. I wasn't surprised. Why would he want a stranger moving into his house?

'Don't you think she should stay here?' said Rosa, turning to him.

'If you think so,' he said unconvincingly.

'But I want to go home,' I said, trying to gauge the distance from the table to the door. My feet hurt in the tight lace-up shoes and the floor was swaying – only gently for the moment, like ripples on the surface of a pond. It really was time to go.

'Wait, don't you want to see our little one?' Rosa took me by the elbow and led me to the living room door that stood slightly ajar. The touch of her hand stung my elbow, but I made a great effort not to flinch.

In the living room, where there used to be a table with a potted plant, stood a baby's cot. I stepped back.

'This is our Mira.' Rosa bent down to the cot.

At that's when it dawned on me. Karásek and this child had robbed me of Rosa.

I turned on my heels and shuffled off.

Terezín, Summer 1943 - Autumn 1944

A few days after I was discharged from hospital I found a fusty straw mattress on my bed instead of the nice mattress and blankets my mother and I had sewn before leaving for Terezín. It was obvious that I would never see my stolen possessions again, so I went to ask our *Zimmerälteste* for a new mattress.

'You should have looked after your things,' she said, fobbing me off, but later brought me at least a blanket riddled with holes, so I had something to cover myself with.

I returned to our dormitory.

People in the ghetto didn't see anything wrong with stealing communal property, everyone tried to survive any way they could. This kind of theft was called "organising" or "swiping", and everyone did it, given the chance – including me. But stealing from another prisoner was seen as immoral, even in Terezín.

'Any idea who could have taken my mattress, Mrs Reissová?' I asked the woman on the neighbouring bunk, but she shook her head and shrank back from me.

'It's all right, I'm not contagious anymore.'

I meant it as a joke but Reissová wrinkled her nose. 'Oh, I don't know. Loose morals do seem to be catching.' She glanced at the woman on the bunk next to her and went on, encouraged by her approving expression. 'Let me give you a piece of advice, Hana. You shouldn't be friends with Jarka. You know what people say – birds of a feather...' And she turned her back on me.

I could feel myself blushing. I looked around. For the past six months no transport had left the ghetto and the occupants of our dormitory had stayed more or less the same. Thinner, paler and more tired every day, but usually friendly and willing to help. I wondered what Jarka and I could have done to make them turn against us?

'Jarka is a good girl,' I said while pretending to straighten out the musty straw mattress.

'Hah!' said Reissová, ending the conversation. I curled up into a ball on my bunk with my back to the world and stared at the wall.

'They're just jealous,' said Jarka when I asked her some time later what Reissová had against us. We were sitting on the top bunk sharing a cucumber I'd smuggled out of the SS vegetable garden in the concealed bottom of my knapsack that Jarka had helped me to sew. At first I was scared but the Czech gendarmes supervising us weren't very thorough and I was able to smuggle something out every day. I would share everything fairly with Jarka and Leo, and that, according to her, was the main reason why the women resented us – her in particular.

Because she knew which side her bread was buttered.

'If they were younger and found a man who wanted them, they would also get laid,' she said but that was a step too far, even for me. Getting laid? Was that what I was doing with Leo? I looked around uneasily to make sure no one had heard us.

'Stop making faces. And anyway, it looks like we'll be out of here soon.'

I was horrified. 'You think there will be more transports?' I didn't consider that grounds for rejoicing.

'Quite the contrary.' She sidled up to me and lowered her voice. 'There is a transport coming. Apparently, it's bringing kids from Poland. Jakub said that those houses they've been getting ready on the edge of the ghetto are intended for them. The Germans want to swap the kids for gold or prisoners of war, I've no idea which. But the main thing is, they're looking for nurses and carers to look after them. Only women without any relatives here can apply. And do you know why? Because they'll be sent to Switzerland along with the kids. You get it? Not just far away from the ghetto but also far from the war. I told him to add our names to the list.'

'No,' I blurted out, 'not me, I don't want to go.'

'Are you out of your mind? This is an incredible chance to get out of here and you don't want to go?' Jarka stared at me as if she had never seen me before.

But I couldn't leave. I was the reason my mother had ended up in the east and Rosa was somewhere in hiding, with strangers – if, that is, she was still alive. I had sacrificed them to my romantic infatuation with a man whose face I could no longer recall. Terezín was the punishment for my stupidity.

Nor did I want to leave Leo. Although our meetings were only fleeting and mostly consisted of what Jarka had referred to by that horrible term, I thought of these encounters as lovemaking and even began to enjoy them. And sometimes we would also talk. Leo told me about his life before the war, his family and the town where he was born. He said that once the war was over, we would move to Prague together and would go to the theatre and cafés, and on Fridays to the cinema. I knew it was just a daydream, but Leo's promises helped to keep me going.

'You want to leave Jakub?'

Jarka gazed at me for a moment, eyeing me up and down as if I were a complete stranger.

'You still don't get it, do you? This is a prison and if there is a chance of getting out, you must take it. And this is it.' Jarka was now sounding tearful and I didn't want to listen to her anymore. I wanted her to be once again the strong Jarka who could solve any problem. 'Maybe it's just rumours and there will be no exchange. Maybe I won't get out of here and will be stuck wiping snivelling little kids' noses, but what do I have to lose?' She gave me a defiant look, but I saw that she was on the verge of tears. 'Jakub would get out of here too if he could. Everyone would.' She took my hand and squeezed it hard. 'You're my best friend. I don't want to lose you. I'll stay here with you if you want me to.'

I was petrified. This would mean being responsible for the fate of yet another human being, something I couldn't possibly have on my conscience. 'You have to go. You'll send me a parcel from Switzerland. You know the address.'

Jarka popped the last piece of cucumber into her mouth. 'I'll send you a new pair of shoes. Your old ones look really tatty.' And she added: 'But do think it over, please.'

That night I couldn't sleep. The straw in the thin stinking mattress pricked my skin just like the ravenous insects, and thoughts raced helplessly through my head. I knew that without Jarka my days in Terezín would be even more lonely, but decided to stay nevertheless.

At the end of August a special transport from Poland did indeed arrive. It was an endless, sad procession. We were not allowed to go out as it passed through the ghetto, not even to stand by the windows. Even so, word soon got around that there were no adults on this transport, only school-age children, over a thousand of them, frightened, emaciated and in rags. After putting them through disinfection, the SS-men billeted them in the barracks at the edge of the ghetto and announced that nobody was allowed anywhere near their dormitories. Anyone trying to talk to the children would be shot.

The strict orders served only to increase our curiosity. We knew that the train had arrived from the east, presumably from the places where many of our families, friends and acquaintances had ended up. The ghetto was awash with rumours and speculations of every kind.

Some claimed that the children were from Polish orphanages. Another rumour had it that their families had been shot by the SS. But we couldn't believe that. Why would they have done such a senseless thing? we asked. As long as we were useful and able to work, they would surely let us live.

Jarka packed her suitcase and moved to the barracks with the children. We didn't even say goodbye, for it never occurred to us that we wouldn't see each other again. But neither the children nor the nurses were allowed to leave the dormitories. I knew from Leo that the children were receiving bigger food rations and were recovering. Apparently, the SS wanted to fatten them up before handing them over to the International Red Cross. Six weeks later the children left and Jarka went with them. We hadn't met once during this time. In fact, we were never to meet again. And I waited in vain for that parcel from Switzerland.

In the autumn, work in the garden and in the fields came to an end and I was reassigned to the uniform repair workshop. The doctor who discharged me from hospital warned me that I would probably never fully recover but the fatigue I struggled with day in, day out was soul-destroying and things only got worse in the spring. I had absolutely no strength left, not even for the occasional meeting with Leo. At the end of my shift I would just slump onto the bunk bed wearing all the clothes I had and lie under the blanket shivering.

I lay on the bunk feeling nauseous and on the verge of retching. I didn't move because, for one thing, I didn't want to throw up the bread I'd had for my dinner, and for another, I was scared of wandering through the impenetrable darkness that reigned in the dormitory and the communal rooms. For the second week running we were not allowed to put the lights on, as a punishment for someone's transgression. There was only one toilet for the whole floor and, try as we might, we couldn't keep it clean on those dark nights. The stench carried to the far end of the dormitory.

'I told you to keep away from that girl.' I recognised Reissová's cackle. She must have heard the retching noises I was making. 'Here, so you don't mess up your bed.' I felt something poke me in my side and found it was a tin bowl. It came not a moment too soon. I felt a little better. I just lay there for a while resting and taking deep breaths. 'What's this got to do with Jarka?'

'If she hadn't taught you those bad habits of hers you wouldn't be knocked up now.'

'I'm not knocked up.'

'Listen to me, my girl, I've been through six pregnancies, you can't fool me. But beware of the *Zimmerälteste*, she'd have to report you.'

'I'm not pregnant,' I repeated but more to convince myself than Reissová. My periods had stopped after three months in the ghetto and I thought that meant I couldn't get pregnant. Now it began to dawn on me that I'd been wrong. The nausea, the loss of appetite, the weakness, the bulging belly. I touched my breasts in the dark. They were fuller than ever. Just at that moment I thought I felt something stir inside me. Gently, like tiny fish that happen to brush against a swimmer. I curled up in a foetal position and began to cry.

I'd never seen a pregnant woman in Terezín. All women arriving in the ghetto were subjected to a gynaecological examination and those that were pregnant were made to have an abortion straight away. According to an order issued by the camp commander in the summer of 1943 every pregnancy had to be reported under threat of the harshest punishment. An abortion would follow. I pressed my hand to my stomach. I had no idea how long I'd been pregnant but since I hadn't noticed until now and as, I hoped, no one apart from the nosy Reissová had noticed either, I could pretend I wasn't aware of it until it was too late for an abortion. Terezín may not have been the best place to give birth but surely we wouldn't be here forever. Maybe there was something to the rumour that the Germans were losing the war. Maybe I'd be lucky and the war would end before I gave birth.

I was no longer crying. I pressed both hands on my slightly swollen stomach. I decided not to mention the pregnancy to Leo for the time being. What if he wanted me to get rid of the baby, which I wasn't prepared to do, and that would be the end of us. I didn't want to lose my only friend.

I wondered what people might say back home if I

returned with a baby and no husband. I could say that the child's father had died. There was so much dying all around. People died of the most ordinary diseases, injuries, old people were dying of starvation, exhaustion and the cold. In Terezín dying was more common than living.

Two months later, when the *Zimmerälteste* reported me and I had to go for a gynaecological examination, I could no longer claim I had no idea I was pregnant because my bulging belly on my emaciated frame was glaringly obvious. I could just about disguise it under the loose cardigan I wore in the draughty workshop. Leo hadn't noticed during our occasional brief bouts of lovemaking on the hard floor in the dark stables, when we pressed our bodies together without taking our clothes off. And it would also have gone unnoticed by the *Zimmerälteste*, if I hadn't fainted right by her bed on one of my night-time visits to the toilet. She unbuttoned my cardigan to help me breathe, paused in surprise, felt my belly, and straightened up. She towered above me for a while, watching me come to, then she gave me a kick in the side with the tip of her shoe and went back to bed without a word.

The next day I was summoned for an examination.

I was frightened but I told myself that my pregnancy was so advanced now it would be too late to have an abortion. It was indeed too late, so they decided to induce premature labour instead.

They declared that I had behaved immorally, as I'd got pregnant out of wedlock. Did I even know who the father of the child was? 'Of course I know,' I shouted. 'Leo loves me, he's going to marry me.'

'Leo who?'

'Leo Gross, who else. He works in the kitchen.'

I struggled, I fought, and I pleaded, but the doctor just took notes without looking at me.

'I have to report this to headquarters,' he said. 'It's up to them to decide.'

When my baby boy was born, he was so tiny he would have fitted into the cupped palms of my hands. But he never lay there, I caught only a glimpse of him as the nurse carried him away. He wasn't crying or moving but I knew he was alive. The nurse returned empty-handed, bent down towards me, stroked my arm and whispered that I'd just been saved from a transport. 'Pregnancy is a certain ticket to the east, my girl.' I didn't care.

Sometimes I picture the soul as a sugar loaf, a white loaf from which slivers of sugar are carved off. With every terrible thing that happens to you in life a thin slice is peeled off. The loaf gets smaller and smaller until one day there is nothing left of it at all. When this happened, my soul had been badly battered but it was still holding together. The day my son was born, the son I wanted to name Leo, the chunk that broke off the loaf was so big that my soul broke in two, with one half tumbling down from a great height, shattering into a thousand tiny fragments when I learned that while I was recovering in hospital, Leo Gross had received the summons for the first transport of the autumn, and was sent east.

And the nurse in hospital was mistaken. I received the thin strip of paper with my name on it from our *Zimmerälteste* the very next evening.

CHAPTER TWENTY-FIVE

Meziříčí

In the early days Rosa came to visit me every day. She would bring baby Mira along but then she realised that I couldn't take the child's crying and started coming alone. Admittedly, the crying did bother me but what bothered me far more was seeing Rosa's loving gaze as she held Mira tight and comforted her. Mothers with babies were sent straight to the gas chambers from the ramp, it flashed through my mind, as I staggered to my bedroom.

Rosa tried to draw me back into the world of the living, forcing me to go out and expose myself to people's furtive glances and listen to them complain about the hardships they had suffered during the war. Food had been scarce, they said, averting their gaze. You never knew when they'd come for you. And those dreaded air raids towards the end of the war – but you just had to grin and bear it. Actually, you don't know how lucky you've been. In the camps you were safe from the allied bombing, you can't begin to imagine the horror of it, how we feared for our children's lives. You have to pull yourself together, they kept saying, get a grip, stop feeling sorry for yourself and get on with life. Blah blah blah... I said nothing and they began to give me a wide berth.

Nor did my body heal, but I wasn't tormented so much by the pain caused by every sudden movement, change of weather or burst of excitement, as by surges of anxiety. I saw no reason to keep on living, but I wasn't able to die either.

For a long time Rosa did her best to try and lift me from the void. She didn't understand that she was doomed to fail because all that was left of me was a husk. My soul, the soul that makes a person into a human being, was no longer there. It had travelled east along with my family, had lost its way in the streets of the Terezín ghetto, remained trapped in the cattle trucks heading east, mired in the mud of the camp, and incinerated in the furnaces of Auschwitz.

After a while Rosa started to take me to see doctors. Men in white coats merely shook their heads and spoke of patience. When the word institution started cropping up with increasing frequency I refused to set foot in any doctor's surgery, although Rosa tried to cajole me in the same affectionate tone of voice she used to comfort her little girl.

There was only one way I could get through yet another day. I would take it minute by minute, one step at a time. Get up, get dressed, eat breakfast, tidy up. Monotonous chores had a calming effect on me. They kept my hands busy and didn't stir up memories and take me back to the barbed wire fence, preventing the voices from the other side reaching me.

That was how I survived the next few years. Rosa realised that instead of regaining her older sister she had acquired another child that depended on her love. I was aware of her affection and even if I wasn't capable of repaying her in kind, I was grateful to her, although I couldn't put my gratitude into words.

Rosa's family grew. First there came another girl, followed by a little boy, and my sister continued to come and see me quite often. However, my visits to her new home in the tall house above the river were rare. Karel Karásek couldn't stand me and the feeling was mutual. Furthermore, the cold house was a constant reminder of the days I used to climb the wooden stairs to keep old Mrs Karásková company and of the evenings when I would walk across town back to our flat, which then still felt like a real home.

The world around me changed but it didn't change me in any way. The stationer's was requisitioned by the state and Mr Urbánek went back to his old job at the factory. I didn't care but Rosa was cross because, unlike Mr Urbánek, the state didn't pay any rent and I was left to manage on the few crowns the authorities allocated me when they discovered that I was good for nothing. Mind you – how much does a person actually need?

A bite to eat and some warm clothes to wear in winter.

And a reason to be alive.

I tried, I really did. I tried for nine whole years. I really wanted to clamber out of the deep well of my memories, to come up to the surface, and once again take a deep breath. I longed for it, for Rosa's sake, but I failed. My feet remained firmly mired in the past.

And then Rosa turned thirty.

The nine years of my life after my return to town are a single, vast, white blur, the memory of Rosa's birthday looming above them like a mountain peak. That day I remember in every detail and if I could paint, I could paint every single minute of it. My last day with Rosa.

She showed me to a seat at the festively laid table and went back to the kitchen to fetch the soup tureen. Karásek and the children were already in their places – Karásek wearing his usual bored and disdainful expression, Mira unusually tongue-tied. Mira's younger sister, whose name I couldn't for the life of me recall at that moment, and Rosa's youngest son, Otto, cast furtive glances at me because they saw me only a few times a year. I slipped my hand into my pocket, broke off a bit of bread and put it in my mouth. The taste of the crust calmed me down. I rolled it around on my tongue and looked out of the window. The day was as cloudy as my thoughts.

I forced down a few spoonfuls of Rosa's soup and, just to make her happy, I even tasted some of her hunter's stew. Then, to my surprise, Rosa placed a cream puff on my plate. I didn't think that one of the pastries would be for me, as I could barely stomach even plain boiled potatoes.

Just then Mira started screaming about something or other, Karásek became much louder than usual, and Rosa had to gently remind them that it was her birthday. Mira pushed her chair away and hared off. I felt strange, as if this was all my fault. Head down I carefully picked up the pastry, squeezed it between my toothless gums and the sweet taste of vanilla flooded my mouth. I finished the whole cream puff. As did Rosa, Karel Karásek, the little girl whose name I couldn't recall, and their youngest, Otto.

Within a week we all fell ill with typhoid. I was the only one who survived. The doctors said the only reason I didn't die was that I'd had typhoid before.

Terezín, October 1944, Auschwitz, October 1944

Once again, all of Terezín lived in fear of the transports. Their resumption caught everyone unawares, as it had been a long time since May, when the last trains had left the ghetto for the east, and people began to believe that those of us who had escaped the transports so far might just manage to stay in Terezín until the end of the war. The ghetto was run by the SS, it was filthy, disease-ridden and plagued by hunger, but at least it was familiar. Word went around that the Allies had liberated Paris and the Russians were approaching the river Vistula. Germany's defeat seemed imminent. How much longer could it be before the fighting was over?

I was standing in the sluice with the others who had received the summons. They included Reissová and a few other women from our dormitory who had volunteered as their husbands or sons had been sent off on the first transport of the autumn. The men had been told they would be building a new camp near Dresden and would be back in Terezín in six weeks' time. A few days later the ghetto administration allowed their wives and mothers to join them.

I remembered my mother telling me to try to stay in Terezín for as long as possible and wondered if anyone had warned these women, but their frightened yet determined faces told me that their desire to be reunited with their loved ones was stronger than fear.

After an interminable wait with endless roll calls we were shoved into the trucks of a waiting train. Squashed among strangers I had to gasp for air and tried to elbow my way to the wall to have something to lean against. I felt a hand grab hold of me, pull me through the crowd and push me in the direction of the wall. People grumbled disapprovingly but Reissová snapped at them. 'She's just given birth, she needs to sit down.'

I sat down on my rucksack, leaned back against the wooden wall of the carriage and concentrated on trying to breathe. The air was stale and saturated with the odour of bodies.

The train set off, its wheels clanking rhythmically. During the seemingly endless journey I thought of Grandpa Bruno and Grandma Greta who had left Terezín with a high fever, and mentally said farewell to them. The sick and the old couldn't possibly have survived a journey like this. I needed the toilet but was scared to leave my spot. Also, in those days, I was still ashamed to relieve myself in front of others. Men, women, children...

Soon it transpired that I wasn't the only one with this problem. Three people positioned themselves around a bucket that served as a toilet and held up a blanket to provide some semblance of privacy and we all took turns behind it. But soon the bucket was full to overflowing and when someone tried to empty it out of the tiny window covered with barbed wire, an unbearable stench filled the whole carriage. I closed my eyes and told myself over and over again that I simply had to keep going. Maybe I'd be lucky and meet my mother or Leo wherever it was that we were headed. I just had to survive this journey. Then everything would be all right again. How much worse than Terezín could other ghettos be?

The monotonous rumbling of wheels and the piercing sound of the train whistle echoes in my head to this day. I still feel the horror swelling in the carriage with every kilometre. Because, after we passed Dresden and the train turned east, we all knew that our men and some of us, too, let ourselves be fooled by false promises and the hope that this train was headed for a new ghetto similar to Terezín. We passed through Wrocław, Opole, Katowice and after travelling for more than thirty hours, the train came to a halt in the middle of the night on a siding in the Auschwitz concentration camp.

The carriage was dark, except for the cold light of streetlamps filtering through the barbed wire-covered windows. We heard noises from outside. Steps, shrill German commands, but also Yiddish spoken on the other side of the locked doors. We clutched at the tiniest shred of hope. We would get out before long, breathe some fresh air, quench our thirst and, with a bit of luck, we might soon be taken to our living quarters.

The carriage doors started to clatter open against the backdrop of the barking of dogs and loud yells. *'Schnell! Schnell!* Leave your luggage on the train.'

Spilling out on top of each other we looked around in bewilderment. Low buildings enclosed by high electrified fences and watchtowers. Barbed wire. A sea of mud under our feet. A stench emanating from the darkness. The train surrounded by armed guards with dogs. Screaming and wailing.

Emaciated men wearing caps and striped uniforms unloaded our luggage into piles.

They pushed us forward, whispering the words 'Auschwitz, Birkenau, Auschwitz, Birkenau.' I must have been moving too slowly because a blow landed on my back. This was the first time I was hit with a stick in Auschwitz, the first time in my life anywhere, for that matter. I hurried to catch up with a group of women, and the second blow just glanced off my coat. Men to one side, women to the other. The pace slowed and I wondered if I'd ever see my luggage again. I had brought some spare underwear, winter clothes and a family photograph. The line inched forward, slowly approaching a group of SS-men in neatly pressed uniforms. One of them prodded my shoulder with a small whip.

'Age?'

'Twenty-five.'

'Healthy?'

What might the right answer be? I asked myself. If I told them I had just given birth, perhaps they might assign me to lighter work alongside the children and the elderly. I heard shouting and desperate crying around me. Why are they separating families?

'Healthy,' I said decisively.

The whip pushed me to the left and then pointed at Reissová.

'Age?'

'Forty-two.' There were no further questions. I turned and saw that Reissová was sent to the right. Had I made a mistake? The group on the right was much bigger and moved off slowly somewhere behind me, while we were driven in groups of five between the barbed wire fences and towards some brick buildings.

Now I know that I did make a mistake. Had I been sent to the right I could have died that very day and my ashes would have mingled with the other flecks of ash spewing from the chimneys of Auschwitz's crematoria in thick, acrid clouds. I would have dissolved in a cloud of smoke as did Leo, who had arrived in Auschwitz a week earlier. Despite being young and strong, he was killed immediately because he'd been sent to the camp as punishment on a *Weisung*, a note that meant a death sentence. Leo, happy-go-lucky Leo, who had survived three whole years in Terezín, had to die simply because I had desperately shouted out his name in the hospital, insisting that he would look after me and our child.

My ashes would have settled on the barrack roofs, mingled with the mud on the roads, and maybe the wind would have blown them over the far side of the camp fence, as it did what remained of Jarka, who had believed that she was going to Switzerland with the Polish children. Only in Auschwitz did I learn why that parcel from Jarka never arrived. The train carrying one thousand and two hundred children from Białystok, together with their carers, ended up in the gas chambers of Auschwitz on the very day they arrived, without even going through selection.

Had I been sent to the right I would have died instantly and wouldn't have had to die minute after minute, hour after hour, and day after day. And no one would have died instead of me.

After a few minutes' walk we found ourselves among some barracks and piles of luggage. We looked around fearfully and entered one by one a large cold room in a brick building. We speculated in low voices where they might be taking us and the braver, or maybe the more desperate, ones among us dared to approach the soldiers who escorted us from the train and now stood guard by the door, to ask what would happen to us and where our relatives were. They put their questions in German but the soldiers didn't respond or just said grumpily that we would be joining the others later.

Female prisoners with a red stripe on the back of their civvies took away our knapsacks with the remaining food. A few women tried desperately to hold on to their bags but after the intervention of an SS-man who hit them across the back of their hands with his truncheon they handed over what was left of their belongings, in tears but without protest. I had nothing left to hand over. In the scrummage as we got off the train someone had yanked my knapsack off my shoulder.

Several SS-men entered the room. The tall man with the whip who had stood on the ramp and sent me to the left was standing in front. He looked around and shouted in a voice used to issuing commands: 'Get undressed!'

We took off our coats and looked at one another, uncertain what to do next. The SS-men started to yell and drum their truncheons impatiently in their palms, as if trying to decide which one of us to hit first. 'Didn't you hear? *Herr Obersturmführer* told you to get undressed. Come on, *schnell, schnell*! Chop-chop! You're going to take a shower.'

We looked around uncomprehendingly. Some of the women started to cry. Did they really want us to undress in the presence of all these men? Prisoners in striped jackets and officers in their neatly pressed uniforms. We took a step back. The SS-men started yelling even more loudly, waving their clubs about threateningly. Some of us were dealt more blows. Weeping tears of humiliation, I tried to hide behind the others but in the end I had no choice but leave my clothes in a pile and, wearing nothing and carrying only my shoes, appear in front of a table where those of us who still had anything left were stripped of their last possessions. A thin silver chain, a hairpin...

As we stood in line trying to shield our nakedness with our hands, the prisoners rummaged through our things, picking out anything they could use. We tried to object but more blows and screaming followed. 'None of this belongs to you anymore, you'll get all new stuff after disinfection.'

Naked, we had to file past the *Obersturmführer* who observed the proceedings as if they didn't concern him. He gestured to some less fit-looking women to move to one side.

I got through. Despite being exhausted and weak after having recently given birth, I'd been able to sit on the train and must have looked strong enough to last for a few more weeks of labour.

After the small batch of rejected women had been herded out of the door, the rest of us were pushed and prodded into the adjoining room, where some women prisoners with electric razors were waiting. I was one of the first in line. As the razor ran across my head, my hair fell to the floor. The women around me were changing beyond recognition. We had to take a cold shower and were left to wait in a freezing cold room for what seemed like an eternity before some dirty rags were thrown on the floor in a pile for us to fight over like dogs. There was no underwear whatsoever among the lice-ridden clothes. All I managed to dig out was a summer dress, a short jacket and a pair of stockings. Still wet, I got dressed and instead of my shoes, which had been stolen while I was in the shower, I tried to find at least a pair of wooden clogs roughly the same size.

A Polish woman prisoner tattooed a number on everyone's arm with a needle soaked in ink. Within a few minutes all our past and future lives evaporated and we were reduced from human beings to numbers on a list. Our lives no longer belonged to us.

We spent the night in an empty room on a cold stone floor. Tired as we were, none of us was able to sleep. We huddled together to try to keep at least a little warm, shivering with cold and weeping tears of helplessness, humiliation and fear.

A woman next to me was praying. Her name was Truda and her enormous eyes reminded me of Rosa. Was my delicate little sister still alive, I wondered, or had she met this same fate? Had she found shelter in the town we had to leave? The town with the tumbling river, paved streets and houses that preserved the memories of people who had died long before I was born. I drew my knees up to my chin. I, too, would die, but alone and far from home. I would never learn what had happened to those I loved and who loved me.

It was still dark when we were chased out for the roll call, hungry and numb with cold. The stench that had filled our nostrils ever since our arrival in the camp grew more intense and mingled with the smoke rising from the low roofs. Barely able to stand upright, we found ourselves in a wide, open space outside the barracks. By the time the roll call ended it was light. We were herded back into the barracks and were finally given some bitter dark liquid to drink. The women pushed their way to the prisoner dishing out tea from a bucket on a cart and showered her with questions but she just shook her head and said not a word.

Truda, the woman with the beautiful eyes, grabbed her by the wrist and shouted: 'Tell us where they've taken our families, tell us where our children are.'

The woman looked at the hand gripping her emaciated wrist, then raised her eyes to Truda and motioned with her head towards the dark smoke billowing from the chimneys at the edge of the camp. 'Gone up in smoke. They've all gone up in smoke.'

After a moment of shocked silence there came the first sob and the room filled with the sound of desperate lamentations. We had seen enough to believe her. I was glad that I'd been alone when I arrived in Birkenau because the worst moment for the women separated from their families was when they realised that the omnipresent, nauseatingly sickly, sweetish smell that we had been inhaling ever since our arrival at the camp was all that remained of those they loved.

Chapter Twenty-Six

Meziříčí

I bring bad luck to those I love and those who love me. I've known this for a long time. My mother died because I kept delaying our departure for England. I condemned Leo to death because I couldn't hold my tongue and named him as the father of my child. In so doing I issued his ticket for Auschwitz. And I couldn't save our baby son either.

People stronger and more determined than me perished in Auschwitz, yet I have survived. But now, all of a sudden, Rosa and her family were dead while I was still alive.

Have I really gone on living only to bring misfortune to others?

The first days after I learned the news of Rosa's death are one enormous smudge of black. I lay on my unmade bed, empty of head and heart. Every time I closed my eyes, an avalanche of guilt engulfed me, sweeping me out of bed. I sat down at the table, fished a slice of bread out of the drawer, broke off a bit of crust and stuck it in my mouth.

Rosa had devoted nine years to trying to heal my shattered soul. She picked it up fragment by fragment, piecing the shards together and sewing them up with the thread of her love. She might never have been able to heal all the wounds and help me to return fully to life, as some of the pieces had been lost forever, but the fog no longer felt so dense and the voices of the dead reproaching me no longer rang out so loud. But the thread holding my soul together was thin and not strong enough to contain all this pain. The stitches came undone under the burden of guilt and again I toppled headlong into a wasteland of anxiety.

I was sitting at the table waiting for death to come knocking when the sound of the doorbell penetrated the fog. I raised my head but didn't bother to get up. The door seemed too far away and there was no point in making the effort. Then the bell rang again.

Resigned, I pushed my chair back and went to the door.

There was a familiar look in the eyes of the man standing on the cold tiles of the hallway. It was one of shock, pity, sorrow and revulsion all in one. When others looked at me in that way it didn't bother me, but this man, of all people, had no right to give me such a look... Because he was to blame for everything that had happened to me, and for what is left of me, for the way I look now.

He stepped back, repelled.

'What are you doing here?' I asked, shaking with fury. I could hear his voice through the stormy sea rumbling in my ears. It gained in height and volume, churning in the air before landing heavy on my shoulders. I was to come and get Mira, he said. Rosa's Mira? Yes, she was at the Horáčeks. Why hadn't anyone told me? Why hadn't she come to me a long time ago?

Long after Jaroslav Horáček had bounded down the stairs, I was still standing in the doorway pondering what to do. The only thing I was sure of was that I wouldn't leave Rosa's daughter with Jaroslav and Ivana.

Auschwitz, October 1944 - January 1945

A roll call in the *Appelplatz* at four in the morning, brown water instead of tea, more endless lining up and being counted, freezing cold, wind, nothing to eat but some thin soup for lunch and a hunk of bread in the evening. Three-tier bunk beds on which we had to lie on our sides, jammed in like sardines. A bucket by the barrack door for a toilet. Cold, hunger, thirst, dirt, lice and exhausting roll calls. There were fewer of us left after each one.

On the fifth day some numbers were called out during the morning roll call. One of them was mine. By then it had been tattooed into my brain as well as onto my wrist. Eight of us had been chosen and led between the electric fences twice the height of a human being to the gate of the women's camp, where a bizarre orchestra of women prisoners in blue skirts and white blouses was playing.

At the gate our small group merged with a bigger contingent and we were all marched, in lines of five, to some brick warehouses and storerooms. The floors were covered with huge piles of clothing that the SS-men had stripped from the new arrivals as soon as they reached the camp. Those in a decent condition were sent to Germany. Evidently, German women didn't mind wearing clothes that had belonged to Jews. Clothing that was too damaged to send off was cut by up the prisoners into three-centimetre-wide strips and women in other workshops sewed them together into longer bands, for use as insulation in German submarines and military vehicles.

At the storerooms we were handed over to an SS-man who assigned us work. Together with two other women I was taken to a workshop where the cut-up material was being plaited into ropes, like women's braids, and then wound onto huge discs. At the sight of the SS-man the women leapt up from their wooden benches and stood with their eyes firmly fixed on the tables in front of them.

'Keep at it,' the officer commanded. The workers moved up to make room for us, and we set to work straight away. I couldn't believe my luck. I'd been assigned light work which was done seated and with a roof over my head. All of a sudden, something jabbed me in the back. It was the

SS-man prodding me with the tip of his whip. '*Du* – you.' I jumped to my feet and stood to attention.

He took out his watch. 'At the word go, start working. Go.'

I was shaking, but my hands were still quite nimble in those days. They recalled the many metres of curtains and tablecloths I had crocheted, the dozens of cushions and blankets I had knitted, and swiftly plaited the material into a long rope.

The SS-man picked it up, pulled at it and placed it back on the table. 'You filthy Jews,' he yelled. 'This girl has only just arrived and she's managed to plait a rope this long in a matter of minutes. This is how fast you must all work! Anyone who makes a piece that's shorter will never see the light of day again.' He took out his watch and slammed his whip down on the table.

The women were in tears but did as they were told, resignedly, as if accepting a long-awaited sentence. Ever since, the eyes of the three women who didn't manage to work as fast as me have stared at me every single night.

The SS-man left and we continued to work in silence. No one said a word to me for the rest of the day or during the march back, the roll call, or in the barrack I had been assigned.

They all refused to look at me and gave me the cold shoulder.

When the barrack doors closed behind us, a blow landed on my back, winding me. I clutched my chest and could hardly breathe, as the *Blockälteste* held me by the throat. 'You've had it,' she hissed into my face. She was purple with rage and had tears rolling down her cheeks. That was how I learned that one of the women who hadn't returned to the barrack because of me was her sister.

From then on, I got the blame for everything. I became a pariah with no right to protection or friendship in the barracks that resembled a horse stables where hundreds of women were crammed into three-tier bunks when I arrived. Those who wanted to curry favour with the *Blockälteste* would hurt me quite openly, the others were simply scared of getting into her bad books.

I had to lap up the evening soup from the cupped palms of my hands because none of the women would share their bowl with me. I was one of the last to get to the food and if I didn't shove a bit of bread into my mouth fast enough, the *Blockälteste* would steal it from me. I had to sleep on the floor and only occasionally, under cover of darkness, could I creep onto the lowest bunk and squeeze in between the sleeping women.

For a while my nimble fingers offered me protection. I was the fastest and the workshop *Kapo* knew very well that the more skilful workers she had, the safer her own job would be. Except that within a few days I grew so weak that I was losing the strength in my fingers and my pace of work slowed down.

In the mornings, on our way to work, we saw the bodies of prisoners hanging from the electric fences. No longer willing or able to endure life in the camp they had decided to take the final decision into their own hands and throw themselves on the fences. I resolved to do the same one day. Once I couldn't take it any longer, I would choose my own death rather than suffocate in a gas chamber. Having taken this decision I felt liberated and my spirits lifted.

The *Blockälteste* would not leave me alone and if the barrack leaders hadn't lost some of their powers by then and if she'd still had the authority to beat me to death, she would have done so in a heartbeat. But the Germans sensed that the end of the war was drawing close and reserved the privilege of killing prisoners for themselves. I fell into a strange kind of lethargy. I clung to the idea of death and in my darkest moments pictured myself approaching the barbed wire calmly, one step at a time, head held high as I reached for the fence. In my imagination the sky was blue and my soul floated about like a tiny balloon. I saw myself slowly rising skyward, feeling nothing. Neither guilt nor pain.

After a while I became so weak that the boundary between the real world and the world of my imagination became increasingly hazy. My body trembled with exhaustion, my thoughts drifted in and out of the fog and the only thing I was still aware of was the cold and the cramps in my stomach. My mind had lost control over my body and my movements became involuntary.

I was no longer affected by the weeping of women eliminated in the selections. I knew that what it meant was more room on the bunk beds and more food from the cauldrons. I felt only numbness at the harrowing sight of carts carrying emaciated dead bodies that had been collected by equally emaciated prisoners behind the barracks and wheeled to the crematoria. They were dead and no longer suffering from cold or hunger.

My toes had turned black, my joints were swollen, and I was plagued by a hacking cough. I had lost two of my teeth and the ones that remained were coming loose. Every morning I gazed at the electric fences and mentally took my last steps towards them. I will do it on the way back, I told myself, I'll reach out for them on the way back. In the workshop my hands were kept busy while the fog in my head grew ever thicker.

I barely noticed that in early December, my second month in the camp, the heavy air in Auschwitz suddenly thinned out and the viscous black smoke stopped billowing from the chimneys. The SS-men were more and more irritable and yelled louder than ever. Lists of the living and the dead were set on fire outside administrative buildings. Lorries and trains were loaded with looted objects and prisoners started to leave the camp, on their way to clear rubble in Germany's bombed cities. There was nothing left to weave ropes from and we were made to clear out the storehouses. We would sort things into crates, which were then carried out by the male prisoners.

'Don't hurry,' the men urged us. 'Once we've finished this job they'll shoot us. They'll do away with the whole camp. The Russians are getting closer.'

They won't shoot me, I thought. My head was about to explode and excruciating spasms convulsed my stomach. Tonight will be the night I will reach out for the fence and drift up into the sky. I walked through the mist, squelching through the sludge and counting out the last steps of my life. I joined the other women for my final roll call and my eyes started to search out the place where I would die. That night I didn't even try to squeeze myself onto a bunk bed. I sat on the floor and reached into my pocket for a last crust of bread. Someone grabbed me by the wrist and the *Blockälteste* yanked the bread out of my fingers. 'You're not going to need that anymore, you stinking filthy bitch. There's a selection tomorrow morning, and you're not going to get through. You'll kick the bucket.'

I lay down on the cold floor with a smile on my face. I should have been freezing, but my whole body was on fire. The *Blockälteste* was right. Right about everything. I was filthy because for several days now I hadn't been able to make it to the washroom, I had absolutely no strength left in my body. I stank, because we all did. And I was going to die.

But not tomorrow morning. Tonight.

The barrack was pitch dark as I dragged myself out of the door. I looked around and started walking towards the fence. I'd never realised it would be so far away. First the left foot, then the right...

'*Halt*! Stop!'

Why? I wanted to keep going but a fierce blow across my calves knocked me to the ground. Then came a kick to my side. 'Get up.' I started to retch.

I recognised the sound that came next. I knew that it would be followed by the sound of shot. And that this would be the last sound I'd hear. I closed my eyes.

'Save your bullet. She's a goner anyway. She's got typhoid. Take her to Barrack 25.'

No, anything but Barrack 25. Shoot me or let me crawl to the fence. That's what I would have shouted if I'd had any strength left to shout. Number 25 was known as the Barrack of Death, where the women condemned to die were left to rot. It was emptied out twice a week and anyone still alive even despite getting no food, ended up in the gas chambers.

I felt hands take hold of my ankles and wrists and toss me onto the cart used to distribute food and carry bodies to the incinerators. That's the last thing I remember.

I came to on a plank bed in another barrack. Outside it was already light but this place was still in semi-darkness. I raised my head and looked around. Some twenty bodies were lying on the other planks. A shadow by the door stirred and approached me. Its hands felt my body and searched through my pockets. 'Bread, do you have any bread?'

Heads rose from the bunks moaning softly. 'Drink. I need something to drink.'

I tried to push the woman away, but the sudden movement made me sick and I retched. A stream of blue liquid erupted from my throat. The woman hovered above me for a while and then returned to her place by the door.

It was the middle of January when I was sent to Barrack 25. I know this because I remember the other women's prayers as they had recently welcomed in the new year. They prayed for their loved ones and to get out of the camp alive.

Their wishes came true. As I lay on my deathbed in the Barrack of Death, SS guards were hounding the other prisoners out of the gates and sending them on their final march. The only people left behind were the ones who didn't take to heart the warnings that the whole camp had been mined, and went into hiding, as well as those who were too weak or too sick to move. Once the SS were gone the prisoners stormed the camp stores and someone had the idea of breaking into Barrack 25. They found the bodies of eighteen women, and two who were half-dead: me and the woman by the door. It wasn't until we were taken to a makeshift hospital that I discovered who she was: Truda with the beautiful eyes.

I spent several months in the camp hospital run by the Soviets and the Polish Red Cross. They cured me of typhoid and fattened me up from thirty kilos to forty-two. My shinbones, smashed by the guard who caught me as I tried to approach the fence, never healed properly, nor did my frostbitten feet. I lost all my teeth and once my hair started to grow back, it was thin and completely white. Pain has lodged permanently in my joints and muscles, but it is never as intense as the torment caused by the broken shards of my shattered soul.

I was told to forget it all and start life from scratch. I might have been able to forget the hunger and the freezing hours spent on the *Appelplatz*. I might have been able to forget the pain in my broken bones. But how could I ever forget the people I saw dangling from the electric fences, the bodies ripped to shreds by dogs, and the dislocated shoulders of men and women executed for no reason, as a warning to others? Or the never-ending processions of children, women and men headed for the gas chambers straight from the trains? How could I forget the despair in Truda's eyes when she learned that her children had been gassed?

I was told to forget because people didn't want to hear what I had to say. They needn't have worried. I wasn't able to forget because the memories have been tattooed into my brain in the same way as the number on my left wrist. I just could not speak of them.

Chapter Twenty-Seven

Meziříčí

Mira stood cowering in the hallway looking no less lost and frightened than I felt. Her clothes and hair were a mess, as if she had just tumbled out of bed, and her eyes, as big as Rosa's, were red from crying. She hid behind Ivana, the woman who used to sit next to me at school in my previous life, when we whispered our girlish secrets into each other's ears and shared dreams of our future happiness. Though I was better at reading and history, Ivana excelled at maths, which was why – unlike me – she and Jaroslav could work out what would be more to their advantage.

Neither Jaroslav nor Ivana bore responsibility for the war that had wiped out my family but their lies were the reason we didn't leave for England in time. They are the reason I am left here eking out this miserable existence while death screams its reproaches at me.

'Let's go,' I said.

Ivana reached out to give me a hug and was about to explain something to me. But the rage I felt was more powerful than my tiredness. I shouted at her, grabbing Mira by the shoulders to drag her away. Mira started to bawl. I stopped at the bottom of the stairs. I took my hands off Mira's shoulders and began slowly walking home. Let Rosa's daughter go back to the Horáčeks if she wanted to. Let Ivana take her, just as she had taken the life that should by rights have been mine.

To my astonishment Mira came after me.

I had come to collect her from the villa that resembled a boat sailing out to sea, where after the war there lived Dr Lewy's brother, the only one in his family to survive, thanks to his non-Jewish wife who would not divorce him and thus saved him from the transport. I had come to take her away from the family of the man who could have protected me in the same way but chose not to. No, Mira couldn't stay with the Horáčeks, of that I was sure.

But I wasn't sure of anything else. I had no plan.

It was so hard to make sense of the world, to concentrate on what other people were saying, to remember what needed to be done.

I tightened the scarf around my head to stop my thoughts from scattering to the winds.

What was happening to me?

I looked back. Maybe this was all just a dream, another figment of my confused imagination.

But Mira was still there.

That was how I came to bring Rosa's daughter to live with me. I had to do it – I owed it to Rosa.

I did want to look after Mira and give her a home, but looking back I can see that Mira was far stronger than me. I gave her my mother's old bedroom. I had been wary of going in there because this was where the voices tormented me more loudly than anywhere else, but the minute Mira filled the drawers with her things and sat a shabby teddy bear on the bed, the voices in the bedroom stopped – except for Mira's.

At first she would tiptoe around me carefully but in a few weeks she found her bearings and settled in the flat where her grandparents had lived and her mother had grown up as if it had always been her home. In fact, she was the one who made the flat in the Square feel once again like a home. She filled it with the sound of her booming voice and her ringing laughter, telling me everything that happened to her and reading out to me from her books. Mira had a penetrating voice from which there was no escape. Sometimes it was too much for me and I had to retreat to the silence of my bedroom.

I did want to look after her but everyone I have ever loved had abandoned me in the end. I didn't want to relive yet again the horror of losing someone I loved. To worry that she might die or just abandon me to start a life of her own.

But I knew from the beginning that it was a futile hope. Mira had stolen into my life, ensconcing herself and forming the new core of my existence. I only realised how vital she was when she got cross with me on her thirteenth birthday, accusing me of not caring for her and stayed out all night.

I sat up and waited for her, and when she came in at dawn, I felt something close to happiness.

How was I to explain to her that I never remember the dates of any birthdays or anniversaries – and have no wish to remember?

I didn't want to tell her that her mother Rosa used to bring me a present on every birthday and every Christmas, while I never gave any presents to her, nor to anyone else for that matter.

Although Rosa had made sure that all the important dates were marked in my calendar, even when I had money to spare I couldn't make the mental effort to leave the house, go to a shop and buy a present.

That February of 1954, as winter was drawing to a close, I gathered from the way Rosa talked about her thirtieth birthday that it meant a great deal to her. And I knew that I owed it to the only person in the world who cared about me to show her that I cared about her, too. Suddenly, for the first time in ages and without noticing how it happened, I was able to think ahead.

Normally, I left the house just once a week, on Mondays,

to buy a loaf of bread and a few other staples. Back at home I would cut off a few slices of the bread and put them away, some into the table drawer, some under my pillow and a few into the pockets of my thick cardigan. That was my safety net.

That Saturday, when the snow on the ground started to turn into a crunching sludge, I left the safety of my four kitchen walls, passed the bakery I knew well and the little grocer's and stopped at the patisserie under the arcades to buy a box of cream puffs. The next day I gave them to Rosa as a present.

The cream puffs with their custard filling and white icing, the cream puffs that harboured death.

I couldn't tell Mira that I had killed her family.

That I have survived only to keep spreading death.

I cherished my solitude but, at the same time, I started looking forward to Mira coming home.

For nine whole years I waited every day for Mira to come home from school and looked forward to her welter of stories about what had happened to her and her friends during the day, before she picked up a textbook or a novel and settled down on the windowsill or her favourite place on the sofa. Sometimes she would read out a maths equation or something else from a book.

Mira's wedding and her moving out caught me off guard but there was nothing I could do. At first it bothered me that she married the young Horáček but after a while I found that many events and things that had once seemed important no longer mattered very much. I still felt a deep aversion to Jaroslav, but Mira's husband wasn't anything like his father. I didn't go to their wedding, oh no – that would have meant going out and letting people gawp at me – so I was surprised when Mira and her new husband came to see me straight from the register office.

'Please forgive me, Auntie,' she whispered. 'I couldn't talk him out of it.' I could see that she was uneasy. She must have been expecting a scene. I was so stunned that I didn't even get up. Gustav pulled up a chair. 'I've come to say thank you for having given Mira a home.'

He continued to talk but I wasn't taking it in. I just nodded and stared at the table. Mira stroked my hand and before I knew it they were gone. The table-top started to dissolve before my eyes and I felt something warm running down my cheeks. Tears welled up just like the time I had said goodbye to my mother at the sluice in Terezín. With these tears I bade farewell to my family, to Leo and to our baby boy.

That afternoon my tears washed away everything that had accumulated inside me over the past twenty years. I knew that Mira would have deserved a better home, more affection and a warmer welcome but there was a limit to what I could give her, and I was happy that Mira understood that. Her husband knew it too because, as Mira made for the door, he bent down to me and whispered: 'Mira needs you very much, don't abandon her.'

She needs me. The words stuck in my mind.

That autumn Mira gave birth to a baby boy and she was no longer able to come by every day. Instead, I've taken to visiting her in the old, cold house above the river. The tall house still looks distinctly unfriendly but when a fire is burning in the hearth, it thaws out and becomes much more welcoming.

It is a draughty building, so Mira asked me to teach her how to knit. Little Otto needs lots of baby hats and jumpers.

Mira is really bright, she's read hundreds of books and I'm sure she will make it to university because she always achieves whatever she sets out to do. But working with her hands is not her strong suit. If Grandma Greta could see the tangled tatters hanging from her knitting needles she would be horrified. I've forgotten many things and many other things have got muddled up in my head but the moment my fingers pick up the needles, they remember.

And so I sit in the armchair where old Mrs Karásková used to sit, my eyes fixed on the needles. I am still visited by memories. Many of them are still bleak, but the number of those that make me want to keep on living continues to grow by the day.

PARTHIAN TRANSLATIONS

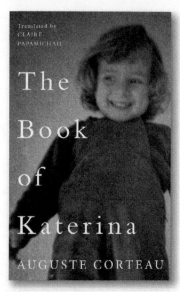

THE BOOK OF KATERINA

Auguste Corteau

Translated from Greek
by Claire Papamichail

Out 2021

£10.00
978-1-912681-26-6

HANA

Alena Mornštajnová

Translated from Czech
by Julia and Peter Sherwood

Out October 2020

£10.99
978-1-912681-50-1

Creative Europe